Praise for *Close to the Soul:*

M000252002

Close to the Soul offers a beautiful escape to a simpler time where God is first and family is a close second. Thayer's debut explores the resiliency of family bonds and the grace of God when those bonds are tested. With equal measures of heartbreak and joy, Close to the Soul is a gripping novel that strikes every emotional chord. Fans of Francine Rivers will flock to this one! **Lori Nelson Spielman, NYT's bestselling author**

Close to the Soul is a beautifully written novel that weaves the story of redemption through every character on every page. I have spent my life grappling with the questions this novel boldly addresses. Mary Jo Thayer passionately portrays the way faith, family, and courage shine a light even in the darkest circumstances. **Pam Stenzel, MA, Enlighten Communications**

When I started reading Close to the Soul, I wasn't sure how Mary Jo would approach this difficult topic, especially from a young woman's point of view. What I found was a beautiful and inspiring story written in such a refreshing way that celebrates life, faith, love, redemption, strength of spirit, and family amid a devastating challenge. I felt honored to read Close to the Soul and pray that many readers will share this story. **Jim Sano, author of the *Fr. Tom* Series**

What an uplifting and hopeful story! I have to admit that it brought tears to my eyes more than once while I was reading it. I loved the solid and unwavering faith displayed by the Fandel family. The story definitely brings out the truth of God's wonderful and mysterious ways and his constant care of us even when we are going through rough times that we cannot understand. I thoroughly enjoyed reading it. **Linda Etchison, author, *Sr. Aloysius Comes to Mercyville***

Mary Jo Thayer has written an uplifting tale, dealing sensitively at each step with the challenges and trials faced by women raising their children alone. Mary Jo's deep faith is obvious, shining through her main character, Carolyn Fandel. Carolyn's resignation to the situation she finds herself in, along with the decisions she makes in the wake of her trauma, would certainly provide encouragement to any Catholic woman in any state of life, and indeed to anyone who picks up the book to read it. **Veronica Smallhorn, author, *A Channel of Your Peace***

Wow! What a powerful and moving story set in the 1950's. The story is of great value for readers today. This is an amazing read. And an incredible debut novel. Christian fiction at its best. Excellent Catholic literature. **Steven McEvoy, Book Reviews and More**

CLOSE TO THE SOUL

A Novel

by Mary Jo Thayer

All of life is a gift!

Mary Jo Thayer

Full Quiver Publishing
Pakenham ON

This book is a work of fiction.
Characters and incidents are products of the author's imagination.

Close to the Soul
Copyright 2021 Mary Jo Thayer

Published by
Full Quiver Publishing
P.O. Box 244
Pakenham, Ontario K0A 2X0
www.fullquiverpublishing.com

ISBN: 978-1-987970-23-4
Printed and bound in the USA

Cover design by James Hrkach and Mary Jo Thayer
Background image copyright Amanda Worrell (Stocksy)
Image of woman: copyright bilanol (Adobe Stock)

NATIONAL LIBRARY OF CANADA
CATALOGUING IN PUBLICATION

Published by FQ Publishing
A Division of Innate Productions

Dedication

*For all the babies—born and unborn—since the
beginning of time till the end.
And for their mothers—those who have rejoiced,
those who have grieved, and those who could do neither.*

You are loved forever by the One Who Is Love.

PROLOGUE

Back then, no one talked about such things. It wasn't polite to speak about them freely. It happened at a time when real men stood up, and boys disguised as men went on their way without as much as a backward glance. Girls in such circumstances were labeled as if humans could read not only minds but also hearts and souls.

The young woman often got saddled with the total responsibility—even by her parents—which she accepted without choice. Most practically, the young lady had to go into hiding—and out of town was preferable. "It" was discussed in hushed tones, cloaked terms, and shared with a select few. The key players, which generally involved those needed to help conceal the incident, were informed on a need-to-know basis. If word got out, an embarrassing black mark might be cast upon the family name.

It was a natural set-up for stuffed emotions and a gigantic web of long-running lies. Lifelong secrets were kept hidden close to the soul, often only between the young woman and God.

At least, that's how Carolyn thought it would go—especially being raised in a conservative Catholic bloodline and given a classical education, as if this somehow made her immune to the ugliness of the world.

***

It must have been cold that winter yuletide the nine months before Carolyn Joanna Fandel emerged into the world. An abundance of babies was born that September. The Christmas lights, decorated with the emotions of the war waging in Germany and Poland, brought couples together in their marriage beds to renew their vows of free, total, faithful, and fruitful love.

Baby Carolyn burst forth in the peaceful twilight hours on September 16, 1941, which is interesting because she was sixteen when "it" happened, a detail she could never forget. After all, how could she? The event would change the course of her life and the lives of countless others, forever, some of whom she would never meet.

1

CHAPTER ONE

October 1954

On a corner lot in Grand Lake — a smallish village on the shores of Lake Michigan — stood the Robert S. and Dana R. Fandel farmhouse-style home: a turn-of-the-century slate-gray, asbestos-sided, four-bedroom, two-story with no garage and one compact bathroom off the recently remodeled kitchen.

Crisp eyelet café curtains with embroidered yellow daisies hung at the windows. The lemon-yellow hue of the walls gleamed in fashionable contrast to the dark brown quarry tile floor and freshly painted, high-gloss white cabinets that extended to the ceiling.

Carolyn was showing it off to Phyllis Norton, her best friend since forever. "Don't you just think the world of our new Formica table and chairs? My dad snagged them as a lucky bargain from the warehouse where he works."

"They're the bee's knees!" Phyllis exclaimed. "I adore the pale blue color. So modern."

The Fandel kitchen was where folks naturally gravitated for meals, conversations, and games. Carolyn was most at peace when her home was crammed with people, enjoying food and fun. The loud laughter and lively discussions provided some of her dearest memories, especially if Phyllis was there. The friend was bookish smart, had a free-wheeling personality, and was apt to say anything that popped into her head.

"Let's play cards! I'll kick your fanny." The two sat across from each other for a speedy game of war.

Surprisingly, only-child Phyllis was unfazed by the commotion at the Fandel house. She simply shouted over the clanging of pots and pans in the kitchen. Toys strewn about on the living room floor and a cold egg with dried toast still on the table from breakfast didn't seem to bother her. Children running up and down over laundry on the stairs appeared to be instant amusement, as Phyllis grinned wide.

"Your house provides hours of entertainment. Mine is so boring. And you're lucky to have a sister."

Carolyn and Adeline were sandwiched between the oldest boys as children numbers two and three. They shared a bedroom that faced the

2

front of the house. From the sole window, the sisters could see the houses and yards of the entire block. At the end of the Fandel front walk next to the street was a rectangular-shaped concrete hitching post with an iron loop set in one end.

Staring out the window, Phyllis pointed, "Remember how we all used to sit there on our way home from primary school?"

"We used to pretend our bikes were horses and tie them up." Adeline chuckled.

The friend laughed. "The lemonade stands were the best. We thought we were rich. We'd walk to the penny candy store on Turner Street and blow the whole wad."

"Or save it to pay five cents for psychological services, pretending to be Lucy from the Peanuts comic strip. I could hardly wait to rotate into the roster and take my place to solve problems," said Carolyn. "I still play the psychiatrist with the elementary kids sometimes."

Silvester yelled through the wall from the next room. "That's right, Doctor Miss Perfect."

"Quit eavesdropping! And stop calling me Miss Perfect. I hate that!"

Phyllis offered a buffer. "Take it easy, Carolyn. You're lucky to have your band of brothers. I wish my parents had had more children, but my mom wanted a law career more, I guess. You and Adeline at least have each other."

Being a year apart, Carolyn and her sister did enjoy a close relationship. They shared chores, secrets, and even friends. "Come on, Adeline, push with me to slide our bed over so we can set up a cot for the overnight."

Hearing Phyllis resent her family stirred up gratitude in Carolyn. "I suppose you're right. No matter how much we tease and fight with each other, I can't imagine even one of my siblings not being here."

She pitied her friend and recalled something her parents had taught for as long as she could remember. "God has given us this house and these things to lead souls to heaven." Phyllis had become not just a best friend but someone Carolyn wanted to help. She carved out a place for her in her heart, planning to keep her friend there forever.

The Fandel parents readily accepted Phyllis or, for that matter, any other kid who wandered into their home. Carolyn's mom didn't care if she had given birth to the person or not. Her rules applied to everybody. If a visiting youngster was out of line, she let them have it. If a neighbor child was invited for a meal, they assisted with the dishes. Or when it was a house-cleaning day, like this one, Carolyn's mom held out dusting rags and said, "Here you go, girls. Show Phyllis what to clean."

Phyllis, a rusty-haired blonde with cornflower blue eyes, award-winning dimples, and a million freckles, was a good blend of the sisters' personalities. She was Carolyn's best friend but enjoyed hanging out with the boys, as Adeline did.

Carolyn was a tall, willowy blonde with hazel-green eyes. She gravitated toward academics, performing arts, and fashion. She tended to pray her way out of stress and hold firm once she had made a decision. She was averse to being challenged about her choices.

Adeline Catherine was an athletically built, blue-eyed brunette. She was fantastic at math facts, inclined to make a mess in the kitchen, and could climb trees better than the guys. She had a sentimental side as well and took disappointments ridiculously hard.

The four Fandel brothers occupied the largest of the upstairs bedrooms. The oldest child, Silvester James (Sil), gloried in having a twin bed to himself, although he did not, on most days, glory in having to share a room with the little guys who, in his opinion, were loud, annoying, and occasionally smelly when Frankie wet the bed.

The three youngest—Augustine Sidney (Gus), Wallace Howard (Wally), and Frank Stephen (Frankie)—shared a double bed. Frankie squeezed himself in between his older brothers, which had the automatic benefit of keeping the two elders from having kicking fights over mattress territory. Carolyn adored Frankie's smug grin as he wriggled up the middle and boasted an endearing smile that would later melt into tears of embarrassment.

"Frankie peed again!" cried Wally.

"Gross!" yelled Gus.

"Ditto," agreed Phyllis.

"I dread changing those sheets," said Carolyn. "I practically have to hold my breath."

The friend agreed again, "Pee-yew!"

The two brothers banished him from the bed for the next couple of nights. Frankie was mortified and crawled under. He would only come out with Carolyn's coaxing. "Come on out, Frankie. It'll be okay."

Carolyn was fond of all her brothers, but she had bonded with Frankie almost as a second mother. At the young age of ten, Carolyn had stepped in to provide Frankie with extra cuddles, baths, and rocking on colicky nights. It was what needed to be done, so her mom could regain her strength from a rough labor and delivery.

Sil took mercy and said Frankie could sleep in his bed but not before he sternly admonished him, "Frankie, if you pee in my bed, I'm gonna clean your clock."

A crackly voice from the other side of the landing spoke, "Silvester, I am not sure cleaning a clock is the most effective way of taking care of one's brother."

"Yes, Ma'am."

Carolyn's never-married great-aunt occupied the tiny bedroom across the hall over the attic. Occasionally, Auntie Dora would go off for a few days and live with her other nieces and nephews, but for the majority of the year, she lived with the Fandels. She often allowed the children and their friends into her room.

"Auntie Dora, may we come in?" asked Carolyn.

"Of course! Hello there, Phyllis!"

"Hello, Miss Dora."

Dora allowed them to look around and examine her odd assortment of things. A faded chenille bedspread in graduating shades of blue adorned her wrought iron bed. Under it was her old black carpet bag containing rolls and rolls of fabric scraps, each held tight by a straight pin. Carolyn recognized some of the remnants in their aunt's wardrobe, as well as in some of her own. A gold-trimmed mirrored tray held a milky-blue container of dusting powder and a few atomizers of perfume. When the girls read the words, "Toilet Water," they raised their eyebrows at one another and stifled giggles.

On the creaky dresser sat two statues. Somehow St. Joseph was missing a chunk out of his arm. The Blessed Mother had a broken nose. A dog-eared leather-bound prayer book lay next to the black rosary on a narrow wooden bedside table. The room held a lot of intrigue. To both of them, every single thing in it seemed ancient, just like Dora. Next to her petite floral-tufted chair, where she was sitting, was an opened Dutch Masters cardboard cigar box with an expanded rainbow of colored thread.

"Auntie Dora taught me how to embroider by the time I was eight," Carolyn informed.

"That's a gas!" Phyllis tittered.

Dora's eyebrows jumped to the sky from shock over Phyllis's moxie, but she still indulged the friend with a cursory lesson before the teens went across the hall and hopped into bed. Adeline took the cot.

Phyllis was honest. "Your aunt smells funny."

"Shh! She might hear you," Carolyn chided. "My dad said it's her toilet water."

"No wonder!" Phyllis roared.

"Shh!" Carolyn giggled, "It's another word for 'perfume.'"

They awoke to baking day—a fine Fandel production. Wafting aromas drew in the neighborhood kids from a two-block radius. Even though Carolyn and Phyllis were in eighth grade, they still waited eagerly for the goodies. Being fall, Carolyn pulled a jug of Farmer Momber's cider from the fridge.

"Ooh, Momber's cider, I dig that stuff!" declared Phyllis.

"Me, too. We picked up a few bushels of crisp apples from his orchard on Fruit Ridge Road last Saturday." Carolyn poured them all a glass to take to the dining room table while they waited.

First out of the oven came homemade cinnamon rolls loaded with butter, Schilling's cinnamon, and raisins. Warm and dripping with white glaze icing, Carolyn unfurled her cinnamon roll and picked out all the raisins, eating them one at a time. She savored the pungent sweetness of each plump raisin on her tongue. Then she rerolled the pastry and ate it from the bottom up, saving the icing top for last. Licking her fingers was a must. No spot of frosting went to waste. Phyllis and Adeline did likewise.

Back in the kitchen to make the mashed potato donuts, Carolyn's mom was pointing to the counter that held a bunch of ingredients. She handed Carolyn the hand beater. "Here, you girls mix." Carolyn and Phyllis surveyed the flour, buttermilk, sugar, eggs, and nutmeg to add to the leftover spuds. Phyllis read the recipe while Carolyn measured amounts.

The dough was turned out onto a wooden board. Auntie Dora wielded a rolling pin like a magician and formed the goo into a circle the size of a huge pizza crust. Then she employed the donut cutter and began making round shapes.

Never having been present for a donut day, Phyllis wrinkled her nose. "Do those even taste good?"

Carolyn promised her friend, "Wait until you eat one. You'll never crave store-bought again."

Carolyn's mom plopped the thick, sticky circles into a vat of blistering hot oil on the gas stove and fried them on each side until they were golden brown. Auntie Dora lifted them out with long-handled cooking tongs and placed them on layers of old newspapers to drain, leaving dozens of ring-shaped grease stains.

While still warm, they were put into one of two paper sacks by Adeline and shaken until coated with either cinnamon sugar or powdered sugar—both amazingly delicious, in Carolyn's opinion. She could hardly imagine anything better than a fresh warm donut served with a cool glass of cider. Nothing could beat that culinary combination of tasty goodness.

Carolyn and Phyllis carried a heaping tray of donuts outside to the waiting kids and sat with them under the maple tree. Carolyn took a donut in her hand and placed her tongue on the powdered sugar, only to have it dissolve immediately.

Phyllis took a huge bite of a cinnamon one and exclaimed, "You were right! These are unreal!"

"Told you so."

Via the open kitchen window, they and the others listened to Auntie Dora and Carolyn's mother exchange stories of long ago.

"How long is she going to live with you?" Phyllis asked.

"Probably forever. She fits right in. She still makes us fairy-dusted butter and brown sugar sandwiches on freshly baked bread when we come home from school on Fridays. And she lets us girls go in advance of boys because she favors us," Carolyn teased.

"There you go again, Miss Perfect," muttered Sil, hanging upside down from a tree branch.

"I'm not perfect!" Carolyn wailed up the maple. If only her siblings knew the struggle inside her head to feel good enough.

"Silvester!" their mom shouted out the window, "Quit picking on your sister."

"Sorry, Mom. Sorry, Miss Perfect."

"Ugh! Why are you SO annoying?" Carolyn huffed and crossed her arms, stomping her foot.

Phyllis acted as if she were watching a performance, snickering and stuffing her mouth with donuts. She helped carry in the empty tray and cups. "Thank you so much for having me over, but I had better get going. My parents are expecting me." She dipped her fingers in the holy water font by the front door and made the Sign of the Cross on her way out. She hopped on her bike and tore down the street.

7

To an empty house, Carolyn surmised. Dousing herself with a reminder of God's baptismal grace, she offered up a prayer for her friend.

CHAPTER TWO

1955

Carolyn took immense pride in her Fandels, as she fondly referred to them, and was partial to having friends over to her house. They often paused to look at the religious artwork in the rooms of her home. "Man, you guys are super Catholic—gobs of kids and churchy pictures everywhere. Catholicism must course through your veins or something," Phyllis had said recently.

"My parents believe people should be able to tell when they walk in the door if someone is Catholic. They said we ought to be more than mere Sunday obligation types."

"I guess. Maybe I'll suggest that to my mom when she's not busy."

Recalling this conversation prompted Carolyn to find her mom, who was in the parlor. "Hey, Mom. Why is it that we have so many kids?"

Her mom put down a *Reader's Digest* magazine. "What do you mean?"

"Well, Phyllis is an only child. She said her mom wanted a career more than kids and called us super Catholics. So, I was wondering about that."

"I can't speak to the intentions of the Nortons. What I can say is that your father and I follow the Church's teaching, which is opposed to contraception of any ilk. Children are manifestations of God's providence, and He chooses us to become co-creators with Him. The more children, the more love."

"So, the Nortons are missing some love?"

"That's not what I meant. I was only saying that we are blessed to have all of you." Her mom threw her head back and joked, "At times, though, it did feel as if my babies would never come out."

"Did you ever get tired of being pregnant?"

"Sometimes, yes. I would get anxious to hold the infant I was carrying. I tried to offer up any discomfort and be thankful for the ability to conceive, bear, and birth my numerous children. Other women aren't so lucky."

Carolyn then realized that being pregnant was a blessing that not all women received. She grabbed her baby album out of the bookcase, opened it, and sat on the couch with her mom.

"What day of the week was I born?"

"Tuesday. A few months before the Japanese bombed Pearl Harbor. It was a starry, peaceful evening. I'll never forget it."

Carolyn was touched. "How long was I in there?"

Her mom chuckled. "Forty-two weeks! I envisioned you taking a vacation."

Carolyn, humored by her mom's comedic line, pointed to one of the photos. "Look at how fat I was!"

"Not fat. Beautifully chunky. You were full of happy life right from the beginning—all nine pounds of you. You smiled at three weeks. Your eyes twinkled. You were destined to be a sweetie."

Carolyn grinned and sidled closer. Even as a high schooler, she enjoyed being nearby. "I love you, Mom."

"I love you, Carolyn Joanna." Her mom traced the picture with her finger. "Look at all that buttery-blond hair. Grandmama Fandel claimed you were an angel. Your daddy dubbed you 'Doll'."

"So, that's where my nickname came from." Carolyn adored being called Doll. No matter what was going on in her life, hearing either of her parents call her that stirred up tender emotions.

"Your dad was pretty sure you were perfect."

Carolyn sobered up. "Is that why Sil is always calling me 'Miss Perfect'?"

"Not at all. It's just what brothers do. It pleases him when you react to it. Most men relish getting reactions from the females in their lives."

The kindred spirits laughed together before Carolyn's mom went to the kitchen to make dinner. Carolyn perused her baby book a while longer and then put it away, cherishing the cozy chat.

The gems of wisdom her mom offered were hers for the taking, and she tried to incorporate them during a phase that did not endear her to her siblings. Her newfound motherly disposition had quite the opposite effect and was met with utter disapproval.

"Wally, Gus, pick up your stuff from the dining room," Carolyn commanded.

"You don't have the right to boss us, Miss Perfect," they complained.

She heard her mother shout from wherever she was, "Carolyn, they have a mother."

Not to be deterred, Carolyn said, "Adeline, come help me fold the sheets."

"In a sec."

"No, now!"

"Do it yourself, Miss Perfect, if you can't wait."

"Don't call me that!" shouted Carolyn before turning her back on Adeline. "I can't stand that name."

Carolyn could tell by the shift in her sister's tone that Adeline realized she had hit a nerve. "The boys do it all the time."

Carolyn turned back to face her. "It bothers me, especially when you say it. I'm just trying to teach you how to do the right thing."

Adeline was annoyed by the justification. "Teaching us is Mom's job, not yours. You're too bossy and a real bear sometimes."

"Copy that." Carolyn felt the sting but could see her point. "I'll work on it, but please stop calling me 'Miss Perfect.' For one thing, I don't think I am perfect. I never have. For another thing, it's just me and you against all those boys. We girls have to stick together."

By this time, sentimental Adeline was crying. "I'm so sorry. I didn't mean to bully you." She grabbed her older sister in a big sloppy hug.

"Stop crying. It's fine. Let's make a pact to always be a team. No matter what, we stick together."

Adeline stuck out her pinkie, and Carolyn wrapped hers around that of her sister. "It's official; we have pinkie-swore."

CHAPTER THREE

What Carolyn kept hidden was that she was afraid to make a mistake. A pang was always lurking, searching for an opportunity to darken her life. It crept up even when she wasn't expecting it—even at fifteen. She thought about it so much she convinced herself that she might be adopted. Intellectually, this did not make sense at all. But, emotionally, she conjectured there was a reason she felt pitted against her siblings.

She had once confided this adoption theory to Phyllis. Carolyn had said, "I feel I'll never be good enough."

Phyllis had hastily replied and ended the conversation, "Don't be ridiculous. Your family adores you, and you're the most virtuous friend I have. Prideful but virtuous. Besides, you share too many recessive genes with Wally and Frankie."

Carolyn sat on the floor of the living room, revisiting these ominous feelings. It plagued her whether these were glimpses into her past or hints about her future. She replayed all those times she had poked around in the drawers of the china cabinet, snooping for evidence that her parents planned to extradite her. She was jostled into the present by the buzzing of the vacuum. Her mom was on another cleaning frenzy.

For years, she had daily observed her energetic mother whirl through the house, mopping on her hands and knees, hanging laundry on the clothesline, folding it meticulously, and whipping up hearty meals in the kitchen. Carolyn asked her mom why she worked so hard every single day.

"Your grandparents, as you are well aware, are immigrants. They practically had to claw their way here from Germany. I have learned to appreciate all the things I have been given and to work hard for the things I want."

Her mom—a whiz at math and talented musically—had to drop out of school to lend support and get a job. She completed the tenth grade before recognizing that she could not finish her education. Great empathy stirred within Carolyn. "Mom, you're so smart. You should go back to school and get your high school diploma."

"Thanks, Doll. I've contemplated it, but—" she said jokingly, "I'm a tad busy at the moment raising you kids." Carolyn wondered if she were truly light-hearted about it. She couldn't even fathom not being able to finish high school. To her, that seemed about the worst thing for a teenager. "I'm content with where I am, Carolyn. I wouldn't trade it for a minute. Besides, it was the right thing to do at the time. The necessary thing."

Carolyn's grandfather used to suffer from the bottle, which was largely responsible for the lack of sufficient family funds. Her mother's words made an impression. "You must be careful with alcohol. It's not the solution to any problem. And it's a tricky thing. One minute you're fine, and the next you could be drunk or—worse—craving it."

Her mom put enough fright into her that Carolyn was sure she'd never have a problem with booze. *I'm never going to drink,* she promised herself.

"Pa was always a good man who worked hard. But when the drink got the better of him, he hardly worked," her mom said.

"Uncle Lou has the same problem, right?"

Carolyn's mom had explained it was partly because of her brother Lou's downward spiral into the abyss of alcoholism that her father was able to turn his own life around. "It's a true manifestation of God's mercy and the ability of a person to change a vice into a virtue. Long-time prayer went into that effort."

"Is that one reason you and Dad insist on saying the rosary as a family?"

"Yes. It always straightens our paths and helps us hold one another accountable."

Carolyn internalized these words and imagined incorporating a nightly rosary into her own clan someday. She vowed to God that she would pray it more often starting now.

That night, she grabbed her rosary off her nightstand and pulled it near. Making the sign of the cross with the crucifix, she began her prayer. "In the Name of the Father and the Son and the Holy Spirit. Amen." After kissing the feet of Jesus, she shut her eyes and tried to picture the life of Christ as she prayed.

When her old fears crept in, she pulled out her rosary and prayed. When she was worried about a test at school, she did the same. She was proud of her attempt to make this powerful spiritual weapon her own.

Every facet of Carolyn Fandel's life was infused with Catholic culture—whether she was attending Mass, hanging with friends, volunteering at functions, you name it. Her parents had seen to that. It seemed the only practical way to organize a large brood, which fell mostly on her mother because her dad worked as a salesman and could be gone for a week or more at a time.

The Fandels had one car, a 1953 maroon Chevy Townsman, so Carolyn's mom would drive her dad to the Greyhound depot at the edge of town, giving her use of the station wagon for the duration. The bus would take him into Grand Rapids, where he caught the train to major cities in the Midwest. From conventions and door-to-door, he and his team sold a variety of brushes, cleaning supplies, magazine subscriptions, appliances, and home improvement products.

He had begun working for Standard shortly after a stint with the National Guard. He had often told the story that during a convoy to Grayling, the guys were playing poker, and he was winning huge. His buddy, Cotter—exasperated from seeing Robert take another haul— said, "Pokerfaced Fandel, you ought to go into sales. You could sell hairbrushes to a bald guy!" Her dad had said that, at first, he laughed but later gave it serious consideration. As soon as his assignment with the Guard was over, he set out searching for a solid sales company. He had recently been promoted to management. Her mom said it was his integrity and business acumen that had won it for him.

Carolyn thought her father—a top rep for Standard Goods—was handsome as he headed off to work. A tall and muscular man, he carried himself upright. In cooler temperatures, he donned a khaki-colored trench coat over his suit and tie. And always, no matter the weather, he placed a chocolate brown Hipster Fedora on his head as he went out the back-porch door, briefcase in hand, doffing his hat to her mother and making a miniature cross on the foreheads of the children with his thumb. "Be the light," he would say, as Carolyn and her siblings craned their necks to look up at their dad's face and receive his blessing.

During his absences, Carolyn's three younger brothers invariably forgot to "be the light" as they worked their testosterone magic. One Sunday morning, Augustine and Wallace wrestled on their shared bed so aggressively that the heel of Wally's foot put a hole in the plaster. Silvester jumped in to break up the raucous fight.

Carolyn warned, "Better cut it out before one of you gets hurt."

"You're not our parents!" Gus yelled as he held Wally in a chokehold.

"Yeah," wheezed Wally, barely able to breathe.

Suddenly, Sil was screaming in pain, "Ouch! Oh my gosh, oh my gosh!"

"Now you've done it," Carolyn scolded, leaving Gus and Wally sitting there in silence with their mouths agape and terror in their eyes. She left the room with Sil.

The two instigators forthwith hopped off the bed and scampered behind them, going down the stairs. "Sorry, Sil. Sorry, Sil." He ignored them, tears in his eyes. He held up his disjointed, misshapen finger to their mom in the kitchen. Carolyn cringed at the sight of it. No finger should look that way.

"Oh, dear. Let me see." Their mom examined the finger from every angle. With their dad out of town and no doctor readily available, their mom fashioned a splint out of two wooden Popsicle sticks, hidden in the kitchen drawer from summer delicacies. She wound masking tape around Sil's broken finger to hold it straight, then gave him two Bayer aspirin for the pain. "There now, you go serve Holy Mass. If it still hurts tomorrow morning, I will take you to see Doc Imthum."

The boys ushered in another catastrophe later that week. Wally and Frankie bathed the pet hamster, nearly drowning it. Gus rescued the poor thing and then tried to dry it with their mother's hairdryer, coming close enough with the heat to cause the animal to cry out in pain. Carolyn watched Wally and Frankie cry their eyes out, while Gus—the oldest of that trio—tried to comfort and keep them hushed so no one would find out. It was an unsuccessful venture.

Punishments would be dispensed pending their father's return and their parents' thorough conversation. If they disagreed, they usually halted these "discussions," until they retired to their bedroom and decided upon a compromise.

One can't grow up in a large clan without several tales of adventure and woe. Add Catholicism to the mix and factor in high ideals, guilt, and hilarious stories of habited sisters and foreign priests, there was rarely a dull moment. Sometimes they got irritated with each other, but they would remain comrades forever. It was a good way to grow up, and Carolyn knew it. She appreciated everything about her life: her home, her Fandels, and her school.

CHAPTER FOUR

1956-57

For one year, the three older Fandels attended high school at the same time—in twelfth, tenth, and ninth grades, respectively.

Adeline, the math whiz, tested out of Algebra I and moved right into geometry, the upper-level math class for freshmen. Adeline, the athlete, settled on cheerleading as an activity—the thing closest to a female sport at Grand Lake High—ideal for the boy-crazy sister.

Carolyn threw herself onto the stage as a cast member of *Our Town* and dove right into her favorite class—American Literature. She couldn't wait to read Twain, Steinbeck, and Hemingway. Her passion for sewing was carried out in home economics. She relayed to her mom, "I'll have to submit a garment for my final exam. This is one sewing project we can't do together."

Her mom drove her into Grand Rapids to shop for fabric at Wurzburg's. They were having a sale on broadcloth cotton. "The navy polka dot print will make a beautiful dress, Carolyn."

Sil, an excellent athlete, was thrilled to see his name in print on the varsity football roster. He was also excited about being able to take a woodshop class his senior year. By the end of twelfth grade, Sil proudly carried home his masterpiece with the assistance of his sisters.

"It's beautiful, Sil," said Carolyn.

"Mom will be flabbergasted," Adeline added.

"Thanks. I'm pretty eager to show it to her."

The three lugged it up the hill on Maple Street to their house. Adeline held the door, while Carolyn helped Sil carry it inside to the living room, where their mom was enjoying a cup of tea. He proudly presented his mother with the long sofa table constructed from hickory that he and his grandfather, known as Pa, had sawn and planed from a tree on his grandparents' farm.

"Oh, Silvester! It's gorgeous!"

The beautiful golden-grained piece was henceforth situated in their spacious living room between two windows. It held their father's sales awards and a plethora of past and present photos. Carolyn often admired the fine finish of her brother's work, along with the memorabilia stationed on top.

Upon Silvester's graduation from high school in June, he obediently registered for the Draft. But, since the Korean War had passed and there was no imminent threat to national security, he was able to avoid being called into the military. Instead, he chose to accept an academic scholarship to Aquinas College in Grand Rapids. The radiating smiles of pride on her parents' faces told Carolyn they were immensely proud of their son for pursuing a degree, an opportunity neither had. It put in Carolyn's mind that maybe she, too, could go away to college when the time came.

By the summer before her junior year, Carolyn measured five feet, nine inches—tall for a girl—but that didn't stop guys of all heights from trying to capture her attention. She had overheard her grandfather use the word "fetching." Her father had commented to him, "The sheer number of them nearly warrant a revolving door."

Her mom had admonished her not to get a big head about it.

She counted four males who vied for her affection that summer. They often stopped on a bike ride under the guise of looking for Sil. Since he could tell that they were there to see his sister, he always called for Carolyn to join them as soon as he spotted one of them round the corner.

Adeline mused out loud. "I dream of the day when boys come looking for me." She confided in Carolyn that she had ranked the guys in a hierarchy. "Can I have your second choice?"

"Maybe. When and if I make a choice."

Sil and Adeline tried to pump Carolyn for information on her true crush, but she would not show her cards. "Don't worry. You'll be among the first to hear if anything turns into a dating relationship."

"Slim chance," said Sil.

"Yeah. Dad will probably never let me date, even after my Sweet Sixteen in September," opined Carolyn.

Their dad was protective of both his daughters. He had instructed Sil to remain present when boys came calling with their "arsenal of pick-up lines," he had said.

***

March 1958

The Junior-Senior Spring Formal was on the horizon. Carolyn dreamed which of her many suitors might issue an invitation. She hoped it would come from Paul Johns, a lanky Lebanese-American basketball player with dark wavy hair, friendly brown eyes, and an academic demeanor. She had secretly admired him since the eighth grade when the Johnses moved to town, and Paul began attending the same Catholic school. He was smart and seemed shy but always had an amiable smile or cordial word. Carolyn, never one to be too interested in athletics, suddenly became an avid fan of both basketball and baseball—the two sports that Paul Johns happened to play.

On the first day of spring, as she headed to Magistra DePue's Latin class, Paul trotted up behind and tapped her on the shoulder. She turned to face him wide-eyed. "Hi, Paul!"

"Would you accompany me to the Spring Formal next month?"

With great enthusiasm, Carolyn readily accepted. "I'd love to!" And then she wondered how in the world she was going to talk her father into letting her go on a date. She had a valid argument, though. Sil was allowed to go his last two years.

It was Sil, home for his first college spring break, who came to her defense. Carolyn, sitting on the upstairs landing, overhead him pleading her case in the kitchen. He gave it one more try. "Dad, the Johns family goes to our church. Paul is one of the best guys around. I think you should let her go. After all, you let me go."

Carolyn smiled, but not for long.

"Son, I've already told you that I am not interested in a debate," she heard her father say curtly.

"Okay, Dad. I'm sorry if I went too far. Good night." Silvester headed up the stairs to bed and found Carolyn on the landing, straining to hear the conversation. "You better go to bed, Sis. It doesn't look good."

Her faced drooped. "Thanks for trying. Good night." She retreated to her room, where Adeline waited for the verdict. The younger sister had a stake in the outcome, too, for she would be a junior the following year. Carolyn shook her head "no" to indicate their father had not granted permission.

She could hear her parents talking privately that night through the floor heating vent. She couldn't make out what they were saying, but it did sound as if they were disagreeing. The sisters finished their prayers—tossing up one last heavenward plea for an affirmative on the formal—and went to sleep.

Good news was delivered the next morning. "You can go to the Spring Formal with the Johns boy."

Carolyn hugged her dad, grinned from ear to ear, and bolted up the stairs to tell Adeline. Peals of joy rang from them both as the sisters jumped up and down in their room.

She overheard her father as he walked out the door for work. "I hope I haven't made a mistake by letting her go."

"She'll be fine, Robert. Let's chat with Matt and Carol Johns this weekend at Mass to make sure we're all on the same page."

CHAPTER FIVE

Carolyn's closest friends—those she had retained from her days in Catholic school—each received invitations from boys who appeared to have good intentions. High thrills were in the air, as they either shopped for the fabrics to make their dresses or borrowed dresses from one another's older sisters.

Carolyn's mom had torn apart one of her formals and restyled it to fit the fashion of the fifties. The outcome was a dark lavender taffeta A-line with a tulle overlay. The vibrant color contrasted nicely with Carolyn's shiny blond hair, and it made her green eyes sparkle. She twirled around as she examined herself in the mirror. "I'm ecstatic, Mom! Thank you!"

"You are beautiful, Carolyn. It fits you to a tee. I hope you have a marvelous time." Her mom applied a light amount of rouge to Carolyn's cheeks and dabbed her lips with Avon candy pink. She tucked in a few bobby pins to keep the Doris Day hairdo in place. Then she grabbed her can of Aqua Net and sprayed the curls. "There you are, Doll. All set."

"Thanks, Mom." Carolyn swooned. "My first date. And with Paul. The dance is going to be the living end!" Carolyn glowed and imagined herself a princess.

"You're blushing!" Adeline announced.

The female Fandels stepped onto their front porch to wait for Paul. He arrived shortly with a corsage in hand. Her mom snapped a few photographs after he had pinned it on Carolyn. She wore the flowers proudly, as Paul held the door to allow her to step into his father's sedan.

The school gym was decked out in crepe paper streamers, and dozens of pink and blue balloons hung from the folded-up bleachers. "Mambo Rock" by Bill Haley and His Comets could be heard blaring through the gym. The principal of the school had schlepped in his stereo and positioned a microphone near the speakers to blast the music. Dressed-up teens in ties and corsages danced in their socks to Perry Como, Rosemary Clooney, and Patsy Cline. They enjoyed hot fudge sundaes prepared by the school secretary and counselor.

Paul and Carolyn left the gym hand-in-hand at nine, along with dozens of their schoolmates. Post-formal plans had been made, and the teens did not want to miss a minute of it. They toted the balloons to the next location and hung them from the rafters in the hayloft.

Hank Starrett, who was Phyllis's date, had convinced his parents to open their barn for continued dancing and late-night snacks for the hungry crowd. Hank's parents had set an eleven-thirty curfew. Everyone in Grand Lake was acquainted with Emmett Starrett. After all, Starrett Brothers' Farms supplied over half of the milk to the village. What neither they nor the Starrett parents realized was that Hank, with the purchasing power of his older brother, also supplied pilfered vodka to the unsuspecting party guests.

The barn was more crowded than Carolyn and Paul expected, but it was a gangbuster! The Starretts had a jukebox in the far corner. The teens had fun selecting songs from popular singers. Carolyn felt treasured when Paul pulled her onto the dance floor for "The Stroll" by the Diamonds. She and Phyllis winked at each other as they were spun around by their guys.

The kids were parched, so Paul went to grab some lemonade for Carolyn and himself. After getting the drinks, he turned and saw her on the dance floor with one of the senior boys, Skip Jergen, who had come stag. Paul gave Carolyn a wave. *He's cool with it.* She and Skip were bopping up a storm to Little Richard's "Tutti Frutti." Skip played basketball with Paul, so the two guys nodded to one another, indicating all was fine.

Although she had started to have true affection for Paul based on their growing friendship since junior high, Carolyn was also proud to be dancing with Skip. He was super popular, charming, a great athlete, and admired from afar by most of the girls. He had steel gray eyes that drew in the ladies, a quick wit, and fantastic dance moves. He seemed to have a radar for those with silent crushes on him. Carolyn was one such infatuated female. After another song, they exited to the side.

Thirsty from dancing so much, Carolyn smiled at Paul and downed the lemonade in appreciation. "Thanks." She and he were able to get in another slow dance together before Paul was beckoned up to the Starrett farmhouse for a phone call. It was his parents, who were at a work dinner for Paul's dad, the vice president of a small-scale brick company. They explained that they had come out of the event to find one of their tires flat. They could not change it in time to meet the curfew of the sitter they had hired for Paul's younger siblings. Therefore, Paul was going to have to leave the barn party.

Carolyn preferred to milk the entire late-curfewed evening and stay with her friends, and she told Paul as much. Hank jumped in and said he'd take both her and Phyllis home. Paul accompanied Carolyn when she made a phone call to her dad and mom to get their permission to stay. Knowing both Phyllis's and Hank's parents, they agreed.

Her dad apprised her, "No later than midnight, and a few minutes earlier is preferred."

"Yes, Dad. I'll be in by then."

Carolyn accompanied Paul to his car. "Goodbye, Paul. I've had a spectacular time!"

Paul took her hands in his and stared into her eyes. "Me, too, Carolyn. I look forward to more dates soon." When he hugged her, it felt safe and right. It felt even better when he kissed her. The two parted, still gazing at one another. Teenage romance was in the air for Carolyn Joanna Fandel and Paul Joseph Johns.

She returned to the barn, lonely without him. She spotted Phyllis, Julia, Nancy, and Patricia whirling to Dale Hawkins' "Susie Q" and joined them. Grabbing more lemonade and chips, the five giddy juniors huddled in the corner so Carolyn could fill them in on what was happening with Paul.

"He's a dreamboat!" they gushed.

Carolyn could only agree. "I've had a crush on him since eighth grade when I first saw those dark curls peeking out from his baseball cap."

More dancing and more lemonade took effect. And Carolyn's bladder was about to burst. She grabbed Phyllis by the crook of her elbow and led her away from the group. "Come with me across the field to the bathroom."

"Not right now. I'm having too good of a time. You just go."

"Please. I'm afraid to go by myself." Whispering in her friend's ear, "Are you snockered? I think I might be." Carolyn felt tipsy. And the vodka she had drunk became partly responsible for her forgetting, at least temporarily, that she was a good Catholic girl with impeccable morals, who ought to have left with her date.

Giggling, Phyllis whispered back, "Kind of. Hank's brother put a lot of vodka in it. And I don't want to leave right now. Hank asked me to slow dance."

"All right," Carolyn sighed and scanned the barn, trying to get the attention of one of her other girlfriends. With his suit jacket slung over his shoulder, Skip offered to walk her up to the house. It was a good two hundred yards and a few rolling hills from the barn. Carolyn, thankful for the escort, vowed to her friend to be back soon.

In the moonlight, the two teens disappeared over the hill. It was then that Skip offered that he'd always had his eye on Carolyn. He said he had selected her to be his girlfriend. With her head spinning from both the lemonade and what Skip, the school's biggest hunk, had just vocalized, she felt flattered.

"Come on," Skip said with a leer in his eyes, ogling her up and down. "You were flirting with me on that dance floor." He leaned in and stole a kiss from her, and she kissed him back. Pulling away, she smiled coyly as she floated into the house to use the restroom.

She noticed herself in the bathroom mirror, causing her to come back to her sensibilities. She took a couple of deep breaths, trying to clear her head. She was being unfair to Paul and untrue to her feelings for him. She had to tell Skip that she did not return his sentiment and planned to do so immediately.

When she emerged from the house into the dim porch light, she caught a glimpse of Skip's face. He seemed extremely determined, as if he had a plan. Her brain sensed that he had an unhealthy desire toward her, but she could not think the worst of him. After all, he had offered to walk her to the house when Phyllis refused. *It's fine. Skip wouldn't hurt me. He told me he wants me to be his girlfriend.*

Still processing Skip's earlier pledge of interest, she decided to put distance between them to try to send him a polite message that she could not be attentive to him in that way. Yet, no matter which way she veered, Skip did not miss a beat. He stuck uncomfortably close. Something in his eyes frightened her. She could no longer deny that he was every bit a man in conquest. It made her extremely nervous— freaked her out, actually. She knew she ought to do something. *But what?*

She finally spoke, trying as hard as she could to remain calm. "Skip, I…I got carried away by the lemonade. I think Paul and I might have something, and I need some time to sort out my thoughts." His fiery, steel eyes burned straight into hers. "Skip, you're frightening me."

"Oh, come on, Carolyn, why were you flirting with me then?!" he shouted, startling her. She shuddered and instinctively wrapped her arms around herself.

Confused, she tried again to explain, "I'm sorry; it was the lemonade." Her brain tapped her instincts, indicating she was in danger. She began to panic and hurried her pace back to the barn. *I just need to get over that hill.*

Skip stepped in front of Carolyn to block her. "You're not going anywhere," he hissed through his gritted teeth.

His formidable voice, and a frame to match, caused Carolyn to obey. She halted to a full stop. As soon as she did, he grabbed her arm and leaned in for another kiss. She turned her head to the side in time to avoid it. A quick scan made her realize that she was too far away from the barn and too far away from the house. She concentrated hard to find a solution, but her brain was swirling.

She writhed and writhed to break free, but he was too strong. "Skip, please don't," she entreated, but his hand went up as if he were going to strike. Fear gripped her, and she whimpered, "Please let me go!" She was shaking and beginning to cry, but he did not care.

Her attempts to call out were stifled partly by the music blaring from the barn but mostly by her fear. Her throat stuck as if she had not had anything to drink in ages. There was a giant lump in her windpipe. She tried to swallow it, so she could scream, but it was a vacant attempt. She froze in fear. Stiff and still and silent, she was no longer under her own power.

Skip's large hand came around the back of her neck and over her mouth. She was unable to breathe, let alone cry out. With his other hand, he slung his coat open on the grass.

Her eyes wide, she almost vomited when Skip's mighty arm reached around her waist and pulled her slowly onto the coat as if he were trying to be noiseless.

Carolyn tried again to break free. She struggled and thrashed, but her head was spinning. It was unclear to her whether it was the lemonade or the fear. She kicked and tried to push him off as he pulled her panties to the side, but he was much stronger and heavier than her lean frame. He was on her, and she hated it. She lay on his coat with her legs in the field. She was powerless. She was doomed. She squeezed her eyes shut and wished—no, pleaded—for it to be over. No tears came, and she dared not to say a word, but inside, Carolyn Fandel was screaming louder than she ever had in her life. And even though not a living soul could hear her, she prayed that God did.

In what seemed like an instant and at the same time forever, it was over, but the pain lingered. She had never experienced such pain. Skip dusted her off and picked the straw out of her hair, as if nothing had happened, all the while professing sentiments in a tender –yet eerie – voice. "Now, you're mine. Johns won't want you." And Carolyn knew it was true. All hope was lost.

No one would believe her, especially Paul. Not after the way she and Skip had been seen dancing together. Besides, her clothes weren't torn, and she bore no visible bruises. She concluded what had happened would have to remain a secret for the rest of her life.

Skip walked her back to the barn with his arm still around her, and oddly Carolyn let him. He then made a hasty excuse to Phyllis, Hank, and the others on why he had to get out of there. Something about going somewhere early in the morning. Carolyn could barely even look at him as he jogged off to his car. Her eyes widened. She couldn't believe he was leaving her there.

She was so confused. Her hands shook, and her soul ached more than her body. She wove her fingers together tightly to keep them from trembling. She managed a few deep breaths, inhaling and exhaling slowly to calm her racing heart. She bit down on her lip to keep from crying. *Please, God, don't let Phyllis or the others notice that I'm upset.*

Phyllis clung to Hank, both waving goodnight to the rest of the teens as they piled into vehicles and left the countryside. Hank hopped into the driver's seat, while Phyllis slid in next to him from the passenger side. Carolyn hoisted her leg up and sat near the door.

Phyllis eyed her inside Hank's pick-up truck.

Carolyn turned her head to gape out the window, rolling it down. "I'm desperate for some fresh air." She could sense that Phyllis was still staring at her. She knew her friend surmised that something wasn't quite right, but Carolyn didn't dare turn her head to look. She could not take the chance.

Phyllis finally whispered in her ear, "Did you get your period?"

Carolyn let out a huge sigh. *Thank you, God.* She continued to stare out the window and pretend she was enjoying the breeze. "No. I'm just tired, and the vodka got to me. I have to pull my act together before I get home." Phyllis readily accepted the excuse. She suspected that her friend was so wrapped up in her new-couple bliss that she couldn't have cared less about Carolyn right then.

Her friends dropped her at the curb. "See you guys later," Carolyn mumbled as she descended from Hank's truck.

Phyllis yelled, "Be sure to dream about kissing Paul Johns tonight!"

Carolyn exhaled a cavernous sigh and lumbered across the patio up the back steps. She paused for a few minutes at the top, trying to get the courage to go inside. She peeked through the back door past the laundry room and into the kitchen, relieved that her parents were not in there. She turned the knob as silently as possible. Slowly she cracked open the door and listened. She could hear them talking in the living room. She carefully shut the door behind herself and offered a perfunctory greeting toward the front of the house, as she made a hasty retreat into the bathroom. She prayed that Adeline was already asleep and that her mom wouldn't come to inquire how the evening had been.

She stared at herself in the mirror over the sink. She blinked a few times because she barely recognized herself. She heard herself ask the girl in the mirror, "What should I do?"

Carolyn paced back and forth in the compact space, silent tears rolling down her cheeks. She ripped all the bobby pins out of her hair and angrily threw them in the sink. Her fingers reached up under her hair and onto her scalp, forcefully rubbing out the fancy hairdo. She could not get clarity in her head no matter how many times she shook it. She realized she was taking a lot of time in the bathroom, but she wasn't anywhere near ready to escape its confines.

She decided to jump in the shower. After turning on the water, she reached behind her to unzip her dress, which made her bristle. She unhooked her garter straps and pushed her nylons down around her ankles. Holding onto the sink with her left hand, she pulled off the stockings one by one with her right. It took great effort to remove her garter and panties, yet she longed to step into the steamy haven.

She gingerly removed one shoulder of her dress at a time, as if it hurt. It fell around her ankles, leaving her fully exposed. She stepped one leg over the tub and spotted a streak of dried blood on her thigh. She nearly fell over from the shock. Visions of terror flooded the bathroom. *I just need to get all the way in!* Carolyn pulled the rest of her frame inside and wrangled the shower curtain closed. In the nick of time.

Her mother rapped gently at the door. "Carolyn, is that you?"

"Yeah, Mom."

"What are you doing in the shower?"

"Um, I was a sweaty mess from dancing so much. I didn't want to crawl into the clean bed until I bathed."

"Okay. But we want to hear about your night."

Carolyn gulped. *No, you don't.* She pushed the plug down in the tub to let it fill with the shower water, as hot as she could stand it. She grabbed her washcloth and scrubbed herself as hard as she could. *I have to get him off of me!* It was to no avail. She could not rid herself of Skip Jergen, no matter how long or how hard she ran the soapy washcloth over her arms and legs. She cranked up the water as hot as it could go and sank into the tub. She closed her eyes and banged her head against the tile. *How am I ever going to get out of here?* Not wanting to face the "how," she opted for soaking until the water was tepid.

She knew that the longer she stayed in there, the more suspicious her parents would become. She finally fished into the water and yanked the plug. She watched until the last bit of suds had spiraled down the drain. Starting to shiver, she reached over the edge and lifted an aqua terrycloth bath sheet to her chest. It seemed heavy. She desperately yearned to cover herself from the shame. And from him. The images of Skip were so clear it was as though he were standing there watching her. She wrapped the towel tightly around herself, taking extra care to make sure none of her private parts were showing. She instantly hated her body. It had betrayed her. She was no longer a beautiful princess. She was dirty. Filthy.

She managed to dry off before the urge to vomit hit her. She turned the water back on in the tub and the sink faucet, too, to drown out the sound of her throwing up. She rolled over onto the cold brown tile, clutching herself between her legs. The mental pain was worse than the physical. Or was the physical pain worse?

With her head lowered, she saw her underpants out of the corner of her eye. They were bloody. *I have to wash those out.*

Her mom was at the door again. "Did you have a good time?"

Carolyn bristled but managed to answer, "Yes. Paul was an exemplary gentleman." Carolyn wanted to add, *Skip wasn't,* but she kept that to herself.

"Glad to hear it. Hey, sweetie, your dad and I are tired. You took way too long for us to hear all the details. We're headed to bed, okay?"

"Fine, Mom. I'll hurry so you two can use the bathroom."

"That'd be great. See you in the morning."

"Mhmm," muttered Carolyn. She scrubbed her panties clean, wrung them out, and stuck them under her towel. She finished brushing her teeth and checked her beleaguered face in the mirror. *Oh well, here goes.* She peeked through a slit and saw her parents walking into their bedroom. She waited until she heard their door close. Then she quietly escaped, bound in her towel, and tiptoed up the stairs and across the landing to her room—her formal wear in hand. She hid her underwear in the back of the closet to dry.

She put on clean panties from her drawer, along with a nightgown. Folding back her side of the covers, she carefully climbed into bed, trying not to wake Adeline. She could never hide the facts from her sister. She'd want every single solitary detail. Carolyn couldn't bear to tell her the truth.

Clean as she was, she still felt scummy and swore bugs were crawling over her. She rubbed her legs as if to send them off in a different direction. Her side of the bed was icy cold, and she struggled to get warm. She finally got up and grabbed another blanket. She spotted her childhood teddy bear in the corner, so she grabbed that too. Back in bed, she hugged the stuffed animal, begging it to bring her comfort.

After a fitful night, Carolyn awoke later than usual and was relieved to discover Adeline's side of the bed empty. *Thank God she's already up.*

Wounded in places she never knew could hurt, she lay in shock—as if she couldn't move. Her groggy brain was jumbled and only partially there. Any thoughts were incomplete and fragmented, as though she had been drugged. She didn't recognize anything she was sensing. Nothing looked the same, and everything looked foreign. Her room appeared gloomy, even though the sun was streaming through the windows. The statues of saints that sat on the shelf were no longer heavenly friends. Instead, Carolyn absorbed their judgment.

She shook her head in doubt. What had happened the previous night couldn't possibly have happened. And, yet, it had. She lay there, shaking her head as if attempting to undo the events and eject them from her brain. She became acutely aware of the impossibility of that. It *had* happened, and she had no one to blame but herself. Skip had called her out for flirting with him on the dance floor, and she had. She had kept drinking the lemonade, even after she realized it contained alcohol. It was clear to her now that drinking was a costly mistake. Yes, it was all crystal clear now. But it was too late. She made two fists and slammed them as hard as she could against her mattress.

She was broken, smashed to pieces, and her well-ordered life had dissolved into an unsolvable jigsaw puzzle. She lay flat on her back, staring at the ceiling, replaying the bad turn of events over and over in her head, feeling addled and foolish. *How could such a superb night have ended up so terribly wrong?* Stinging tears welled in her eyes, and she pounded the mattress over and over again, whimpering softly, NO! NO! NO! *My mom was so right; consuming alcohol comes with a cost.* She felt deep regret for so easily abandoning her vow never to drink.

In hindsight, Carolyn had an uneasy sensation about Skip the first time he asked her to dance, but she disregarded it when Paul gave the nod. She also ignored it when Skip no longer asked her to dance but rather demanded it, even pulling her onto the dance floor at times. She loved to dance, and Skip was a magnificent dancer. She had just wanted to have some fun at her first grown-up party.

Instead, she was assaulted. *That's what it was, right?* She wasn't sure what to call it. She knew it wasn't romantic, as Skip had intimated. At least she was hoping it wasn't. She'd give anything to rewind the clock and undrink that lemonade, but she couldn't. It had happened. To her. And she needed to accept it. No one else had to be burdened by her dumb error in judgment. She beseeched God to wipe it from her memory.

CHAPTER SIX

Carolyn lay motionless in her bed, sending up pleas that she could forget that awful thirty minutes of her life. *Please, God, please.*

To block it all out and attempt to ignore the growing mud-filled chasm in her core, she tried to focus all her energy and attention toward what was left of her junior year, especially the homework she needed to tackle the remainder of the weekend. Her efforts that morning were to no avail. Her body felt like it weighed a ton, and the images of last night were too raw. Her mind was a runaway train. Her heart thudded as she saw the locomotive of her life run off the rails.

She was consumed with how stupid she had been. Skip had accused her of flirting with him. She didn't realize she had, but maybe he was right. After all, she did enjoy the dancing, and she did allow him to escort her in the dark. *Was that flirting? It must have been. I must have been sending all the wrong signals.*

The mental tape of the night replayed on automatic rewind. On and on, the horror movie swirled in Carolyn's head, and Skip's accusations began to seem as if they were facts. She was a trapped creature with nowhere to turn. After all, who could she tell? Not her parents. Not Adeline. *It would flatten them.* Certainly not Phyllis. *Whatever would she think of me?* Although the two were best friends, Carolyn had learned a long time ago that keeping secrets was not her best friend's forte. Probably the first thing Phyllis would do is run and tell Mrs. Norton, who had a reputation of gossiping around town and acting as judge and jury of everyone. Carolyn could not afford this.

Alas! The horrible encounter with Skip Jergen must have been *her* fault. Her own damn fault. She was going to have to deal with it. Alone. Her soul ached while her heart pulsated inside her chest. The rest of her registered as raw and vacant.

Robotically, she sat up and swung her legs over the edge of the bed. She stared blankly off into space, occasionally blinking and then shaking her head again and again as if to toss out the horror. Her gut was in knots and, although she was usually starving in the mornings, food was the farthest thing from her mind. *I never want to eat again. Ever!* She wanted to scream, but her emotions were frozen inside of her. She was desolate. Her soul seemed missing.

***

She barely remembered Saturday but must have fielded questions and performed her obligatory duties as best she could, since no one called attention to anything amiss. She had put all her best acting skills to the test. *I deserve an Oscar.* She spent most of Sunday after Mass digging into homework and trying to disregard what had happened, but that was impossible. She would have to hide this for the rest of her life. She certainly did not want Paul to find out. That would be unbearably humiliating, and he would never want to be anywhere near her after that!

***

On Monday, Carolyn went to school per protocol, both hoping and not hoping to see Paul and expending great energy trying to avoid Skip Jergen. She was able to do the latter quite readily.

Phyllis was already waiting at her locker. "Skip Jergen left."

Carolyn was shell-shocked but managed to ask, "What do you mean 'left'?"

"Hank heard a rumor that Skip left on Saturday to join the military. Not only that, but his whole family has also packed up and moved back to their home state of Kansas. Not one Jergen remains in Grand Lake."

Carolyn's face sagged. Her brain wrestled as she tried to develop this news. He was gone, along with the rest of the Jergens too, but that didn't change the fact that she had been defiled. This grieved her soul like no sin ever had. *At least I won't have to look at him.* "Well, good for them, I guess."

She gritted her teeth and plastered a fake half-smile on her face as she walked down the halls, hoping no one noticed that she was now a devastated and tainted young woman. She longed to seek out her favorite counselor, but she couldn't do that. Mrs. Johnson would call her mom. A forlorn Carolyn sauntered by the counseling office a few times, longing to go in, but she couldn't. *What would I say anyway? I got drunk at the post-formal party and was intimate with a boy?* That was the ugly truth.

She suffered the hours in silence. She searched for some relief that her assaulter was not in the vicinity, but no reassurance came. Behind her Latin book, and again behind her U.S. History book, she shed soft tears and blamed it on a cold when she searched inside her purse for tissues. *I'm such a fake. Nope. Moral fraud is more accurate.* It was the longest day of

31

Carolyn Fandel's entire life, and she could not even confront her assaulter nor get the apology she was due.

It was feasible that she might never see his face again. She stared into her locker at the end of the day. She pictured him, and it terrified her. The image of his face appeared huge, looming. Those eyes were no longer gorgeous. They were sinister. The memory of him gyrating inside her made her gut churn. She recalled his smell and wretched from the Old Spice memory. She darted into the bathroom closest to her locker.

Carolyn shook her head, which was awash with a staggering concept: *Skip has skipped town. How ironic, that name!* She never had to see him again. She could go on pretending to everybody that she was the same Carolyn Fandel they had always known. She made a concerted effort then and there to throw herself into her academics and her play rehearsals.

CHAPTER SEVEN

Life almost got back to normal—except for the nightmares. Their intensity, despite Carolyn's most fervent wish, did not abate. She caught herself instinctively bringing her knees up to her chest, pulling her nightgown down around her ankles, and wrapping her arms around her shins. She rolled onto her side in a tucked fetal position and pulled the covers close under her chin for safety. Sometimes, she inched as close as she dared to Adeline merely for the warmth of another human. No matter what she did, she felt cold and bare with no one to care about her inner cries.

The hellish visions had begun right after the incident and haunted her every night since, sometimes so forcefully, they catapulted her awake. On occasion, her upright jolt roused Adeline. "What is going on, Carolyn?"

She was able to thwart her sister's curiosity because Adeline fell right back to sleep. Thank goodness for that, because Carolyn had no idea how to explain—although she ached to.

Panic attacks appeared out of nowhere. When out for a stroll along the beach, one minute she was fine, and the next minute, her throat shut tight as if someone had tied a rope around it. The weight of this great beast within her seemingly sat on her lungs and constricted her breath. *Is this how a heart attack feels?* The only thing she could do was suffer in silence. And berate herself. *I was SO stupid!*

She wanted to blurt it all out as a way of unloading it. But she couldn't tell anybody. *Please, God, have no one inquire about the status of my relationship with Paul.* They were still friends, but the spark had died out. At least for Carolyn, and it depressed her.

She now lived her daily existence with heaviness, along with tight lips, something that Carolyn could tell her mother noted. Her mom often looked at her expecting a conversation, but Carolyn had become accustomed to saying nothing, if possible. Gone were the typical teenage details of who said what to whom at school, who was wearing what, who was dating, who was not. She knew her mother wasn't oblivious. During the weeks following the formal, her mom kept asking what was wrong, but Carolyn did not disclose any of the rotten details.

"Okay. I'll stop pestering you. I recall what it's like to be sixteen. Remember, though, I'm always here for you, Doll."

Grateful for this reprieve, she said, "Thanks, Mom."

"But is everything okay with Paul?"

Ugh! The question she dreaded most was upon her. "Not so much. I'm trying to figure it out."

"I'm sorry to hear that. He's such a nice young man."

Conflicted, Carolyn rolled her eyes. She was glad that her mom was willing to let the conversation fade so quickly, but she desperately yearned to tell her everything.

The days continued with Carolyn longing to confide in someone—anyone—yet she could not breathe a word of this horrible event to one living soul. Revealing her secret would cause scandal to her family. She might lose friends. She might lose everything and everyone she loved. Tormented, she tried in vain to equalize her reality with her faith. Her introspection concluded that her life, as she knew it, was void of hope.

She had been to Confession to rid herself of the sin of flirting and leading a boy on but neglected to tell her pastor all the details. Full disclosure was too painful. It was a real struggle for her to align the bad angel dressed in red on her left shoulder with the good angel dressed in white on her right. They were constantly fighting, and Carolyn was on both sides, often at the same time.

She came close to telling the good Father one other Saturday morning in the confessional. Embarrassed, she lost her nerve at the last minute. Her mouth would not form the words. She knew she wasn't being forthright, but saying it made it too real. Too raw. In her fear, she had forgotten that she was confessing to Jesus himself. She justified that God would forgive her sin of omission. She calculated that He already knew the details anyway. *No reason to say it out loud.* Therefore, without full disclosure, she prayed her Act of Contrition, and the priest absolved her sins with the beautiful words:

"God, the Father of mercies, through the death and resurrection of His Son, has reconciled the world to Himself and sent the Holy Spirit among us for the forgiveness of sins. Through the ministry of the Church may God give you pardon and peace, and I absolve you from your sins in the name of the Father, and of the Son, and of the Holy Spirit."

Carolyn exited the confessional. *It's settled then. God has forgiven me. At least I have restored order with Him.*

She would probably never reconcile with her assaulter, for Skip was off training for the military. An image of him flashed briefly, causing panic to rise. She hid behind the mammoth bur oak on the church property until she could pull herself together. Reluctantly, she returned with hidden shame to her porch, feeling unforgiven, striving to convince herself that all was well. Putting the fake smile back on her face, she resolved once again to move on with her life.

***

Paul expended great energy trying to keep a relationship with Carolyn alive, but he had perceived a change in her. She could detect the confusion in his tender brown eyes, though he never voiced it. Instead, he continued walking her to class and sitting by her in the library whenever the chance arose. He didn't know it, but his attention afforded her an element of safety she craved. She honestly didn't know what she would do without it. Nor did she want to try.

Carolyn sensed deep in her being that Paul was falling in love with her. She willed herself to return the affection and did so, in part. But she maintained a cautious reserve, built by the wall that had been erected and doused with guilt on that fateful night. For her, Paul represented a glimmer of assurance that all was well. She found comfort in having his arms around her when they hugged—especially after one of their walks along the lakeshore. In those moments, she could almost relate to her old self.

Paul seemed to have decided to be satisfied with what they had. Carolyn had made it clear they were remaining at the "good friends" level. He had no idea that she yearned to be attached as more than friends. She wished she could let down her guard. But the dark formal night had built a barrier she had no idea how to tear down, and she was petrified to try. She feared losing the one person with whom she could be most herself.

A month passed, and then two, and thankfully the nightmares and flashbacks lessened. Carolyn had been able to go about her life and revisit the assault only a few times each day—which she counted as a victory. She was regaining her confidence, and the fake smile became a more genuine one. She had started to find moments where she could relax with Paul, and she had hope for growing the relationship. They had even gone on another date, and Carolyn had a great time. The Lord was blessing her, and she was aware. *Thank you, God.*

She breathed a contented sigh as she stepped into the girls' bathroom. She even smiled at herself as she passed the mirror on the way into the stall. Pausing to ponder her image, she saw beauty—something that had been hiding from her for many weeks now. *It's been a long time since I've felt attractive.* The fresh notion surprised her, and Carolyn realized that she was happy. Suddenly having a desire to look her best, she undid her ponytail and neatened it up, making sure it was flawless. *That looks good, if I do say so myself!* After another satisfactory grin, she entered the stall. Smiling, she shut the gray door and slid the barrel lock closed.

CHAPTER EIGHT

Carolyn had been so busy trying to regain normalcy that she hadn't had time to notice one major thing. While sitting on the toilet, it dawned on her, and her mouth fell open. Any happiness immediately vanished.

Calculating backward, *I haven't had a period since before the spring formal.* Instant impending dread set in, as if someone had placed an enormous chunk of concrete against her ribs. She knew very well what this might mean and leaned back against the toilet tank. She struggled to breathe. Her throat went dry. Her chest ached. Her forehead broke out in a sweat. She was suddenly so hot everywhere—inside and out. She pivoted, knelt, and heaved up the contents from her lunch. Robotically, she finished in the stall, spit into the bowl one more time, wiped her mouth with toilet paper, and flushed the commode. At the sink, she splashed cold water on her face and swished some around in her mouth, bending over to spit it out. She straightened and rubbed her abdomen back and forth directly over her womb, staring blankly into the mirror. She barely recognized the pallid, paralyzed face staring back. Carolyn's spirit was in shambles, matching the feelings in her stomach.

Her heart drummed through her light green blouse with the realization that she probably now had an even bigger secret to keep. A new, awful reality came into focus, and it scared her so much that she shouted out loud, "NOOOO!" She gasped and turned around to make sure she was still alone in the school bathroom. Through an exhaled breath, she begged God to give her something many girls her age beg Him to take away: her period. *Please, Jesus!*

She noted the time on her watch. Late for her last class. She contemplated leaving school property and hiding out until it was time to go home, but her conscience wouldn't let her do that. Instead, she stayed in the bathroom until some color came back to her face. *Where can I go? The school office? No. Too many people in there who will ask questions and call my mom. I'll go to the counseling office and tell them I'm not feeling well. Mrs. Johnson will let me stay in there and rest until it's time for play practice.*

Carolyn suffered through drama rehearsal, getting reprimanded several times by the director to put more emotion into her lines.

During the next few weeks, she expended a lot of wasted effort hoping against hope, endeavoring to stay in her preferred state of denial. But late one evening, she realized she had missed a third period and knew for sure that she was in trouble. BIG trouble.

With Adeline already asleep in the double bed the sisters shared, Carolyn sat on the edge of the mattress, feeling alone. Three missed periods. *Three.* A sick, sinking feeling took up residence in her body and seemed to emanate into the room. She swung her feet off the floor and onto the bed, laying her head on her pillow. She pulled the covers up around her and panted quietly in fear. It was a matter of time before the whole world found out what she had done. Or what had been done to her. It was hard for her to tell the difference. She tucked herself in the familiar fetal position and tried not to shudder nor cry for fear of waking Adeline. She lay balled up as if the wind had been knocked out of her, feeling vulnerable and stupid. Her face was hot with embarrassment, even though no one could see her in the dark of the bedroom. And when she finally fell asleep, she had a new nightmare—one that included a screaming baby.

Morning knocked Carolyn awake with the realization she could not hide this secret forever unless she ran away and never came back. *But how would I survive without my Fandels?* Maybe Phyllis could help. *The Nortons have connections.* Phyllis's parents were well-off and had a lot of acquaintances Carolyn's didn't.

She recalled once last summer when she was over at Phyllis's house. Mrs. Norton was on the phone talking to someone, going on and on about Phyllis's cousin, who had gotten herself "in trouble." Not only had Mrs. Norton called her niece a bunch of unflattering names, but she also said something that Carolyn, at the time, didn't quite understand. "I told her flat out that she ought to go see the old doc up north and get it taken care of. Then it would be over, and no one would ever have to know it happened."

Carolyn had asked Phyllis what her mother meant. Her friend had said that her mother knew a doctor in northern Michigan who could bring on a girl's period if she needed it done. Carolyn was confused but didn't dare ask any more questions.

Carolyn told her mom about the incident later and vividly remembered her mother being shocked that Mrs. Norton had said such a thing. Her mom had let out an audible gasp and a "Lord, have mercy!"

Then her mom told her that sometimes girls got pregnant out of wedlock and that some people believed it best to end the pregnancy by abortion. Carolyn was still naïve enough not to be able to put all the pieces together, but she knew her mother did not approve of Mrs. Norton nor her advice. What she remembered most was her mom saying, "That new life is a baby who does not deserve to have its life ended, no matter how it began."

Carolyn had never forgotten those words, and they echoed loudly now inside her. *On second thought, the Nortons aren't the ones to go to for guidance.*

She counted on her fingers nine months from the spring formal. Sometime around the New Year, she would be a mother. She froze as veracity whacked her. *I already AM a mother!!!* Thrashing, painful panic moved in. It throbbed in her throat and her ears. She felt pinned in place with no way to escape.

She had to tell someone now, but who? *How will my parents react? What is going to happen to me? Will I be able to graduate? What does this mean for Paul and me?*

Too many questions. Too few answers. One thing was certain. She had a baby growing inside of her.

One probing question looped: *WHY, LORD?*

One prayer of supplication did the same: *LORD, HELP!*

CHAPTER NINE

Trying not to think about what was happening inside of her, Carolyn strove to put aside her aching gut for the sake of the success of the play and finish her junior year strong, which she was barely able to accomplish. She managed to make it to the end of the school year without breathing a word to anybody. This took substantial effort, especially listening to Phyllis, who constantly babbled about how the formal was the beginning of her great relationship with Hank. In some ways, Carolyn supposed she should be glad for Phyllis's running mouth. Not being able to get a word in edgewise definitely saved her from divulging the secret.

The only topics Phyllis yakked about were her romance and to express curiosity about whether Carolyn had let Paul get to second base. "Have you let him put his hand up your shirt?"

"No!" Carolyn shuddered. She realized her best friend was going down a path she had never considered with Paul, especially after what had happened. Carolyn had to fight to keep the horror of the memory from showing up on her face. Now was not a good time to spill.

Nothing connected to that awful ordeal was easy. That it had happened in the first place. That she was stupid. That she was pregnant. That she was constantly trying to hide her morning sickness. That she had spent hours crying and knowing she could tell no one. That she had to come up with a plan to solve this all on her own. That Paul would dump her like a hot potato if he found out the truth.

Her entire being was consumed by this skeleton in the closet of her soul. Prayer granted her a modicum of comfort as she became more resigned to her reality. She thought about a dozen times a day, *Mother Mary, make haste to help me.* The dispirited teen desperately wanted to believe that the Mother of Christ would somehow come to her aid and take her sad prayers to her Son, Jesus. Carolyn Fandel couldn't see much hope beyond that.

When the waves of nausea hit, she spiritually sensed someone with direct connections to God assisting her to keep suspicion at bay. The vomiting came when no one questioned why she was ill. When Auntie

Dora was visiting other nieces and nephews around the state and not there to keep her eagle eye on the children's every move. Or when it might seem she'd been bitten by the same spring flu bug that had stricken some of her siblings. Or at school in the girls' bathroom at the end of the hall when miraculously no one else was in there. Oddly, these signs encouraged her to keep her faith strong in those early weeks. She even prayed that God continued to allow her to puke under cloaked explanations. *I'm the lamest Christian alive to bother God with my half-witted requests*, brooded Carolyn. Her reality and her faith continued to battle one another. *Please, God, if You can hear me, clear up this mess.*

She desperately hoped even her weakest prayers would add some weight to her anchor in this turbulent storm. But the anchor had a very short rope, and her ship of life continued to thrash about in the tempestuous sea no matter how sincere her anguished cries.

During her silent bedtime prayers one evening, it appeared that the waves had finally abated. The Holy Spirit alit with surety. It was time to share her secret with her mother. The storm quieted in a way it had not yet been able to be appeased, and her soul settled. For the first time since that dreadful atrocity, Carolyn fell peacefully asleep to the cadence of her heavenward pleas. Her dreams that night were full of normal actions and reactions—the best sleep she had had for nearly three months.

CHAPTER TEN

Carolyn awakened to a dreary, misty day where it seemed the sun had failed to rise. She lay in bed for a long time, seemingly unable to move. Panic had replaced the peace that had lulled her to sleep. Fear had crept back into her heart and darkened it to match her sun-impoverished room. It took every ounce of determination to will herself to get out of bed and face her life-changing task. *Come on, Carolyn, you have to do it.*

Finally, she drew in a huge breath and forced herself to sit up. She was drained, despite the restful slumber. She inched to the edge of the bed until her feet hit the floor. It took all of her strength to stand up and proceed toward the closet to select her clothes. She opted for a baggy summer jumpsuit, one that didn't require a bra. She was going for pure comfort, even though she was anything but comfortable. Her breasts had been painfully tender, something she understood occurred with pregnancy. She let out a long sigh and opened her bedroom door.

Facing the looming staircase ahead, it seemed long and narrow. Constricting. But she had to descend those steps and honestly face her future. She paused at each one, fighting the urge to retreat. Too quickly, it seemed, she reached the bottom and made her way through Bing Crosby's crooning of "You'll Never Know" wafting from the phonograph in the dining room. It irritated her, and she wanted to turn him off but didn't.

***

There would be a window of about three hours that Tuesday morning in late June when all of Carolyn's siblings were out of the house. Silvester would be mowing the neighbors' lawns. Adeline would still be at a friend's house from a summer sleepover. And the three younger boys would be at Aunt Marilyn's all day for Monopoly and Risk battles with their cousins.

Carolyn admired that her mother was such a masterful planner, creating opportunities for one-on-one moments with each of her children—an affectionate message that getting to know them in a deeply personal way was important to her. Carolyn appreciated the effort that was required to farm out her siblings and make these occasions happen. Her mother's outward enthusiasm demonstrated that she prized this one-on-one luxury. In turn, each of the Fandel kids looked forward to spending time with her. Fun facts about her growing-up years with her siblings made for lots of laughter.

Their mom solicited from each child how to spend their together-time. For Carolyn, "bonus bonding," as the kids eventually dubbed it, meant rummaging through Dora's fabric bag for larger remnants and designing a new article of clothing.

***

She turned the corner into the kitchen, all but forgetting that this morning was *her* special time. Then she saw that the sewing machine had already been set up. The fabric choices and scissors were methodically laid out with the pattern they had previously selected. Her heart took an even deeper nosedive and dropped to the pit of her gut.

Her mom sat sipping her coffee, waiting with an enormous smile of Dana Fandel enthusiasm. Her rosary was lying on top of the Bible. It was cracked open to Romans, Carolyn's favorite book of the New Testament. Carolyn heaved a heavy sigh. *Lord, I can't do this.*

On the table was a plate of raisin bran muffins, pats of butter, and a prepared half-grapefruit with sugar on top—components of Carolyn's favorite breakfast. Her throat gulped as she forced a smile of appreciation toward her mother.

It was unconvincing. Her mom took one glimpse at her face and could tell it was serious. "What is it, Doll?" As soon as Carolyn heard the term of endearment, she began to weep.

Her mother stood up and drew Carolyn into her arms. While she sobbed, her mom whispered, "No matter what it is, everything will be okay." For an instant, the comfort of being held by her mother made Carolyn envision herself as a safe six-year-old girl instead of a terrified sixteen-year-old pregnant mother. Her mom continued to hold her, peppering her with questions trying to get to the bottom of it. "Were you not able to get your classes for the fall semester?'

"No."

"Did you and Paul decide to call off your special friendship?"

"No."

She dreaded having to tell her mother. The longer the interrogation went on, the more Carolyn was tempted to turn away, bolt out the door, and never come back.

"Carolyn, something is wrong. I have known it since the night of the dance. You will feel better if you tell me."

Oh, no, I won't.

"Whatever it is, we can fix it."

Oh, no, we can't.

Her gut hurt so bad. She was about to give her mom the shock of her life. She decided to just say it. *Here goes.* "I'm pregnant."

Without saying a word, her mother dropped her arms, turned her back, and walked away from Carolyn. She bent over the record player in the dining room and shut off the music, which slowed to a deep crawl and stopped. A great silence followed. So silent, it was deafening. Carolyn's thoughts raced. Her ears were throbbing. Her heart was hammering so strongly she was sure it would come crashing through her chest.

Her dazed mother returned and wrapped Carolyn in her arms but stood motionless. She seemed unable to breathe. She could hear her mom take in a few quick sporadic breaths as if to bring herself back to life. Her mom still was not speaking, which worried Carolyn. *She hates me. I'm an awful daughter.*

She released Carolyn and pulled away, searching her face. She could tell her mom was hoping against hope that she had misheard. But she had not. A distraught daughter was still in front of her. Her mom reached for and held onto the table. She grabbed Carolyn's hands to join her. They sat down together, both heavy with the world's weight on their shoulders. Her mom held her hands, kept eye contact, and cried with her. Now and then, her mom would shake her head as if trying to make sense of what she had heard.

Carolyn's sad green eyes stared back. "I'm so sorry, Mom. I'm so sorry." In an attempt to make it better, she added that she had been to Confession.

Her mom blew her nose. "Sweetie, I am so sorry for you. Can you tell me how this happened? Is Paul the father?"

"NO!" Carolyn screeched. "Paul would never have done that to me!"

"I'm sorry. I don't understand. How could you possibly be pregnant?"

Carolyn composed herself, trying to be as brave as possible. Throughout the ugly, sordid story, her voice trembled. She melted into sobs of anguish. She hated having to repeat it. Horrific memories resurfaced. She had to stop several times to get herself under control. All the while, her mother held her and tried to soothe her.

"There, there, Doll," her mom said, rubbing her shoulders. "We'll be okay." Carolyn knew her mom well enough to know that her soul ached—both for herself and her daughter's brokenness. Her mom listened calmly to the horror story, but inside, Carolyn was sure her mother was screaming. Her mom's face had a pained expression. She appeared as frightened as Carolyn herself.

Her mom blinked back tears. Now and then, she would open her mouth, only to shut it again. Carolyn was certain her mother must hate her. At the very least, she must be furious. She imagined her mom was trying to figure out a way to kick her out of the house. That's what happened to her cousin who got pregnant. Her old fears about having to leave her family home filled her entirely with dread.

Carolyn examined her mother's face. Her eyes were squinted as if she were trying to get a clearer picture. She watched her mom shake her head from side to side, as if in disbelief. And she took a lot of deep breaths. She could tell her mom was contemplating something—probably whether Carolyn had or had not been the instigator. After all, it was a paradox that had driven Carolyn herself insane. She figured her mom had the same dilemma. Her mom bit her lip as if to hold her tongue. Her silence nearly drove Carolyn crazy. She was ready to answer any question. She willed her mother to say something. Anything. *Please, God, make her talk!*

When nothing came, guilt overcame her. *I'm the worst daughter on earth.* She tumbled out her flirtatious part. "I wanted to dance with Skip. He's so popular. I guess I was sending the wrong signals." As she unfurled those details, her mom's lip quivered. Carolyn wept bitterly. "I'm so sorry, Mom!"

"I can see that you are. I am so sorry you are in this predicament. Right now, to be honest, my head is swimming. I need a moment."

Carolyn nodded as if she understood, but she didn't. She had been carrying the weight of this secret for too long. She had hoped that telling her mom would make her feel better, but it didn't. She began to cry again. Not tears of anguish. Tears of disappointment.

"Oh, Carolyn, now I am the one who's sorry. I don't want it to be worse for you than it already is." She settled her hands around Carolyn's shoulders and gave her a gentle squeeze as if to reassure her. "I am here for you." She offered her best motherly smile. "It will be okay. Our love for you is without limits. We will sort this whole thing out alongside you. I promise."

Her mom sounded convincing. Carolyn wanted to trust the words, as she had been able to her whole life.

For what remained of their private three hours, sewing was cast aside. She and her mother tried to cobble together a plan. Under no circumstance was Auntie Dora to know. At least not for a while. She was too interested in the personal lives of others. Quite the chatterbox, she relished in sharing unfiltered facts about Carolyn, her folks, and the rest of the kids with the other members of the extended Fandel clan. Or with someone she met on the street. Dora wasn't fussy about her audience.

If Carolyn could have her choice, no one would ever find out. She felt terrible for bringing this problem to her devoted mother, risking scandal to her good family. The last thing she wanted was to cause more pain.

Dejected, she sat at the table, picking at her now dried-up muffin. She skimmed over the grapefruit with the back of her fork, scraping the sugar away. *I'm undeserving of anything good.* Amidst copious, soulful sobs, she cried out, "I'm so sorry, Mama! I'm so sorry for doing this to you! I didn't mean to!" She couldn't even bear to look at her mom anymore. In those few minutes, her mother seemed older and more tired. Carolyn dropped her face, shoving her plate out of the way.

Her mom wended her way around the table. From behind her, her mother's warm hands touched her shoulders. She began to rub them. Back and forth, oh so gently. It was something her mom did to try to soothe her whenever she was upset. She heard her mom release another heavy sigh. She could tell that her mom was trying to push aside despair. It wrecked Carolyn how deeply she had upset her. Carolyn knotted up and moved to the side in pain—a pain so engulfing and intense that she doubled over and wept again.

Carolyn had caused her mom tremendous sorrow. She could hear the tears in her mom's voice when she spoke. "Well, there is no way to make this not true. I'm anguished for you. I love you more than you could possibly understand." Her mom sniffled and wiped her eyes with her apron bottom.

Carolyn reached up to her shoulders and put her hands over her mother's. "I love you, too, Mom."

"I'm proud of you for taking this straight to the confessional, but this is not your fault. Nonetheless, the grace of the sacrament and the power of God's forgiveness is healing. Through prayer and listening to God, our mode of action will become clear. One thing's for sure. God loves you. Our Blessed Mother loves you. And your father and I love you. We will get through this together. You will not be alone."

Carolyn nodded her tear-streaked face, willing herself to believe her mother. She gasped out a question through more sobs. "What…am…I…going…to…do…Mom?" She stood up, turned, and clung to her mom like she was at the end of a lifeline. Her mom hugged her tighter and swayed back and forth in the kitchen, humming. The lull helped Carolyn's rigid body to loosen up.

Into her ear, her mom whispered, "Well, Carolyn, you're going to persevere in prayer. And so am I. And we're going to come up with a plan. The sooner we patch one together, the better it will be." She had hoped her mom could figure out what to do. Now she prayed it to be so.

With Auntie Dora away for a few days, the kids out of the house, and her dad away on business, she and her mother brainstormed. What if Carolyn disappeared to take care of a long-lost relative? It was not uncommon for older children to take on such responsibility. While away, she could have her baby, and her parents could adopt the infant as their own. Plausible.

A second plan included going to live with a distant cousin in Detroit. They could tell people that Carolyn had an illness not treatable in a small town. She could adopt the baby out to a family with whom the Fandels had no connection. She could then return to school the second semester of her senior year, healthy, and be graduated on time. A ridiculous plan filled with outright lies, so they scrapped it with the understanding that it might be able to be amended later.

She had to go away somewhere, at least until after the baby was born. Staying in Grand Lake would invite ostracization. Rumors would fly. And the school was not going to allow a pregnant girl in their halls.

"Let's let it go for now," said her mom. "I've got a busy week ahead with the other kids. They must not get a whiff of anything until your dad and I decide on a plan."

"I don't want them to know ever!" shouted Carolyn.

Come Friday, however, she would have to repeat the whole terrible mess and upend her father's world as she had done to her mother's. Her mom would not give him this news over the phone. News of this magnitude should never be uttered on the party line they shared with the neighbors on the block.

On the one hand, she longed for her father to return. Her dad had a level head. He could make everything seem okay. On the other hand, she dreaded it. *It's going to break him. And he'll be so angry about the drinking. And about my behavior.* How angry was yet to be seen. In the meantime, Carolyn offered a silent *God bless my dad.* It had to suffice, for now.

With that, the weight was somewhat alleviated from her shoulders. The hardest part behind her, at least now she had her mom as an ally. She dreaded telling her father but, at the same time, ached to see him. For an instant, she saw her parents as one highly capable unit. She took a cleansing breath, trying to inhale that one iota of consolation.

CHAPTER ELEVEN

The week dragged for Carolyn and her mother like a thousand-pound weight. The burden of keeping the secret was substantial. Trying to conceal the worry and not let it show on their faces was challenging. It would have been so easy to give in to emotion and blurt out the truth, especially in those weak nighttime stretches when the sisters were alone in their room. But Carolyn remained steadfast in silence, offering private rosaries instead, night after night. Little sacrifices. There was no good reason for Adeline to know. *Not yet.* No plan had been decided. *Why upset her?* Carolyn was anxious, yet she remained resolute in holding her plight close to her soul, as she waited for Friday. Her mom had said this would be best, and Carolyn had to dig deep inside herself to trust that advice.

She waded through the living room and sat in her dad's favorite chair. Longing for a big fatherly hug, it was the best she could do. *But will he even want to hug me?* She hoped so. *Or will he be disgusted with me once he learns of my condition? Will he kick me out of the house?* After all, her dad's brother had done precisely that to his daughter. The recollection set off an internal alarm. Once again, she was transported back to her younger days of fear and started to cry. To avoid being seen, she went behind his chair and slithered down in the corner. As tears stung her eyes, strong emotions gripped her throat. She couldn't breathe. A monster had welled up inside her, taking her out of the present. She crouched there for quite a long time, waiting for the enemy to quell.

Shouts of "Bang, bang; you're dead!" brought her back to reality. Wally and Frankie came crashing through the front door playing cowboys and Indians.

She decided then and there that she had to brace herself for the same fate as her cousin, just in case. It wouldn't be her decision to make, and she knew it. From her view behind her father's chair, she spotted his photograph on Sil's table, and she willed herself to focus on what a good man her dad was.

Carolyn esteemed her parents so much—even more so this past week. She admired her mother; revered her father. She needed them both more than ever, and she stormed heaven that she would not be banished.

Please, Jesus, I don't want to leave.

Both she and her mother had understandable trepidation about his reaction. As they washed the lunch dishes one day, her mom admitted, "I'm nearly nauseated myself."

Carolyn apologized again. "Oh, Mom. I'm so sorry." Her thoughts switched to her father, feeling grief-stricken all over from having to disappoint him with such a nasty shock. *He'll never be able to look at me in the same way again.* With his return becoming more imminent, her anxiety got the better of her. She imagined him raging with furor, and her knees buckled.

Her mom caught her under her armpits. Whispering in her ear, she told Carolyn, "Breathe, Carolyn, breathe. In through your nose, out through your mouth. And again. In through your nose, out through your mouth." Carolyn did as she was gently commanded. "There you go." After a while, her nervous system calmed down. "That's a trick my midwife taught me for labor. It relaxes the body, so it can do its job. Remember it when these panic attacks strike. I won't always be with you."

Just before it was time for her mom to leave to get her dad at the bus stop, he called to explain that his train was going to be delayed, putting him in Grand Rapids too late to catch the last transfer. "I'll come to get you," her mom said into the phone. Little did he know this was an answer to prayer. Usually, her mom drove alone to collect her husband, and Carolyn stayed behind to finish dinner. But for this trip, her mom prepped the Friday meatless casserole and told Adeline, "Put this in the oven at five. You're in charge of the younger kids." Calling up the stairs, "Silvester, please make a salad."

The hour-long trek provided Carolyn and her mom an opportunity to talk. As they pulled into the transit station parking lot, her mom said, "By the time we all return, your dad will have had a chance to offer his first impressions about this heavy predicament. That's the best-case scenario."

"I hope so, Mom." Carolyn's eyes pooled.

For now, the two sat with bated breath, waiting for the train to pull in.

CHAPTER TWELVE

Carolyn watched her dad round the corner outside the depot. Her mom stepped out of the station wagon to wave him down. As he neared, Carolyn could tell he had spotted her silhouette by the way he smiled toward the car. "What a pleasant surprise!" He peered through the window to the back seat.

"Hi, Daddy." She tried to sound cheerful.

She saw her father raise his brows in question toward her mother. Carolyn saw her rubberneck the other way, pretending not to notice. Instead, her mom quizzed him as she navigated her way around the hatchback to the other side. "Tell me, how was your week, Robert?"

"Good! But I am looking forward to getting home."

Not for long.

"We're all looking forward to having you home," said her mom in the front passenger seat. Carolyn could tell there was a knot in her mother's throat.

Her dad rotated toward the backseat to see Carolyn unsuccessfully holding back tears. He then turned to face her mom, who was also crying. "Dana, darling, whatever is the matter? Is it Auntie Dora?"

I wish!

It was as if her mother had read her thoughts. "Oh, Robert, I wish it were as uncomplicated as the death of your elderly aunt." She then gave him a tearful, condensed version of the story.

Carolyn sat in the back seat, listening. Her hands wound round and round one another. She wished she could turn out the sound. It was as if her mom was speaking in slow motion. Or underwater. Each syllable was a jab in her gut. *Please stop talking.* Every muscle in her anatomy was tight. She held her abdomen as if to conceal her secret a short while longer. She wasn't showing, but she was sure her tiny bit of bloat must appear huge. Her mom's droning seemed to go on forever, and her dad's immediate silence lasted as long. By this time, Carolyn was hunched over with her hands on her ears, her torso lying across her lap. She was afraid to sit up. She was afraid to see her dad's face, but she peeked.

He sat stunned—open-mouthed—behind the wheel, almost as if the car had just been hit by the train that had carried him. He appeared pinned in place. His eyes fixed forward, staring straight out the windshield. She could see he was grappling with what he had learned. He repeated, through gritted teeth, pounding on the steering wheel with each word, "Carolyn is pregnant because she drank too much at that damn post formal party?!"

It scared Carolyn so much that she shrunk from fear. She had never heard him so angry. Her mom shuddered and then shouted, "Robert! That's not what I said!"

"What, then, Dana?!" Her dad yelled back. He then turned and shot what seemed to be a nasty look at Carolyn, who instinctively put her head back down. She was petrified. "Look at me, Carolyn!" her dad commanded, but she could not obey. She couldn't bear it. "Well, this is grand!" her dad bellowed.

The two women sat motionless in the car, waiting for him to calm down. Carolyn couldn't tell, but perhaps her dad was more sad than angry. Her mom turned back toward her and gave her a tiny nod that everything would be all right. Carolyn was unconvinced. She had heard her dad yell plenty of times, but not like that. In the depths of her being, she felt she had hurt him beyond measure, maybe even beyond forgiveness. *Oh, no, what have I done?* Carolyn wanted to die rather than watch her dad be so upset. "I'm so sorry, Daddy! I'm so very sorry! Please, Daddy, don't hate me!"

She could see his eyes in the rearview mirror. They had welled with tears, something else she had never witnessed. She wasn't sure what to do. So, she did nothing. She didn't dare.

Her mom reached across and took hold of her dad's hand. She massaged his knuckles, white from gripping the steering wheel. He jerked it away and struck the steering wheel again. "Damn!" he shouted.

Time stood still. Carolyn was almost afraid to breathe, let alone speak. After a thick silent span, he cleared his throat. "I'm sorry. Please forgive me. I can't imagine what you two have been going through holding on to his news."

Both Carolyn and her mom exhaled sighs and blew their noses.

Her dad pivoted toward the passenger seat and extended his right hand back for Carolyn to grab. His left locked fingers with her mom's. "I love you both. We will figure this out together." He eyeballed Carolyn and said, "Your version of this story, Doll, will have to wait." He turned toward her mom. "Let's use the time on the road to pray. First, though, I need to collect my thoughts."

He put the car into drive, and Carolyn saw him mouth the words, "All you angels and saints, pray for us." It was a familiar way her dad begged God for mercy and direction. After fifteen minutes of silence, her dad said, "Our faith will get us through this, and I adore both of you."

He could not have said anything better, even though Carolyn was unconvinced her father could ever adore her again. Not the way he used to. She was defiled. Her virginity stripped.

She kept playing with the fringe on her summer top, braiding and unbraiding the rainbow-colored strands. Tying them into bows. Then untying them. It was the only thing she could manage to pass the time. She attempted the Hail Mary but was unsuccessful at keeping track of where she was in her plea. She resumed fiddling with the fringe. It was the longest car ride of Carolyn Fandel's life.

By the time they pulled into their driveway, Carolyn was exhausted. Her father had offered his cursory suggestions. The conclusion had not been decided, but one thing was for certain: her father's life, her family's life, and her life had changed forever. Her ribs seemed crowded. It was as if she were housing the broken dreams of her parents, as well as her own. She wanted to crawl in a hole and be alone, which was impossible.

The house was teeming with hungry, excited children. The three travelers were greeted at the door by Frankie, who still commenced in scaling his father like a tree upon long trip returns. The other kids dashed to acknowledge their father. Sil and Gus were into handshakes. Wally still enjoyed a manly hug. Adeline lingered a while so that she could get the full-on embrace of her daddy. Her dad performed his typical duties, though Carolyn figured he would have rather skipped them this night. She was in awe of her father, who disclosed nothing, either with his actions or his words. *He's hiding his grief. And I'm hiding mine.*

Dinner was the first order of business that evening. While the other kids devoured the casserole, Carolyn picked at her food. She took an ample supply so as not to raise any red flags, but she spent most of the dinner hour moving her macaroni and cheese from one side of her plate to another with the backs of her utensils. Her throat was so tense that it was difficult to swallow.

Adeline and Silvester were too caught up in their after-dinner plans to notice. The other boys were too busy fighting over the one remaining dinner roll.

Carolyn and Adeline cleared the table, then washed and dried the dinner dishes. Their dad took Gus, Wally, and Frankie outside to rough house. "Time to go burn some energy," he called as he shut the back door behind him.

"Whew! It sure is quiet with all those males out of the house. They are so loud," her mom declared with a sigh. "You girls finish up. I'm going to go sit on the front porch with my coffee."

Carolyn swept the floor while Adeline put away the clean dishes in a hurry, clanging and banging as she went. "Be careful, Adeline! You're going to break something!" Carolyn snapped.

"Geesh! Calm down, Miss Perfect." As soon as the words left her mouth, Adeline shouted, "Sorry!" But Carolyn was crying. Adeline went over to offer her a hug. "Sorry, sis. I forgot. I'm in a hurry to get over to Margaret's for the sleepover."

Carolyn did not return the hug. Instead, she exited the kitchen at breakneck speed and ran up to their room. She trekked through their dark closet, all the way to the back, and sat in a corner.

She heard the kitchen cabinet slam shut and figured Adeline had put away the last pot. She could hear her running up the stairs. Carolyn knew she was hunting for her.

"What the heck are you doing in the closet?"

"I wanted to be alone." Carolyn hoped her sister wouldn't turn on the light and was relieved when she did not.

"Hey," Adeline spoke to the back of the closet, "I get that you can't stand that nickname, and I'm sorry. But, did it warrant all those tears?"

The family crybaby is commenting on my tears? Carolyn, who had every right to cry, weighed how to answer. "No, it didn't. I'm being silly. I guess I'm tired from having to help Mom so much this week. Sometimes those boys drive me crazy."

"Yeah. Me, too." She could see in the dim light that Adeline had sat down on the threshold of the closet and stuck out her pinkie. "Re-swear?"

Carolyn inched on her bum along the closet floor toward her sister, her pinkie extended. "Re-swear."

Adeline rose, slung her overnight bag over her shoulder, and tucked her green and blue plaid sleeping bag under her arm before skipping out of their room.

Carolyn got up and followed her down the stairs in time to see her sister slither past her dad and brothers at the door. Their dad was herding Frankie toward the shower. Then Wally. Then Gus. A Friday night routine.

"See you guys later," Sil called on his way out the door. "Hey, Carolyn, no plans tonight?"

"Nah. My girlfriends are on vacations with their families. I'm staying in to work on a little project." *What a gargantuan understatement. Can he tell I'm lying?* She hoped her brother couldn't hear deception in her tone. And how she wished she could trade places. She'd much rather be going to the Sun Theater and grabbing an icy root beer float afterward.

CHAPTER THIRTEEN

"Okay, the trio of testosterone is hunkered down," said her dad. "Let's head into the kitchen."

Her mom poured them each a mason jar of iced tea, and the three of them sat down at the new Formica table. The shininess of the kitchen seemed too bright for the doleful mood. Carolyn wished she could tone it down. Her parents looked as weary as she felt.

Per Fandel tradition, her father began praying. Carolyn and her mom joined in. After an Our Father, a Hail Mary, and a Glory Be in Latin, they concluded their prayers with the Sign of the Cross, marking their bodies with the sign of their salvation as they did so: "*In Nomine Patris, et Filii, et Spiritus Sancti.* Amen."

Her father initiated the weighty conversation. "Carolyn, I am so sorry to make you go through it again, but I need to know how this happened. What went on?" She could tell by his measured tone that he was trying to keep his voice calm. But the way he was tapping his fingers on the table in a rhythmic pattern was a sure sign of distress. She watched his fingers tap on and on as if her dad was mustering up all the patience he could while awaiting her answers.

Her dad stared right into her eyes, which were connected to her soul that night. Now that her misfortune was exposed, she had nowhere to hide. She didn't know how to continue but knew she must, and she did not want to disappoint him. *That's ironic. I already have.* "Well, Daddy, I'm not sure how it happened."

"You aren't?" queried her father in a voice that, to Carolyn, sounded accusatory.

She forged ahead. "Well, we were all in the Starrett barn, drinking lemonade, munching on snacks, and dancing. Everyone was so happy and having a great time." She hesitated. "Um, then Phyllis told us the lemonade was spiked."

Her dad pursed his lips together and bobbed his head in annoyed acknowledgment. "So, there was alcohol? That part is true?!" His voice deepened, moving from shock to anger. "At the Starrett farm, alcohol was served to a bunch of high school kids?!" His fist slammed the table. "Damn!"

Carolyn and her mother jumped.

"I'm sorry," he said, "I'm not mad at you. I'm mad at the Starrett parents for losing control of what was served on their property."

"It wasn't served, exactly." Carolyn corrected. "I mean, we didn't know Hank's older brother had put it in there at first. After a while, I knew something peculiar was going on."

Her dad scowled. "Peculiar?! And you kept drinking it? That seems peculiar to me." He lowered his voice and continued, "Can you please explain why you kept drinking after you knew it was spiked? Were you merely curious?"

Carolyn was hot with mortification. Her father had not accused her, yet she had convinced herself that it was what she deserved. She pushed forward anyway. "Because we were having fun. Everybody was doing it. I didn't even know how drunk I was until I walked to the bathroom with Skip. That's when it happened. Oh, Daddy!" Carolyn sobbed, "It was awful! I didn't…I mean…I had no idea…I mean…I don't know what happened!" She put her head down onto her arms rested on the table and continued to bawl as her shoulders shook.

Her mom must have shot a look at her dad because the questions ceased. Her two parents sat in silence while Carolyn cried and cried. She became aware of her mom's loving hand on her shoulder.

Her father elevated her chin. His eyes revealed sympathy for her—a captured spider caught in a web of big girl problems. His countenance was so forlorn that she imagined she must look pitiful. She pictured red eyes and a puffy, blotchy face.

Her father unclenched his other fist. She hoped it was an indication of diminishing anger. The expression in his eyes made her guess that he was contemplating how one single event had changed everything. *Believe me; I feel the same way*, she wanted to say. She revisited the question she had asked herself a million times: *How did that night turn out so horribly wrong?*

He reached and grabbed hold of both her hands. "Carolyn, I'm quite sure this isn't your fault, and I will be beside you to help carry this cross and see it through."

Carolyn was beyond relieved. *Maybe he isn't going to send me away.* "Thank you, Daddy. I would never have done this on purpose."

"Of course, you wouldn't." Her dad lovingly squeezed her hands tighter.

She squeezed his in return. Any words were stuck inside the huge lump in her throat. Her father made his way around the table to where she was sitting. He pulled her up from the chair and drew her into his papa bear hug. Wrapped within the sanctuary of her father's arms, Carolyn disclosed the other details she could remember.

"We arrived at the barn. It was crowded. We danced to a few songs, then got thirsty. Paul and I had agreed to dance with other people before arriving at the Starretts'. He gave a nod, which told me it was okay to dance with—" Carolyn could not even say his name. She got sick to her stomach and broke away from her dad. She excused herself and went into the bathroom. She sat on the toilet, praying not to vomit. *Please, God, let me get through this night!* Her tummy took a while to calm down.

Back in the kitchen, she continued the story and got up to the part where Paul left, and she had gone with Skip to use the Starrett bathroom. Some of these recollections were so gut-wrenching. They were as painful for her to say out loud as she was sure they were for her dad to hear. He winced. She saw his neck stiffen and observed him trying to relax by taking deep breaths. It seemed as if he were trying to get in all the clean air and expel the dirty air. Her father grimaced. It made Carolyn feel dirty all over again, and she recoiled. The worst of it, though, was she could tell he was close to crying himself a couple of times. She wished he would! *Please let it out, Dad!* It pained her so much to see her father try to hold back his sadness. She bit her lip to stave off her own tears.

"The most important things," her father peered again into her eyes, his voice shaking, "are to keep your faith and to guard your reputation as much as possible."

"My reputation?" Carolyn gasped. "Who all has to know about this?!"

"No one, for now, Doll. But it is pretty clear that this Jergen kid took advantage of you by force."

There was something her dad wasn't telling her, but she was too scared to ask him what it was. She feared he was going to try to track Skip down and force him to apologize. Carolyn was adamant that this could not happen. She couldn't bear it. She had long given up confronting him. Her most pressing concern, above all else, was that no one must ever find out about what happened. She prayed that her dad and mom thought the same.

Her dad noted the daisy clock high on the wall over the sink. "Sil will walk in any minute." Turning his attention back to Carolyn, he said, "We will pick this back up sometime over the weekend, Doll, after your mother and I have some time to talk in private. Tomorrow we will begin making calls to some relatives who might be able to offer solutions. Your job, young lady, is to pray. Stay close to Christ. We love you. Now off to bed."

"Yes, Daddy." She had called her father "daddy" more times in this one night than she had since she was a little girl, but she didn't care. Tonight, she needed her father more than ever. She had felt like a frightened child since it happened and wished with all her might that she was still that small with problems of the same size.

Carolyn would trade anything to be carefree and waiting for one of her mother's delicious baked goods coming out of the oven. Instead, she was pondering the oven of her womb. She instinctively rubbed it and wondered if it was warm in there. She hoped so.

They all made the Sign of the Cross and prayed three more quick Hail Mary's. "Who better to take our prayers to the Sacred Heart of Jesus than His Mother?" her dad said.

Carolyn nodded. In her Old Testament history class in eighth grade, Carolyn remembered learning that a good Jewish king always listens to his mother. *Okay, Blessed Mother, here I am. Beg God for me that I can be patient during this tribulation. And please pray for me.* Carolyn remembered the Latin vocabulary derivative from last week. *I've got a tribulation, all right.*

Her parents gave her another hug, and she headed up the stairs. She could hear them downstairs, opening their dresser drawers. For their pajamas, she presumed. She was going to be the topic of their bedside conversation, so she laid down by the heat register and strained to hear.

Her mom's voice was soft. "What do you think, Robert?"

"What I think is, this is a hell of a mess! And I can scarcely believe that our sweet Carolyn was raped by that Jergen scum of a half-man, but I doubt there's anything to be done about it now."

Hearing the word "rape" sent a shock through Carolyn, and she stiffened. She took a deep breath and focused on the serious implications. She hadn't considered that the term applied to her situation. That was what her dad was trying not to say in front of her while they were in the kitchen. *For all these weeks, I've been blaming myself. I've been so worried about what this was doing to my parents and how other people would label me.* Discerning that her father had called it "rape" caused a new dawn. A sliver of light came back into Carolyn's life. And, for the first time, she allowed herself to think that this whole thing might not be her fault after all.

She continued to eavesdrop. She heard her father say, "Skip Jergen and his part will have to wait until Carolyn is tucked safely away somewhere." She sat upright. She didn't want anything to do with Skip Jergen. Not ever again! *And what did he mean by "tucked away?" Aren't I safe?* Or maybe her dad was going to kick her out after all. Her mind swirled.

She crouched back down to listen some more to see if any other information might be coming via the heating duct. Her mom was saying something, but her voice was so soft that Carolyn couldn't quite make it all out. All she could decipher were the words "Blessed Virgin Mary," "pregnant," and "Joseph." She figured her mom was just praying *like she always does.*

Grabbing her teddy bear for comfort, she climbed into bed and pulled her knees up to her chest. In the dark stillness, Carolyn fought to keep fear from gripping her. She could not stop the tears. She muffled any sobs so as not to wake the younger boys nor cause her older brother to become keen about her new reality. She tossed and turned on her wet pillowcase, trying to feed herself soothing thoughts and be at peace. *Come, Holy Spirit, let me rest in you. Please give us a clear plan. Come, Holy Spirit.*

She fidgeted, trying to get comfortable. First on her side, then her tummy, then back to her side. She mumbled quietly, "Holy Spirit, let me rest in you. Holy Spirit, let me rest in you," over and over again, until she drifted off to sleep.

CHAPTER FOURTEEN

Saturday morning dawned bright. On Confession days, her parents were up way before any of the kids. Carolyn woke up and heard their voices in the kitchen. She was safe. She pictured them sitting at the kitchen table, their hands hugging hot mugs of coffee, making a verbal schedule of activities and chores to be accomplished. This morning she also heard Adeline down there. *She's back from her sleepover. And on time. It's a miracle.*

Carolyn was surprised to find herself famished. She hurried down to the kitchen and dove into her mom's blueberry pancakes. She couldn't eat enough of them. For the first time in months, she was keeping up with her brothers.

They noticed. "Gosh, Carolyn, leave some for us!"

Suddenly self-conscious, she slowed down.

With all the kids' mouths full, she suspected that her parents would use the prime opportunity for a brief catechesis. They made a good team in teaching the kids not merely the how's of Catholicism but also the why's. Although the three oldest could recite from memory the forthcoming lesson, they were expected to appear engaged.

"Quite mysterious. Sinners enter the confessional with the stain of sin on their souls and, by the power of the Redeemer, emerge with clean souls ready to grow in virtue," their father said in an excited tone, his eyes wide from raised eyebrows. "Can any of you tell me why we confess to a priest?"

Gus and Wally turned their heads toward Silvester, expecting him to answer. Silvester shook his head. "Not today. You guys are on your own," he said with college snark.

Wally's eyes lifted to the top of his brain as he tried to recall the lesson from the last time they were proposed this question. "Um, because sin is never private?"

"And?" Silvester goaded.

Carolyn rolled her eyes. *Who's trying to be perfect now?*

"And, sometimes, there's no way to apologize to all the people your sin has affected?" Wally submitted.

"Right!" said their dad. "Augustine, can you give an example?"

"I'll try." Gus paused a few seconds and then continued, "Let's say I have a bad day at school. I enter the house in a sour mood. Wally starts to pester me—"

"Hey!" Wally shouted. "Why is it me?"

"'Cause it always is," Carolyn said.

"Miss Perfect to the rescue!" cried Sil.

There he goes again. Carolyn shot Sil a look and then became quiet. She braced herself for all her siblings to join in but heard her father pipe up in her defense, "Silvester James, I've about had enough of that out of you."

Drooping his shoulders, he answered, "Yes, sir." He hung his head and then turned toward his sister, "Sorry, sis."

With her elbows set on the table, Carolyn leaned toward him and inquired sarcastically, "Is this a real apology or another fake one?" She glared at her older brother, who rolled his eyes and glared back at her. He remained silent, appearing to have nothing else to add. Neither one of them wanted to be the first to blink.

"Moving on," their dad continued. "Finish your example, Gus."

"Yeah, so I've had a bad day, Wally picks on me, and I take it out on Frankie. Frankie's feelings are hurt. He goes to play with Butchy Hodge next door and takes it out on Butchy by grabbing the favorite Matchbox car and refusing to share. Then Butchy punches his sister."

"Let's hope not," their mom said, "but that's a pretty good example."

Her dad concluded the lesson. "Confession is one of the most necessary and powerful sacraments that Christ gave His Church. It gives us cause to rejoice in hope." Carolyn had always relied on this being true, especially in the past few months.

"So, the priest stands *in persona Christi*," offered Sil.

Carolyn recognized the toss-in of Latin as her older brother's way to try to get back into their father's good graces.

"Right. He stands in the person of Christ. You are indeed confessing to Jesus," said their dad. "Okay, hurry up and brush your teeth. We've got to get a move on." Directing his comment to Sil, he said, "Now, young man, clear the dishes for your sister."

Carolyn delighted in her father's command. She pitched in by rustling up the younger boys to meet her parents' goal of standing in the confession line by ten to nine. "Faith first," her parents had said a million times.

She watched Father Fedewa, donned in his white alb and stole, walk through the narthex of the church and past the penitents. Carolyn found it beneficial to have other sinners in line seeking forgiveness. Her eyes surveyed several families, each waiting for a turn to cleanse their souls. She gave little waves to a few friends—Julia, Nancy, and Patricia—who waved back. Carolyn's spirits drooped. *None of them have big, horrible secrets from the formal night. I'm the only one with that sin.*

Out of the corner of her eye, she saw Father Fedewa set foot into the center section of the three-part confessional. He was ready when the first person in line could hear him glide open the window on one side of the box. A green light came on outside the door, indicating he was ready.

The younger two, not as knowledgeable about grave sin, still balked at going to Confession. "Do we have to?" was a frequent whine. Silvester, who was forced to share a room with the younger boys, stepped out of his place in the queue to enlighten them about their sins.

Her dad promptly instructed Sil to back down. "Your brothers already have two parents, young man. They don't need a third. Get back in line."

Carolyn recalled two main things about God. One was that He was a God of justice. She could either pay now for her sins or pay for all eternity. *Paying now seems smarter.* The second thing was that God was a God of mercy, extreme and total mercy. It didn't matter what she had done or where she had been. All that mattered was true repentance and the resolve to try to avoid all future sin. Even though her guilt had wracked her, intellectually, she knew this is what her faith taught. *Lord, I trust in your abundant mercy.* That was her holy grail at this point, and she felt freedom in finally making an honest confession.

Back at home, her dad wasted no time in getting to the chores. Silvester and her dad started heaving various things into her grandfather's old pick-up truck, borrowed for the annual trip to the dump. In went a yellow-stained mattress from the boys' room, a tell-tale sign the bed-wetting had come to an end. *Thank goodness!* A broken chair beyond repair, a rusted-out burning barrel, a few broken dishes, and a blown-out tire followed.

With the truck loaded, her dad and Sil were off, accompanied by one additional passenger. Adeline had climbed into the truck with the guys, squeezed between them. Carolyn had no idea why her sister found the dump fascinating. "Why are you going there, Adeline? You're in high school now, for goodness sakes."

"To add to my treasure trove."

Carolyn put her hands up at the sides of her mouth and yelled as the truck backed out of the driveway, "Your box is already full!" Shaking her head, she muttered to herself, "I will never understand how my sister can stand the rank odor!" It made her nauseous, and she stifled a burp. Then she snickered, visualizing her sister being enthralled that another person's trash could become her treasure. *I wonder what she'll haul in next.*

With Adeline gone, it left Carolyn and her mother to strip the beds. They remade them with clean sheets from the closet and then carried armloads of dirty linens to the laundry room on the back porch. "You take over from here, Carolyn."

Carolyn grabbed the box of Tide and sprinkled some into the bottom of the washer. Putting it back, she spied the jug of Downy and made a mental note to remember to dump some in at the beginning of the rinse cycle. She bent over, grabbed an armful of sheets and pillowcases, and stuffed them into the washing machine. She shut the lid and spun the dials.

One load after another, she lugged the heavy laundry baskets of wet items out the back door and hung them on the clothesline in the backyard, the warm summer breeze serving as the dryer. The truck rumbled onto the gravel driveway, and she turned around to wave. Her dad tooted the horn in response.

"Nice rabbit's foot, Adeline!" teased Carolyn. She followed her sister up the stairs to their room and watched her crouch down to retrieve her special box. The rabbit's foot was placed among three jacks, one marble, a dented tin measuring cup, a Nehi soda pop-top, a Petoskey stone, and a pink eraser. All had value to Adeline, something Carolyn never understood.

Soon they were teaming up on a cleaning frenzy with their mom, putting a shine in every room. Toilet, sink, and bathtub were scrubbed with Comet cleanser. So, too, was the kitchen sink. Their mom did those. "You girls dust the furniture and the hardwood floors." By the time the sisters were finished, their mother was folding the first two loads of laundry.

Carolyn heard her dad instruct Gus and Frankie to remove twigs from the yard so it could be mowed. Soon Silvester was giving the lawn a haircut with the rotary mower. She peeked out the living room window. Her father was on his hands and knees with trimming shears hacking away around the perimeter. Gus had the green wheelbarrow by the handles, while Wally and Frankie scuttered behind, filling it with the clippings.

Upon completion of the yard work, the sweaty men and almost-men sat at the wooden picnic table under the maple tree. Carolyn carried out a tray of bologna sandwiches and chips. Adeline followed with a jug of lemonade and some Dixie cups. Their mom brought out a plate piled high with oatmeal cookies. The eight Fandels marked themselves with the Sign of the Cross and said the blessing, "Bless us, O Lord, and these thy gifts, which we are about to receive, from thy bounty, through Christ our Lord. Amen."

Saturday mornings were hefty work, but it was rewarding work and good bonding time. Today, it had given Carolyn a temporary distraction from her predicament.

The sisters cleared the remnants of lunch, stacking up the dishes and proceeding inside to commence the kitchen clean-up, followed by their mom, who began sweeping the floor. Carolyn let Adeline wash because allowing her to dry meant a future scavenger hunt. Her sister had many talents, but organization wasn't her strong suit. Sometimes she thought Adeline could easily have been a boy.

I wonder if my baby is a boy or a girl. Carolyn grew sullen and slouched her shoulders. She had momentarily forgotten her plight in all the busyness of household chores and lunch. All the while she was stuck inside her own head, Adeline had been staring at her.

"What *are* you thinking about?" Her sister reprimanded, "You're way behind in drying!"

"I have a lot going on."

"By 'a lot', do you mean someone named Paul Johns?" her sister teased.

"Yeah, sort of."

"Well, stop daydreaming about him and do your job, please."

Carolyn turned to their mom as if to say, "Help."

Their mom promptly rushed over and grabbed a towel to help catch her up with the drying. Carolyn glanced over her shoulder to see her mom offer a reassuring smile as she excused herself to go into the parlor behind closed doors. *There she goes to find me a new home.* Carolyn peeked down at her stomach, yet to reveal to the world her secret. *Thank you, God, for getting me this far without anyone but my parents knowing the truth.*

With the dishes put away and the counter wiped down, Adeline announced, "I'm headed outside to play with dad and the boys. You coming, Carolyn?"

"Nah, thanks. I've got summer reading to do."

"But summer vacation just started," complained Adeline.

To be convincing, she picked up her British Literature book and said, "Shakespeare and I have a date."

"Boring!" yelled Adeline as she bounded out the door.

CHAPTER FIFTEEN

Carolyn sat in the chair closest to the parlor to hear whom her mother was calling and what was being said about her. She could tell her mom was talking to Carolyn's grandmother, Ma Wagner. Tears escaped and trickled down her cheeks while she listened. As the oldest granddaughter on the Wagner side, Carolyn held a favorite spot. *Or I used to.* She wondered what opinion her grandma held of her now.

She eavesdropped while her mom described in cloaked terms what had happened. With a party line to consider, privacy could never be assured because a neighbor could pick up her phone any second and overhear the conversation. She was comforted when her mom said into the phone, "Thank you, Mom. I will assure her that you wish her the very best." She hadn't been judged. That's all Carolyn needed to hear from her grandma.

Her Wagner grandparents weren't going to be able to take her in. Her grandfather had suffered a farming accident, leaving his left arm partially paralyzed. And with three of her mother's younger siblings also still living at home, they had a full-enough house.

Carolyn recalled yesterday that her parents decided it best if her dad informed Grandpapa and Grandmama Fandel in person.

"I'll drive over tomorrow afternoon," her dad had said. *I wonder what their reaction will be.* After all, it was their son who had kicked out his daughter, who had gotten herself pregnant. And it was Carolyn's grandpa who suggested it, while her grandma said nothing. *They'll hate me for sure.* It made her sad, but it was never a secret that her father's parents were harsh.

She opened her schoolbook to the table of contents, seeing that *A Midsummer Night's Dream* was on page forty-five. She flipped the pages, saw the title, and launched into the introductory comments. She had no focus. She couldn't have cared less about Oberon and Titania. And she couldn't concern herself with Lysander and Hermia's love relationship. She had enough problems of her own in that regard. She wondered what Paul was doing at his house. *Not this, that's for sure.* She closed the book and leaned closer to the parlor door.

She heard her mother's voice brighten. "Hello, Aunt Hildy, Dana calling." For fifty years, Hildegard Wagner, her mom's godmother, had delivered babies as a trained midwife, which made her the likely and preferred choice for Carolyn. Her mom was checking to see if her aunt was up to having a house guest.

She surmised the question Hildy must have asked when she heard her mom reply, "No. None on the way for me."

Carolyn's jaw stiffened. *Nope, Hildy, not for her anyway.* She inched to the edge of her seat with her hands and sat erect as if to brace herself. She was dying to hear every word that was being spoken.

"Aw, thank you, Aunt Hildy. Robert is well. The kids are all fine." Carolyn heard her mom's voice crack, and she could tell she was trying to hold her emotion in check before continuing, "What about you, Hildy? Have you been well?"

Aunt Hildy was an old, no-nonsense soul yet a generous one. She had achieved bloodline fame by saying she was "fit as a fiddle for an octogenarian." A widow with no living children, Hildy lived alone several towns away on a farm practically in the middle of nowhere.

Carolyn swallowed and was automatically conflicted. She wanted to go away and hide, but she dreaded having to leave the familiarity she had always known. Old disquietude rose in her gut and traveled to her throat, squeezing it shut. Her palms were sweaty. Her current bodily reactions connected to the fears she had had as a young girl. *Maybe God was giving me a premonition. Maybe He was preparing me for this nightmare in my life.* She knew that God did not cause her this trouble, but she prayed *Oh, God, why did you allow it?*

She moved right next to the door to hear all she could. Shaking from nerves, she guided herself down the wall to avoid her quivering frame from accidentally touching the door. She pressed her ear to it and reminded herself to breathe. *In through your nose, out through your mouth.*

"Aunt Hildy, Robert and I were wondering if Carolyn could come to stay with you for a while."

It killed her not to be able to hear the whole conversation, especially the words coming out of her great aunt's mouth. Her mother was listening for a long time before she finally said, "Probably closer to the end of summer."

Carolyn had to get her story in order. Paul deserved an explanation. *What the heck am I going to tell him?* She had kept pretty much to herself, but they were still trying to maintain a friendship. She was lost in her reflections about Paul when her mother opened the door, causing her to fall over in shock. "Sorry, Mom, I couldn't resist eavesdropping."

"I understand, Doll. This is your life we're talking about." She sat down on the floor with Carolyn, both their heads against the wall. Her mother sighed. "As you probably heard, you will be going to your Great Aunt Hildy's for a while."

"Yeah, I gathered as much. For how long, Mom?"

"Well, your father and I need to discuss this first. But if he agrees this is best, you will go there sometime in August before you start to show too much. At least until the baby is born. We will figure out the rest once you decide if you're keeping it or placing it for adoption."

"Adoption?" Carolyn mused out loud. "The idea has appeal. I could give some married folks the baby they've been wanting and then get on with my regular life."

Her mom sighed again and waited to speak. A sign of contemplation. "Yes, that's true. You would be giving a childless couple a beautiful baby, but—" Her mom stopped as if she didn't want to finish the sentence.

"But what?" Carolyn asked.

"But, Doll, nothing in your life will be the same. Once you have a child, even if you place it for adoption, that little person will always be part of your memories. Part of your whole life story. Sure, you will go on with the same activities and keep all the goals you ever had, but—"

Carolyn finished for her, "—but I will be living a new normal, a new reality."

Her mom put her right arm around Carolyn's shoulders and pulled her close. She took comfort in her mother's floral scent. Avon Cotillion. All of the women on her mom's side wore it, including the aunts who had married in. Carolyn breathed in the comfort as she grabbed her mother's free hand. She held it tight. Together they sat and let their tears roll down their cheeks. At that moment, Carolyn felt more understood than she had in several months. Her whole being knew that from this day forward, she and her mom were more than kindred spirits. They were both now mothers.

Carolyn wiped her eyes. She let go of her mom's hand to raise her own and dab her mother's tears away. Her mom pulled her closer. "My sweet, sweet girl. I'm so sorry this is happening to you."

"And I'm sorry it's happening to you, too, Mom. I love you so much.

And, guess what else?"

"What?"

"This," Carolyn said, taking her mom's hand and placing it on her stomach, "this is your first grandchild."

She saw more tears escape from her mom's eyes. "Yes. Yes, it is. Thank you, Jesus."

Sitting together on the floor, Carolyn found her spirits lighter. She could breathe better than she had been able to since that awful night. She loved sharing her innermost self with the woman she admired and trusted more than anyone in the world.

Her mom had been steadfast in helping Carolyn sort out the confounding jigsaw puzzle that had become her life. Settling on Aunt Hildy's place seemed like the right fit. With that piece secured, her mind opened up and allowed some joy to settle in. A happier Carolyn and her mom ventured out to the backyard to join in the competitive kickball game. "I'm on Adeline's team!" yelled Carolyn, running through the backyard toward her sister.

CHAPTER SIXTEEN

Waking on Sunday, Carolyn put her hands under the covers to touch her abdomen. She could tell it was fuller, but she was fairly certain no one else had noticed yet. She pushed her breasts from all directions. Still sore. *I wonder when that will end.* Her happiness from yesterday had waned. Somehow during the night, it had been dampened with harsh reality. She forced a cheerful tone into her voice and nudged Adeline with her left elbow. "Wake up, sleepy. Time to get ready for Mass."

Adeline moaned, "Five more minutes."

"Fine." Carolyn got out of bed and shuffled to the closet. Moving her eyes from one end of her clothes rod to the other, she surveyed options for church outfits. She planned ahead. *I'd better save my dresses for later in the summer. Thank God my mother has always made my clothes big to account for growth.* She lamented. *Not the growth I planned on, though.* Her dresses would have to wait to go to church, but one of them would not be the blue polka-dotted final exam. *No way I'll fit into that. I'm already too fat for it.* Her skirts were getting tight, but it was cool enough for her to put a cardigan over her blouse to hide the skirt's button being undone in the back. She sighed and opted for her periwinkle blue polyester swing skirt, white blouse, and pink cardigan. She examined herself in the mirror from all angles to make sure nothing showed. She didn't realize Adeline had been watching her the whole time.

"You look fantastic as always, Miss Per—" Adeline caught herself in time to avoid the evil eye. "You look pretty, Carolyn."

Carolyn jumped, so startled, she decided to let the slip-up go. Raising her eyebrows, "Thanks. But you'd better hurry up. Your extra five ended ten minutes ago."

***

Carolyn's soul was warmed by the reverence of Mass. As altar boys, her brothers looked dignified in their black cassocks overlaid with white lace-trimmed surplices. In the quiet, she drew close to her Maker. The incense reminded her of heaven. Her prayers were sincere as they floated up with the smoke. She had sandwiched herself between her Mom and Frankie. She leaned into her mom more than usual, as if touching her kept her safe. Kneeling, she sent her intentions to God as the priest lifted the bread and wine toward heaven for the Transubstantiation. After Communion, she offered silent prayers of supplication. *Lord, I believe; cure my unbelief. Safeguard my child, Lord. Please send a clear sign about whether I should keep my baby or choose adoption. Please, Lord, reveal a clear plan.*

***

With each passing day, Carolyn dreaded the end of July. She felt her choices had been ripped away from her. *My singular recourse is to follow through on the Aunt Hildy plan.* She tried not to agonize too much over how she was going to explain it to her close friends. Thankfully, Phyllis had already left with her folks to live at their cottage for the summer in Michigan's Upper Peninsula. Usually, they waited until the end of June, but this year they took off the day school ended. Carolyn was barely able to say goodbye. *All for the better; one less lie to tell.*

Telling Paul was going to be arduous. Her head was swirling with concocted stories about where she was going and why. Whatever she told him had to be convincing. Still several weeks away, she was able to procrastinate devising the final plan for a while. She sat out under the maple tree, revisiting all the what-ifs. She had been what-iffing for months. *What if I had never gone to the formal? What if I had ridden with Paul instead of staying? What if I didn't become pregnant? What if I told Paul the truth? What if I was already at Aunt Hildy's? What if, what if, what if?* Her brain bounced back and forth until she thought her head might explode. She nearly screamed out loud—and would have if her sister wasn't so near.

Carolyn catapulted herself out of the lawn chair. She yelled to Adeline perched high in the tree, "Hey, Sis, I'm taking off for a walk on the beach. Tell Mom that I'll be back to set the table and make the fruit salad for dinner."

She took off her sandals and dangled them to her side. She meandered along until her head cleared. The cool water lapped at her toes. It was as if the waves were washing her uncertainties back out into the enormous lake as they receded from the shore. Renewed, she was determined to focus on enjoying her remaining summer fun with her Fandels. She glanced down and touched her midsection. With her taller frame, she was able to gain some weight without anyone being the wiser. *Except for Phyllis. She would have guessed.*

In a way, Carolyn was glad that her friendship with Phyllis had faded. Carolyn had matured in the past few months and had begun to be bothered by qualities in her friend that she could not appreciate. Even though the two had been best friends for as long as Carolyn remembered, Phyllis was self-centered and judgmental. Her parents were the same way. Both Mr. and Mrs. Norton came from money and acted as if they were above the common citizens in Grand Lake. The two attorneys played judge and jury of the mistakes other people were making. Phyllis had become critical of everything and everybody, even Hank. They had an ugly, bitter break-up on the last day of school, moments before the Nortons left for the Upper Peninsula.

Paul, on the other hand, was a different story. That was one connection Carolyn owed an explanation—even if it was a lie. He had been there for her, and he had exercised great patience in not pushing for more. She had avoided any outward signs of romance, even though she was captivated by him. She could not reveal her life's complications. For her sake. And his. It wasn't fair. Carolyn knew she was taking advantage of him, and her regret surfaced. *Well, he'll be free of me soon enough,* she justified.

Her parents had cautioned her more than once that it was best to break it off, except that Carolyn could never bring herself to do it. She tried as soon as school got out one June night down by the lake. When it came time to recite the words she had practiced, they wouldn't come out of her mouth. Instead, she explained that her parents did not want her to have a dating relationship heading into senior year. "We're going to be graduating. I'll be tied down to a job or maybe college. It's going to be quite a while before I'll be pursuing marriage. That is if the right guy comes along." There, she said it, proud of herself for being clear.

"I'm the marrying type," Paul offered.

Carolyn's face got warm. She kicked herself for not being crystal clear about her situation. *He is such a nice guy. He deserves better.* She could not prolong the inevitable. "Please, Paul, let's leave this thing we have as friends. Please don't phone my house or come around. My parents have requested that I focus on my future."

From then on, he respected Carolyn's wishes and did not call on her. The two still stole glances at Mass and snuck in whispered chats on Saturday mornings in the confession line, but that was it. She desired to be with him more than he knew. There was definite chemistry between her and Paul. *People who don't see this are either blind or stupid. I wish it could be different!* Whatever they still had would come to a screeching halt, and it saddened her.

On the last Saturday in July, the time had come. She could not delay it any longer. She whispered to Paul at confession, "Meet me at the Tasty Freeze across from the park at three?"

Paul smiled and nodded at her invitation.

Not yet wanting her parents privy about her meeting with Paul, she returned from church with an idea. She had saved her babysitting money. "Hey, boys! Adeline! Wanna go get ice cream?" They agreed, and it was then that Carolyn comprehended she might have complicated her plans to talk to Paul alone. But it was too late. The offer had been made, and ice cream was the promised expectation.

The group was about a block or two away when Gus, Wally, and Frankie broke into a run. They would take their ice cream to the park and play on the equipment oblivious, as the frozen concoction melted down their arms. Adeline, however, might be a problem. Carolyn feared she would stick close. She said a silent *thank goodness* when her sister's cheerleading friends showed up. They had gone a long way down the shoreline with their ice cream by the time Paul joined Carolyn out behind the park ranger's shed.

After a brief hug, Paul quizzed, "What's up? Why the secret meeting all of a sudden?"

She dared not to make eye contact lest she'd lose her composure. Instead, she tried to appear nonchalant, glancing around as if checking on her brothers. "Well," she hesitated, "I have to leave for the rest of the summer." She decided to leave it there and not add that she would be gone for much longer.

"How come?" His questioning eyes were loaded with suspicion.

She answered as she had rehearsed—in one huge breath. "Well, my great aunt is ill and lives on this huge farm and needs a righthand man, and since Sil's at college and I'm the oldest granddaughter, I have to go."

Paul squinted his eyes and cocked his head to one side. "What's the real reason?" Her explanation wasn't adding up. While she built up her resolve to keep from enumerating, he continued. "I get that your parents directed you to slow things down and keep us as friends, but this sudden having to leave town is difficult to swallow."

"Well, I don't know what else to tell you." *Liar.* Carolyn felt like a dishonest rat and hated having to lie.

"You can tell me why your voice sounds funny." He paused before accusing her. "You're hiding something."

Not something. Someone. She couldn't risk being honest, so she repeated her story in what she hoped was a more convincing tone.

Paul's next question indicated a failure. "What's the matter, Carolyn? Don't you like me anymore?"

Her heart thudded and sank to the bottom of her stomach. "Oh, Paul, that's not it at all. I care for you a ton—more than I do anybody." She saw that her words rang true to him when his face brightened.

Paul put his arm around her shoulders and said, "Okay, Carolyn. We'll play this your way. No doubt, there's a lot more to this, but I'm going to respect your privacy. I take it that this is a pretty serious family business."

"Yes. Yes, it is, Paul." Tears appeared out of nowhere, and her voice wavered. "Please, can we leave it at that?" She was proud of herself for not blurting out the whole story. Her parents had told her that her strength and reserve was for her good and his. She could see now why that was true.

After some silence, Paul touched her hair, and his brown eyes met hers. "Without a doubt, I'm going to miss you and those sparkly green eyes for the rest of the summer. Who's going to almost get me into trouble at confession, and who's going to peek at me at Mass?"

Carolyn forced a laugh, but she could have melted from his gaze. She felt some relief for having told him face to face—even if it was a lie.

"I can't wait until school starts, and then I'll get to see you every day," Paul said, changing the subject.

No, you won't. "Yes, that'll be great," she said, forcing a smile to avoid any further suspicion. She had already stirred up plenty. Paul presumed this aunt thing was a short-term arrangement. She didn't have the nerve nor the emotional stamina to set him straight.

CHAPTER SEVENTEEN

The following Monday morning, Carolyn was surprised to see her dad sitting at the kitchen table. Knitting her eyebrows, she inquired, "Dad? Good morning. How come you're not at work?"

"Well, I figured since you're leaving soon, you and I should have some father-daughter time. Maybe start with a long walk on the beach. Okay with you?"

She wasn't buying it but couldn't question him right then. Her younger brothers were up and about rummaging through the cupboards for their favorite cereals. "Okaaay," Carolyn hesitated. "Um—that sounds nice— I guess." She eyed her mom at the other end of the table. Her mom grinned and nodded. A positive sign for her to go with her dad.

They sauntered along the shore, letting the Lake Michigan waves rinse over their feet. Carolyn lowered her head to see the sand ooze around her toes, leaving a momentary footprint anticipating the next wave washing it away as if it had never been there. "Okay, Dad. Let's get to the point of this father-daughter walk."

He sighed. "Let's do that at the next bench where we can take a break." She knew the topic was serious. Her dad always insisted on sitting down for important chats. Soon they were veering away from the water toward the boardwalk and a bench.

She scooted back on the seat against her dad's shoulder, breathing in the lake air along with the security her father rendered.

"There's no easy way to tell you, but remember when I said I spoke with my old friend, Jerry?"

Carolyn searched her mind. She remembered that name. Jerry Edmonds was a lawyer. He and her dad had been friends for years. The Edmondses had a pack of kids, the same as the Fandels. "Yeah."

"What I didn't tell you was that I called him not just as a friend but also for some professional legal advice." Carolyn wrung her hands together, nervous as she waited for her dad to say more. He put his arm around her for comfort. "It's nothing to worry about, but you have a right to know the context of the conversation."

"Such as?"

"I talked to Jerry because he could offer advice on what we should do about Skip Jergen and his part in your dilemma."

Carolyn pulled away from the weight of her dad's arm and sat on the edge of the bench, ready to bolt. No longer secure, she shrieked, "You talked to him about me?! About Skip? Daaad, why would you do that?" Tears of betrayal rolled down her cheeks.

"Doll, please hear me out. You can trust me. I'm your father." When she saw the hurt in his eyes, she softened. She repositioned herself close to her dad as he continued. "I talked to him about your being raped, Carolyn, and to see if there was any legal recourse to hold that Jergen kid accountable. I don't want him to do this ever again to any young woman. I did not protect you from him, but I sure as hell want to shield others." She could hear him choke up and take a deep breath.

"Dad, you did nothing wrong. Please don't add your guilt to the weight of this. You're the best father a girl could have." She let her words sit a while. "So what did Mr. Edmonds say?"

"Unfortunately, with no evidence besides your pregnancy, there is nothing to be done. You had no visible injuries. You had no witnesses. You told no one for months. We did not take you to the police. The short story is: there is no legal recourse."

"I see." She sighed, taking a minute to process it all. "Okay, then." With sudden clarity, she added, "That part is settled. And truth be told, I'm glad. I'm prepared to put all this behind me. If I never lay eyes on Skip Jergen again, that is fine with me. This is MY baby, and I'm the mother." She gave a firm nod as if to slam the book on Skip Jergen. *It's just me and my baby now.*

She could tell her dad was observing her, but she kept gazing at the water. Her dad took her hand in his and squeezed it. "Well, Carolyn, you certainly can speak your mind, and I'm proud of you for it. We'll consider this matter closed and never speak of it again."

They sat there, watching the waves roll in and out. It was as if time was standing still. *If I stay right where I am and don't move, maybe my body will never reveal my pregnancy more than it already is.* It was a ludicrous thought, but she earnestly wanted to sit there forever against her dad, never facing what was ahead of her.

They stayed silent. Carolyn watched the lake ripple, mesmerized. The rays peeked through the clouds enough to send a shimmer of diamonds skipping all across the dawning waves. She imagined them making their way west to the shores of Chicago. She had never been there. She wondered whether she would get lost in that big city.

As the glitter on the water rolled in and out and across, a tear full of great sorrow rolled down her cheek. She wiped it with her finger and noticed that even the minuscule salty speckle glinted in the rising sun. Growing philosophical, she mused, "Dad, will I be alone the rest of my life because of this?"

Her dad took a thoughtful breath. "Doll, nothing in life is a sure deal. Our faith is all we have. What I do believe is that God sent to an unwed Mary, an upstanding husband in Joseph. You're a beautiful soul, Carolyn. I'm sure He has a Joseph for you, too."

She rested her head on her dad's shoulder. "I pray it's so, Dad." She tried to picture her 'Joseph.' The vision she got was of Paul Joseph Johns. She rolled her eyes, feeling foolish for dreaming.

CHAPTER EIGHTEEN

Before leaving with her mother for Aunt Hildy's, Carolyn scanned her room one last time. She hesitated for a second and then decided it was a must-take article. She scooped up her teddy bear from the corner and tucked it under her arm. *Gotta have this!*

She hugged all of her comrades goodbye with advice. "Adeline, keep saying bedtime prayers. Gus and Wally, do your homework. Frankie, obey mom and dad. Silvester, cut the little guys some slack."

She teared up when hugging Silvester and Adeline, shed a tear when hugging Gus and Wally, and outright cried when she hugged her baby brother, Frankie. Ten years older than he, Carolyn had spent many hours reading to and playing with Frankie. Many afternoons she watched all the younger brothers, so her mom could go across the street to have coffee with the Protestant neighbor lady, Dorothy. Having to leave her Fandels behind nearly broke her.

"Oh, come on, Carolyn, it's not like you're never going to see Frankie or any of us again. Quit being a baby!"

His teasing stung, but she tried not to show it.

Her father scowled and yelled at her older brother, "Knock it off! I seem to remember you weren't too keen on leaving last August when you went off to Aquinas College."

As grateful as she was for his defense, she didn't need it in this case. She feared that each time her dad had come to her defense over the summer, suspicion increased.

Sil's eyes narrowed, and she could tell he was surprised by their father's sharp tone. "Okaaay, Dad. I was only teasing." Turning to Carolyn, he said, "Sorry, Sis." She could see that Sil was puzzled. After all, their father was a great kidder himself and often played devil's advocate to keep them on their toes. He let them hang in there while being teased to "build character," he had said. She feared that each time her dad had rushed to defend her had made Silvester wiser to the bigger picture at play.

She picked up her things and followed her dad to the car. He opened the back of the station wagon and hoisted in Carolyn's suitcase. She placed beside it her teddy bear and the box of groceries her mother had packed to contribute to Aunt Hildy's household. Carolyn whispered to her dad, "Daddy, Silvester knows something is going on."

"He probably does, but you let me worry about that, Doll. We'll tell him when the time seems right."

"Yeah, okay," she said as she glanced toward the patio to catch Sil eyeing them as if straining to hear the conversation. "He's not going to back down. He knows there's more to this story than he's been told."

"Copy that." Her dad held out his arms to embrace her. He hugged her for quite a while. "It's all is in God's hands. Keep close to Him."

"I will, Dad."

Carolyn's mom had hugged all the kids and had made her way over to the car. "Ready to hit the road?"

"I'm ready. Let's go." Carolyn turned to smile at the comrades she was leaving behind. She slunk into the passenger side of the station wagon, fighting to keep her eyes dry until they were out of sight. Her mother slid into the driver's seat, handing a tin of homemade peanut butter cookies across to Carolyn. They waved goodbye to her father and siblings still standing on the driveway with big "see you soon" smiles. Tears fell from Carolyn's eyes as soon as they rounded the corner onto the main road, which took her out of her hometown and on the way to Aunt Hildy's farm community of Kalkaska.

Her mother patted her leg. "I'm so proud of you. You've amazed me with how you've carried this heavy cross with such maturity and grace." Carolyn smiled in appreciation. Her mom continued, "Hold onto your faith, Doll. Jesus walks beside you, and the Blessed Mother has her mantle wrapped around you."

"Thank you, Mom, for all you've done. I couldn't have made it this far without you."

"Let's pray a Rosary." It was her mom's remedy for everything.

She squeezed her mother's hand, leaned her head against the window of the car, and shut her eyes, letting her mom pray the words for both of them. *Growing an infant is tiring work!*

***

The white Victorian farmhouse was as Carolyn had recalled. Huge. She noted the paint was still peeling in the upper gable. Aunt Hildy presented with open arms on the expansive gray porch. The two females leaned against the car and buttressed themselves for a big German hug, and they were not disappointed. Hildegard made her way toward them, arms still wide. Typical pleasantries were exchanged within the embrace.

Before anyone else could, Aunt Hildy grabbed the suitcase out of the back end of the station wagon. "I'll take that."

Her mom picked up the groceries, and Carolyn followed up the six wide stairs and into the house with her bear and the cookie tin. The living room was as sparsely furnished and modest as she remembered. The same faded wallpaper covered the walls. The same yellowing doilies could be spotted on the wooden end tables. Carolyn set her teddy on the floor next to her suitcase by the stairs.

She walked to the kitchen and set the cookie tin on the counter. Glancing at the stove, she smiled, relieved. Her great-grandmother's tea kettle sat on the back burner as it always had. The bluebird painted on the side was still faintly visible. For some reason, she had always imagined the bird chirping when the kettle whistle sounded. Oddly, the sight of it comforted her. She looked forward to hearing it peep during the last half of her pregnancy.

Aunt Hildy had followed behind, sizing Carolyn up, but not for her growth spurt in height this time. Rather, the aging midwife was staring at the girth of her niece's swollen abdomen. "The baby looks the right size, Girl."

Carolyn blushed and covered her belly with her palm as if to hide her secret. *I guess I'd better get used to that type of attention.* She kept her hand there, wondering when she would feel the butterfly movement inside of her.

She and her mother exchanged rolled eyes at the bluntness of their aunt. Her mother raised her eyebrows at Aunt Hildy, who shot glances back at them both. "Oh, dears, what's the problem? Why the long faces? It's not the first time a young girl has found herself in this situation. I've seen plenty. It isn't the end of the world. Life will get back to being normal. It will just be a new order of normal." When neither Carolyn nor her mom responded, Aunt Hildy continued. "A baby is God's way of showing us how much He's in control. God doesn't will the circumstances of how new life comes about. He leaves that up to us, but He's always there in the creation of life. We have to trust His plan. Babies often bring hope and joy to circumstances such as yours, Carolyn Joanna."

There was no way to argue that. Carolyn's mom had given the same counsel to other Catholic mothers in similar circumstances; yet this time was different. *This time, it's happening to her daughter.* Carolyn noticed the pensive expression on her mother's face and tried to take away some of her concerns. "Aunt Hildy is right, Mother. I have thought a lot about this; trust me. Although I would change in a split second what happened to me, I wouldn't change the new life growing inside of me. I am a mother now."

Hildy agreed enthusiastically. "Oh, Carolyn, that is such wisdom!"

"Well, I learned it from my mom." Smiling, she grabbed her mother's hand and drew it to her abdomen. Her mom closed her eyes and flattened her hand, holding it there. Carolyn waited. When her mom's eyes opened again, Carolyn asked, "Did you feel it?"

"Not yet, but it'll happen." Her mom turned toward her aunt with pride, pointing to Carolyn's womb. "That's my grandchild in there."

Aunt Hildy beamed and nodded.

After a lunch of egg salad sandwiches, pickles, and potato chips, her mother commenced with unpacking and organizing Carolyn's things to get her settled into her room.

An old four-poster that squeaked offered a place of rest. The bedspread was blue chenille, akin to Auntie Dora's. Aunt Hildy had provided three feather pillows for extra comfort. Next to the bed was an end table one of her uncles had made. Neither she nor her mom could remember which one. Carolyn noted how old and wobbly it was when she set her prayer book and rosary on it. The room had no closet, but a large wardrobe could hold all her clothes. It smelled musty when she opened it. Carolyn scrunched up her face from the odor.

"Leave the doors ajar for the rest of the week to air it out," her mom suggested. She then opened the window that overlooked the pasture for a bit of ventilation.

Carolyn turned to breathe in the fresh country air. She noted that the bench under the sill looked comfy with her great-grandmother's old quilt and a throw pillow. *A delightful place to sit and read.* She propped her bear against the pillow. She pictured herself relaxing alongside it in her flowered nighty with a book.

All the women eventually joined at the kitchen table for tea and cookies. Her mom opened up the conversation about expectations. Carolyn chimed right in. "Aunt Hildy, I so appreciate your letting me stay here through the remainder of my pregnancy. I am willing to clean the house, take care of the laundry, do yard work, and share the cooking."

Hildy took hold of one each of Carolyn's and her mother's hands. Carolyn noted the large size and obvious strength. "This is my turf, dearies, so I set the rules. Carolyn's job will be to assist me in my daily duties, not wait on me hand and foot. She is growing a baby, which takes a lot of work, especially in the latter half." She turned to Carolyn and added, "I will let you do all the tasks you desire, Girl, but I call the shots when your resting is in order."

Carolyn nodded in obedience and returned the squeeze of her aunt's hand.

After exchanging tearful goodbyes outside, Carolyn sat down on the white porch swing her Grandpapa Wagner had built. Hildy was his sister-in-law. When his brother—her husband—died, followed a few years later by their only child, Carolyn's grandpa wanted to give her something that might bring her some joy on lonely days. *I hope I can find some joy here.* She remained in the swing while she watched her great aunt walk her mom to the car. Carolyn had hugged and cried her eyes out enough for one day. It would be too hard to be next to the station wagon when her mom started the ignition and drove off to the safe familiarity of home. Carolyn observed they were deep in conversation. About her, she presumed.

She overheard Aunt Hildy ask, "Dana, are you taking care of yourself?" Her aunt's arm was draped around her mom's shoulder.

Carolyn stopped swinging. *Why did she ask that?* The familiar panic rose inside. Concern gripped her.

She headed to the edge of the steps. She saw her mom tilt her head, seemingly puzzled by the question. "I'm fine, Aunt Hildy." Twisting her neck back at Carolyn, her mom offered her an unconvincing grin. Her mom turned back toward her godmother with a fake giggle. "Why ever would you ask that?"

Carolyn ran off the porch in tears. "Mom, are you sick?! Tell me!"

"No, I am not sick."

Her eyes searched her mom's face, which revealed nothing. Turning then to Hildy, the aunt appeared unable to answer the question. Instead, she stared at Carolyn's mom as if to wait for her response. Carolyn's eyes followed.

Her mom heaved a heavy sigh. But she was smiling in such a way that Carolyn knew if something was wrong, it wasn't serious. "I'll tell you what's going on, but there's no cause for worry. I haven't said anything

83

because your father hasn't been told. Having two pregnant Fandel women in the house might have been tough for him to handle."

Carolyn squealed, "Mom! You're expecting?!"

"Yes, she is!"

"Wait. How did you know, Aunt Hildy, if my mother hasn't told anyone?"

Her mom laughed. "She just does. Nothing gets by Hildegard, the midwife." Continuing, "At forty-two, I surely did not anticipate this."

"When are you due?"

"Early February."

"Oh my gosh! Our babies will be near in age! When are you going to tell Dad?"

"I'm not sure, so you two can't say a word." Her mom tilted her head toward them with eyes that elicited a promise.

"We promise." The two replied as if they were teammates.

"Thank you. I have been praying for the right time to tell him. After Frankie's birth, your dad and I waited until I regained my health. We were surprised my fertility didn't return after I stopped nursing. We've always been open to life but, after seven years—" Her mom choked up. "—after seven years, I wasn't sure that God would send us any more."

"Well, He did." Aunt Hildy chimed back in with her straight-shooting German tone, "And you'd better take care of yourself, Girl."

"I will."

"I mean it. Put that Adeline to work."

Carolyn laughed, "Yeah, put that Adeline to work."

"Okay, you two. I'm a seasoned professional at being pregnant, but I do appreciate your concern." Her mom chuckled. "I see you two have already formed an alliance."

By then, the three of them were laughing, sharing another round of hugs.

Carolyn waved and exchanged blown kisses with her mom one last time and watched the family station wagon roll to the end of the driveway, turn south, and head home. Without her.

84

CHAPTER NINETEEN

The first few weeks at Aunt Hildy's dragged slowly, and Carolyn missed her Fandels. She lived for the phone calls from her parents. No one else had yet been told. She longed to be able to shoot the breeze with Silvester and Adeline.

Passing by the bathroom mirror in her mom's old, blue-checked maternity top, Carolyn noticed her slouching shoulders, revealing her slumping attitude. Sequestering herself back in her room, she sat on the window seat. She pulled her feet off the floor, clutched her teddy, and wrapped her arms around her knees. She leaned her head against the pane of glass and had another good cry. Since her arrival, she had shed her private tears time and time again until her eyes had no more to offer.

She did her best to maintain a cheerful attitude around Hildy. Her aging aunt had gone out of her way to make Carolyn feel welcome. From the purposefully placed items in her room to not giving her too many chores to serving her tea every single night after dinner, Hildy had embraced her. Carolyn felt comfortable there.

Strolling alone in the farm fields the next afternoon, while admiring the hints of promising fall colors high in the trees, her mind catapulted back to that horrid spring night. Another panic attack. *Oh, no! Not again!* Her throat tightened. Her heart raced. Her gut clenched. Stark still as if her feet were frozen to the ground, she replayed the rape over and over again. She saw the lavender dress she was wearing. She heard the same music blasting. She had the weight of him on top of her. Searing pain resonated between her legs. The worst of it, though, was what she smelled—Skip Jergen. She bent over and vomited beside the weeping willow as if to cast out the resurgence of Old Spice that had permeated her senses. She attempted to scream but couldn't. It was as if her voice had been stolen along with her purity.

Breathing herself back to reality as her mom had taught her, she headed to the farmhouse. Praying all the way there, she pleaded with God to let her dispel this gut-wrenching memory. *Lord, I beg you to erase my memory. Please, make me forget.* Carolyn trudged up the back stairs into the kitchen in time to hear the phone ring.

"It's your parents," hollered Aunt Hildy.

Hurrying with relief to the living room, Carolyn took hold of the receiver. "Hello?"

Her dad chimed in from the background, "Hi, Doll." She smiled at the pet name. "And by the way, your mother told me her news." She could picture her dad leaning into the receiver of the phone. The enthusiastic tone told Carolyn her dad was happy about the new baby and probably winking when he said it. Their joy was contagious enough that Carolyn temporarily forgot about her panic attack.

"But, what we're calling about," her mom continued, "is that your brother has sorted things out."

"What do you mean, 'things'?"

"Pretty much everything. He will explain it himself when he sees you. He's planning a trip up there this weekend if that's okay with you."

"Sure. I guess." She hesitated. "Actually, it would be great to see him. What about Adeline?"

"No," her dad said. "We haven't told her yet."

***

From the large picture window, Carolyn watched the maroon Chevy wagon meander up the farm's long driveway. She noticed her mom in the passenger seat, her brother at the wheel. She was both looking forward to and dreading seeing Silvester. She sighed with resolve and stepped out onto the porch to greet them, but her emotions got the better of her. As soon as he exited the car, she became too embarrassed by her paunch. *I can't risk being chided by him.* Crying, she turned around and ran inside up to her room and shut the door, his footsteps following.

"Let me in, Carolyn. I know what happened. And it isn't your fault. Please let me in." She remained silent, willing him to go away. But he pressed on, "Carolyn, it isn't your fault. Skip is the scum of the earth."

Hearing his name made her shudder enough to stop the cascading tears. She wiped her eyes, cracked the door a fraction, and peeked through—so exposed, so vulnerable. Sil pushed it open a sliver at a time until she reluctantly stepped backward, allowing him to enter. The first thing he did was embrace her, something he had never done. Carolyn was touched by his compassion. She let down her guard and allowed herself to be held by her older brother. Sil stood still, permitting her to remain in his arms for as long as she wanted. "Sis, I wish this weren't true. But I knew it for sure when I confronted Mom and Dad about it.

86

They were reluctant to tell me, but I could see them eye-talking."

Carolyn had a vision of her mom and dad looking back and forth at one another as if they were having a full conversation with no words. "Yep. They always do that when they're trying to communicate between the two of them and keep everyone else in the dark about the topic."

Sil laughed. "You got that right!"

Carolyn pulled away and pointed to her midsection. "Guess you can see that I am not even close to being Miss Perfect."

"What are you talking about, Carolyn? I don't think any less of you." Carolyn was relieved. "But who told you?"

"No one told me. Listen. At the beginning of last school year, I overheard some junior guys talking about a similar occurrence at the previous Spring Formal party. I didn't go because I had to work the next day, remember?"

"Yeah," nodding for him to go on.

"Well, anyway, these guys were laughing about how drunk this girl was, someone who used to be in their class but who had 'miraculously' disappeared during mid-summer. Then, I heard them say, 'She transferred to another school, according to Skip.'"

Carolyn's mouth gaped open. She slowly lowered herself to sit on the bed. "Did you ever tell anyone?"

"No."

"Why not?!" she yelled, her eyes wide and full of disbelief.

Sil took a seat on the window bench to face her. "Because it was a rumor. I had no way of validating it. What if it wasn't true? The police aren't going to believe a drunk girl anyway. It would be assumed she asked for it."

I wonder if he knows I was drinking? At this point, it didn't matter, so she let her brother finish his story. "We've always been taught to keep rumors to ourselves unless someone was in immediate physical or moral danger." He paused. "Believe me, I have thought about this. A lot."

"Okay. I guess that all makes sense. But why are you telling me all this now?"

"To apologize."

"For what?"

"If I had told someone, this might not have happened to you."

Carolyn noticed his eyes were moist. "Oh, Sil. You're the last person I blame."

"Thank you, Sis. You have no idea how much I appreciate that. I've been going crazy replaying the what-ifs in my mind."

"Trust me," said Carolyn rolling her eyes, "I have what-iffed a trillion times the past five months." Changing the subject, "Are you starving? I'm starving."

The two ventured downstairs and into the kitchen. Their mother and Hildy were putting out a lunch of cold fried chicken, potato salad, and fresh applesauce. Carolyn was famished and couldn't wait to savor the flavors. The chicken smelled so good. Its crisp, salty coating was finger-licking delicious. The creaminess of the potato salad made its way around her mouth. And the chunky cinnamon applesauce delighted her sweet tooth. Most of all, though, she was enjoying the lively conversation. She had missed them. Her mom was so animated in talking about the antics of Adeline and the boys that her eyes twinkled. And Silvester had inherited their dad's brand of button-pushing humor.

Carolyn exchanged smiles with Aunt Hildy, who also seemed to be relishing the chatter. It could get lonesome rambling around that farm.

Her mom redirected the tone of the conversation, and Carolyn found herself nodding with Aunt Hildy. They had been waiting for it. "Silvester, I have news to share with you. You're not only going to be an uncle. You're also going to be a big brother again."

He grinned at his mom and winked. After a slight pause, "So, when will this one pop out?"

Aunt Hildy nearly choked on her chicken.

"Oh, for heaven's sakes, Silvester James! 'Pop out'? Really?!" And then their mother added with a huge smile, "February sometime."

After lunch, and all too soon, in Carolyn's opinion, it was time for her mom and Sil to leave. Hugging her brother, she said, "Thanks for coming. I didn't want you to know, but I am so glad you do. Please do not breathe a word about this to anyone, though, especially to Paul Johns."

Silvester swore that he wouldn't, and Carolyn could tell he meant it.

CHAPTER TWENTY

Summer ended abruptly, as it always does in Michigan. With it came the first day of school and nothing but distress for Carolyn. *My entire class will be there for senior year. Except for me. And poor Adeline is stuck having to field comments from everyone.*

"I'm up for the challenge," Adeline had assured her. Carolyn had no option other than to trust that her sister could handle the barrage of questions.

Resigned to miss her last year of high school and all it held, she let out a deep sigh and cried a few tears. The baby moved—proof again how real this was—and she implored God to get her through this. Her spirits were low. Her days were spent doing chores, tackling the classwork the school was sending, traversing the property. She longed to sit at a desk at school and to sleep next to Adeline. She was miserable and bored out of her gourd. Nothing seemed to appease her. She was alone without her friends and her Fandels—an irritating truth.

Younger women at church had given Carolyn the cold-shoulder treatment. Aunt Hildy urged her to strike up a conversation at coffee and donuts with a few girls her age one Sunday after Mass. She told her niece it would be good for her, but Carolyn would have been fine without the attempt. They were polite enough, but their mothers came to the table and ushered their daughters away. The moms later told Aunt Hildy that they didn't think it was a good idea to have their daughters mingle with Carolyn. "After all, she isn't the model of virtue," they had said. Aunt Hildy, of course, did not repeat these nasty words to her niece, but Carolyn wasn't a fool. She understood.

It pained Carolyn to be shunned. She had plenty of friends at home. She wasn't used to being an outcast, and it caused her a great deal of loneliness and annoyance. *Geesh! They can't get pregnant from sitting next to me. I'm not contagious, for Pete's sake.*

Aunt Hildy had tried to explain to the mothers about Carolyn, but it made little difference. If they weren't glaring at her, they were shooting pitiful expressions, which Carolyn couldn't stand. She became resolved that no friends were going to be made in her new town. She was going to have to be content with her aging aunt and the few old ladies from church who had been hospitable to her. If they judged her, they kept it to themselves.

***

Her childhood images of extradition resurfaced the day two strange men came to Aunt Hildy's. From her bedroom window, Carolyn spied them, pointing toward the farmhouse. They spent a great deal of time circling the entire perimeter of the acreage. Her great aunt was engaging the men in what seemed to be a serious conversation.

When Carolyn asked about it later, Aunt Hildy had stated that it wasn't at all her concern. Carolyn couldn't shake the unsettling trepidation inside herself. *Maybe the men are somehow connected to HIM.* Back in time, she flew. She had to make an unremitting effort to keep herself from being hijacked again.

She took a huge breath and peered out the kitchen window. The day was too warm for hot tea, but Carolyn didn't care. She turned on the burner under the kettle. This was the most expedient way to try to keep the fright at bay. While she waited for the reassuring bluebird to chirp out steam, she shut her eyes and begged the Lord to keep her safe. Carolyn grabbed her cup of tea and went out to the porch swing. With each comforting chamomile sip, her internal alarm dissipated.

She heard the phone ringing and ran into the house to answer it ahead of Hildy. Carolyn was expecting a call from Adeline.

"Boy, have I got news for you!"

"Well, do tell. How is school going?"

"To be honest, trying to run interference with you has been a challenge—especially with Paul."

Carolyn's mood shifted as she lowered herself onto the couch. She was getting nervous. Her legs were shaking. "How so?"

"He's backed off some, but for a while, he was following me around like a dog sniffing for a bone."

Carolyn laughed. "I'm sure he was. What did you tell him?"

"I kept sticking to the story about Aunt Hildy needing a righthand. I could tell he wasn't buying it."

Carolyn sighed. "You've done all you can. Thank you."

"I'd do anything for you, Sis. I miss you so much."

Carolyn could hear Adeline start to cry, causing a lump to rise in her own throat. She choked back the emotion. "I miss you too."

"Will you be back in time for the Spring Formal, so we can double date?"

"Oh, Adeline, I'm not sure. I'm figuring things out as I go along. Let's both try to be patient." She had no idea what else to say. After all, she was barely seventeen with the weight of the world on her shoulders. Taking in a big breath and changing the subject, "So what's your big news?"

"I was voted as captain of the cheerleading squad!"

"That's fantastic, Sis. So happy for you." It was true—at least when she said it. She ended the conversation before Adeline could catch on that her older sister was headed into another downward spiral. She didn't begrudge Adeline anything, but she was jealous. And Carolyn hated that she was. One more thing to berate herself about.

CHAPTER TWENTY-ONE

In the coming weeks, pressure built inside Carolyn, creating additional anxiety. Her life's jigsaw puzzle still held gaping holes with some of its pieces still in hiding. The critical decisions she had to make had caught up with her. Shadows loomed in her soul. *Please, Jesus, send in some light.* She stretched her arms behind her and noted how stiff her neck was from carrying her stress between her shoulder blades. She took in a few deep breaths, breathing in the clean country air and then exhaling as if she was forcing out the dirty parts of her life.

She was aware that she had started to waddle. *Great! I've always desired to be a giant duck.* It was difficult for her to focus on her schoolwork. *What's the point of it anyway?*

Her aunt had offered a lot of good advice during the rich conversations they had had, but any choice going forward was Carolyn's.

By the time October revealed leaves of crimson, amber, and rust, God had revealed answers to Carolyn. She dialed the phone. "Mom and Dad, could you both come for a visit this weekend?"

While waiting on the porch for their arrival, she wondered how pregnant her mom would appear. A sullen mood welled up inside her. *Everyone is excited about Mom's baby, but mine is still a secret.* Carolyn rubbed her mound and spoke softly, "Don't worry, baby, whoever you are. I love you, and soon, the world won't be able to hide you."

Seeing the station wagon wend its way closer, she became eager to hug her parents and share with them her innermost reflections. She descended the porch stairs into their reassuring arms. "It's so good to get hugs from both of you!" Stepping back, she put her hand on her mother's abdomen. "Oh, mom, you have so much going on. I'm sorry you have to worry about me, too."

"Nonsense. I'm doing fine. Aren't I, Robert?"

"Your mom's a wonder. And we're both looking forward to having another squeaker in the house. It's been a while."

Her mom smiled, first down at her midsection and then at her daughter's. "Two squeaking miracles." She winked at Carolyn's dad.

The three of them went into the kitchen where Aunt Hildy was finishing up the lemon meringue pie. She was just pulling it from the broiler, where the pure white tips of the meringue had been transformed into a nutty golden brown. Hildy set the pie on a ledge near the open window to cool. Carolyn's mouth watered as she imagined dipping her fork into the warm lemon custard, wrapping her lips around the tines, pulling it into her mouth—an ultimate fusion of sweet and sour with the flakiest pie crust on the planet. It was hard to wait.

Sitting down at the large oak table, water glasses in hand, Carolyn made eye contact with her parents. "Aunt Hildy and I have been talking about what I should do with the baby. Although she knows a slew of good people who might be willing to adopt, I have come to love my baby so much. I don't see any way clear to give it away and never see it again. I could not withstand that sorrow. I will always wonder how my baby's life turned out, which relatives my baby resembled, or if my baby hated me for giving it away."

"I comprehend that overwhelming love for the new life growing inside," her mom said. "I can tell you've put a lot of time into making the best decision possible."

Carolyn nodded. "I have." She drew in a long breath. "I've decided that since I am wholly capable of being a good mother, and because I'm so blessed to have all of you in my corner, I should keep the baby."

Her dad grabbed her hand for a squeeze. "Your mom and I have talked about this many times. We've always respected this as your choice. We will back you any way we can." Gazing sympathetically at her mom, he said, "Won't we, Dana?"

"Absolutely. You have always had our total support as our daughter, and you have it now as a new mother."

Carolyn exhaled a massive sigh of relief. She had her parents' unconditional love, but hearing their unwavering reassurance confirmed for her that she had made a good, moral decision. "Aunt Hildy said I could stay with her for a while to see how life plays out after the baby is born."

Her dad interjected. "You have time for that decision. But now, of course, we will have to inform your other brothers and relatives."

"Thank you for handling that for me." It was the part Carolyn dreaded, but it had to be done. She might be able to keep herself hidden for a few months, but she couldn't hide a baby. She wondered how they might judge her, but she couldn't waste precious time dwelling on it. She was not responsible for their feelings.

She treasured her limited visit with both her parents. She missed them so much. She missed family confession on Saturdays, she missed family chores, she missed sewing and baking with her mother, she missed summer lemonade stands with the younger kids, she missed rooming with Adeline, she missed Frankie, who wasn't so little anymore, and she missed being with her mom through her pregnancy with Fandel baby seven. She missed them all! She pondered the notion of being separated from her Fandels for even more months or years.

"Mom and Dad? You said we'd talk later about what happens after the baby is born, but I'm inclined to make firm plans now if that's okay?"

"What is it you're thinking?" her mom inquired.

"I don't want to live away from Grand Lake for too many more months. I'd rather the whole world see me with my baby than live apart from you. May I please come home after the birth?"

A tear trickled down her mom's cheek, and she reached across the table to hold the hands of her brave daughter. "Of course, you may! I'm not sure where we're going to put the two of you, but God always makes room."

Her dad gave a positive nod. "And we can subsidize your living expenses until you are finished with high school, get a job, and save some money to finance yourself." The rule had always been that once a child had graduated, room and board must be paid.

"Thank you, Dad. That means a lot."

Carolyn noticed her father narrowing his eyebrows and pursing his lips. "What's the matter, Dad? Are you having second thoughts about me and the baby returning?"

Her dad eyed her mom.

"Go ahead, Robert. If she's going to come home, she needs to know."

"Know what?" Carolyn demanded.

"Paul Johns has been asking about you. He's even been over to the house."

"What?!" Carolyn might be ready for all her relatives to learn the truth, but she was extremely concerned about Paul's perception of her. She was sure he'd want nothing to do with her. She definitely did *not* want him to know. "What did he say?"

Her mom spoke. "Two Saturday mornings ago, Wallace answered the back door to find Paul standing there. As soon as I heard his voice, I went to the door, closed it behind me, and joined him on the patio. He was perturbed and direct. He said, 'Mrs. Fandel, is something wrong with Carolyn?'"

"What did you tell him?"

"I stuck to our storyline about Aunt Hildy, but he wasn't buying it. He said, 'Please forgive me, Mrs. Fandel, but too many things aren't adding up. I respect that it's your call, but please tell Carolyn I hope to see her.'"

"No!" Carolyn argued, "I couldn't bear it! I don't want to see him."

"Eventually, he'll learn the truth," her dad pointed out.

"Eventually, he can, but not yet. I'll figure it out, but having the relatives know about me is all I can handle right now."

Her dad added, "That's fine, Carolyn. You can tell him when you wish. But, with Silvester and Adeline already in the loop and more people coming on board with your news, he might hear it from someone. So, if you aspire for him to hear it from you, I suggest you make it snappy. He's a man on a mission, and I believe he has a flame for you. There's one thing I'm sure about, and that is it's hard to hold a man on a mission at bay."

"Okay, I hear you, Dad. I will work on a plan. I promise."

After her parents left, she went out to the porch swing, happy to have found another piece to her puzzle. She and her baby would be welcomed back, and Carolyn felt lighter than she had in weeks. She caught herself dreaming of what was ahead. She imagined herself and Adeline pushing their double bed over like they had done for many guests. This would make room for a crib next to Carolyn's side of the bed. She couldn't wait for the prayers and late-night chats she and her sister had always shared.

The one thing she *could* wait for was telling Paul. No conversation played out well in her mind. All scenarios ended with him walking away to find a woman he deserved, not one saddled with a kid.

95

CHAPTER TWENTY-TWO

The Sunday before Thanksgiving, Hildy's bellowing voice called up the stairs, "You've got visitors!"

Startled, Carolyn hadn't realized Sil and Adeline would be there so soon. "Tell them I'll be there in a jiffy." Standing in front of the mirror in her room, she tried to make her hair presentable. She settled on a ponytail, tying it with a silk floral scarf. She examined herself, bulging belly and all, in her green pleated maternity top—a birthday gift from her parents. Its long sleeves were ideal for fall's cooler temperatures. She shrugged her shoulders at the image in the mirror. *It's the best I can do.* She tottered down the stairs for a group hug in the living room. "Oh my, it's good to see you guys." She noticed Aunt Hildy had her hands full. "And that pumpkin pie you brought looks delectable."

The three autumn-jacketed comrades sat outside, enjoying the last of the sunny fall days. Sil and Adeline flanked their sister on the porch swing, taking turns tracking their niece's or nephew's kicks. Now and again, Carolyn detected Sil and Adeline taking turns scanning the front yard. She tried to ignore it, but when she saw the two of them link eyes, she, too, scanned the area. "What the heck are you two looking for?"

"I'm not sure exactly," Sil said.

"Me neither," said Adeline.

Carolyn saw them roll their eyes toward each other as if they knew the obvious, but she didn't. "Spill it!" she commanded.

Sil ventured, "We're being watched by someone, but don't panic."

Too late. Terror gripped her. She put her hands down and hugged her abdomen as if trying to bring her baby to safety. Her worst nightmare was about to come true. "Oh, no! How did *he* find out?"

"We're not sure." Adeline said, "Maybe from some conversations at school. I guess he must have followed us."

Carolyn's head was spinning with visions of disloyalty, and her pulse picked up pace. "Wait! *He* was at school?! You were talking to him about *me*?!" Fury rose inside. "Adeline! Why on earth would you even waste your breath on Skip Jergen?!"

"Not *him*!" Sil and Adeline said together.

Poor, pregnant Carolyn had sorely misunderstood. She was so confused. "Then, who?" But as soon as the words were out of her mouth, she knew. "Lord, have mercy!" Carolyn whispered. "What am I supposed to do?" Her heart now thumped for a different reason.

The three sat silent. What should they do? Let Paul slink around in the bushes without confronting him? That seemed dumb.

"Go get him."

"Are you sure?" Adeline asked.

"Well, clearly, he's already seen me now. Better to let him have his say than for him to go running back to Grand Lake with all sorts of news to tell," Carolyn reasoned with a hint of scorn.

"He wouldn't do that," Sil said.

With dripping sarcasm, "What makes you so sure? Don't people eat up this type of gossip, especially when it happens to a good girl from a good background?"

"He's not that breed of guy," Sil defended. "You're imagining things."

Adeline agreed. "That isn't his style. Besides, I think he honestly cares about you. Whenever he asks questions or pumps me for info, he is always sure to do it where no one else can hear us. It's as if he's protective of you."

Carolyn cracked a smile. "Yeah, he would do that. He is an exceptional guy," her emotions flip-flopping.

Sil and Adeline rolled their eyes.

They all sat mute, each waiting for someone else in the threesome to come to a conclusion.

Sil hunted around again, trying to spot him. "He's there all right, biding his time behind those shrubs at the fence near the road." He slunk off the porch and tiptoed toward the bushes. When he got close enough, he shouted, "Hey, Johns!"

Carolyn and Adeline giggled as they saw Paul jump, scared out of his wits.

"I can see you, you dummy. What in the heck are you doing, Johns? Following us? Creeping on Carolyn? You'd better start explaining yourself." Sil was trying to sound as tough as possible.

"I'm sorry, Sil, but you Fandels have been so damned tight-lipped. It was driving me crazy. I had to see her for myself. I just had to."

"Come on, Johns. She sent me out here to get you." Sil slung his arm around Paul's shoulder as a friend would. The two made their way across the dirt driveway to the expansive porch.

Hildy towered on the steps, her arms folded. She was large-boned for a woman, which made her look quite formidable. Having already been made privy by her nieces, she feigned a curious tone, "Well, well, who have we here?"

"Hello, ma'am. I'm Paul Johns. I'm Carolyn's—" Paul stopped for a second. "Um, I'm Carolyn's friend from church and school."

"What brings you to this neck of the woods, young man?" Hildy asked with a wink.

"I'm here to check on Carolyn. I'm sorry for intruding, though. Real sorry. I'll leave now."

"Nonsense! No one comes to visit and gets sent away without eating something. Besides, I get the impression my great-niece is glad you're here. Take a seat," Hildy pointed to the porch stairs with a slight smile, winking at her nieces.

Paul obeyed and took a hasty seat on the first step. He glanced up at Carolyn, who felt her face get warm. She noticed he was gawking at her belly, finding it hard – she was sure – not to stare at the obvious. She drew her jacket around herself. Her face grew hotter while waiting for Paul to say something. Anything. When he did not, she thought she'd bail him out. "Well, I'm sure I'm a sight you didn't expect to see."

Paul shook his head. "It's okay, Carolyn. I'm happy to see you. I've been so worried about you. It's good to see that you're not sick or something."

She was touched. He had tailed her siblings and hid in the bushes to make sure she was okay. "Thank you for your concern, Paul." It pleased her that he wasn't scared off when he caught a glimpse of her enormous paunch. He knew she was pregnant, yet he was undaunted. *He could have easily gotten back into his father's car and driven away.*

No one on the porch offered more to the conversation. They all stared at their feet, unsure of what to do. The silence made Carolyn uneasy, and she was certain Paul must have felt awkward. She threw a glance at Aunt Hildy as if to plead for help.

Sweeping her arm toward the house, Hildy said, "You two come inside while I rustle up some sustenance." Sil and Adeline glimpsed their sister, who waved them in with the back of her hand, indicating she was fine to be left alone with Paul.

He climbed a couple of steps closer. "I'm truly sorry, Carolyn, for surprising you. It was a ratty thing to do." He was nervous, rubbing his hands up and down his thighs.

"It's okay. I should have told you that afternoon in the park, but I couldn't." Pointing to her mounded tummy, "How do you tell scandalous news to someone you care about?"

"I understand why you didn't want me to find out. What I don't understand is—" he trailed off as if afraid to hear the answer to the question he was going to ask.

She finished it for him, "You don't understand how I got this way. Right?"

He nodded. "You're right, Carolyn. I do not understand any of it." He shook his head. She sensed he might have more to say, so she waited for him to muster up the courage. "How far along are you?"

"Seven months."

"Seven months?" Paul paused. His face turned ashen, and he dashed off the porch.

Oh no, he's leaving! "Paul! Come back. Let's talk," she hollered after him, her heart pounding. He turned around to wave her back. He did not want to be followed. She was stunned. Her head was swimming. But then she saw him lean over behind a maple tree and throw up. She saw him spit and wipe his mouth. He fished around in his pocket and pulled out a half stick of Wrigley's spearmint, popping it into his mouth. He trotted to the side of the barn and turned on the spigot. With his hands cupped together, he scooped some water into his mouth, swished it around, and spewed it out before returning to the porch. He had pieced together the 'who' and 'where.'

Back at the porch, Paul's eyes pooled as he gazed at Carolyn's face and then at her swollen abdomen so rich with new life. He stood on the top step, rocking back and forth from foot to foot as if he was contemplating what to do next. "I can't believe it. That scum. I'm so, so sorry I left you there."

"This is not your fault, Paul." She extended him the offer of sitting beside her on the swing by patting the space next to herself. "If it doesn't gross you out or anything by sitting next to a pregnant girl."

He wasted no time taking his place close to her. Wiping his eyes with his sleeve, "Carolyn, don't ever say that again. I could never be grossed out by you." He reached for her hand, and she let him take it. It felt right. They sat there together, swaying back and forth, neither one of them speaking. Somehow, that felt right, too, just to be together. For that moment in time, no words were necessary.

After a while, Paul told her, "I've been praying for you, and now I will add your baby to those prayers."

The words he spoke were balm to her troubled soul. She peered into his brown eyes. *Man, are those eyes piercingly brown.* "I appreciate that, Paul. This baby and I can use all the prayers we can get."

"I will support you in any way I can."

Aunt Hildy emerged, carrying a sturdy stack of plates and forks. Behind her were Adeline and the pumpkin pie. Sil followed with a jug of Momber's apple cider and four cups. The chatter diminished as they enjoyed the fall flavors, indicative of the awkwardness of the whole situation.

Standing in the driveway for their departure, Sil and Adeline took their turns hugging their sister and placing hands on her abdomen, hoping the baby would kick. As they opened the doors to the Fandel car, Paul offered his farewells. He leaned over and gave Carolyn a peck on the cheek. "Don't worry. It'll all work out."

She smiled, but inside she was rolling her eyes. *Easy for you to say.*

As Paul started his slow jog down the drive to his car, hidden near the road, Sil leaned out the window and shouted, "Hey Johns, you'd better stop by our house back in Grand Lake, so you can tell our parents what you did today. Know what I mean?"

Paul nodded. "Copy that."

Sil added, "Are you gonna lead or follow this time?"

Carolyn busted out laughing, followed by her siblings, and then Aunt Hildy, and finally, Paul.

She and Hildy together waved goodbye to the two-car caravan. Her aunt remarked, "He sure is a nice boy."

Carolyn nodded in agreement. *And very good-looking,* she thought but didn't say. She spent the remainder of the afternoon replaying the visit and daydreaming about what-ifs.

That evening, she poured a cup of tea and swiped another piece of pie to take to her room. She planned to savor the pie and the tea's warmth while she finished deciphering the prologue to the Canterbury Tales, her current lit assignment. She changed out of her maternity clothes and into her comfy nighty. She sat on the window seat and opened her literature book:

When in April the sweet showers fall
And pierce the drought of March to the root, and all
The veins are bathed in liquid of such power
As brings about the engendering of the flower

She couldn't get much beyond the word "April." Her last April was too raw still. She read the first four lines over and over, trying to let them sink in with meaning, but the word "April" got bigger and bigger each time she crossed it. As she read, she reflected upon her last March when things were uncomplicated. And compared the showers of April to the water her eyes had shed. And the power Skip held over her. And the result—an engendering flower now within her.

A salty stream cascaded down Carolyn's face, as one had so many times already. What inaugurated, though, as tears of regret, rooted their way in a more positive direction. She found herself smiling now and then in the midst of crying, replaying Paul's words, "Don't worry. It'll all work out." She pondered what he had meant. He said it so convincingly as if he had a plan. If it was what Carolyn hoped it might be, it would shock a lot of people, especially his parents.

CHAPTER TWENTY-THREE

Her folks phoned to wish her and Aunt Hildy a Happy Thanksgiving and informed her they had told the rest of the kids and Auntie Dora the news.

"What did she say?"

"She was surprised. And very empathetic. When we explained we weren't ready to tell the whole world, she winked and said she'd take it to her grave. She's praying for you," her dad said.

Her mom informed, "We plan to tell your aunts and uncles throughout today as we see them at your grandparents' houses. It's up to them how and when they'll tell your cousins."

***

Carolyn was taken by surprise when her dad called again on Sunday. She assumed it was so they could fill her in on the rest of the relatives' reactions. Answering the phone, she could tell right away that something was wrong.

"I've got some sad news, Doll," her dad began. "When we went upstairs to wake Auntie Dora for Mass, she wasn't breathing."

"Oh, no!"

"She died last night. Poor old soul. She was clutching her rosary, so she was praying when she passed."

"Oh, Dad. I'm so sorry. She was your favorite aunt."

"She's with God, and it was a peaceful death. That's all that matters. And for once, she kept her word not to spread our family business," joked Robert. "She took your news to her grave. She kept her promise not to blab for once." He was laughing.

"Dad, what a thing to say! But it's sort of funny and true." Carolyn giggled. But then she grew somber. "I won't be able to come to the funeral, will I?"

"Not enough people have heard about your condition yet. A funeral is no place to explain such a thing. It will take the focus off celebrating Auntie Dora's life. She would understand, Doll. You and Hildy can pray from there."

***

On the day of the funeral, Aunt Hildy and Carolyn offered a Rosary for the repose of Dora's soul. Carolyn spent time alone in her room, reminiscing. *I'm going to miss those butter and brown sugar sandwiches. No more baking days with Auntie Dora.* Carolyn sighed.

In her sadness, she realized Auntie Dora's funeral wasn't the only family gathering she'd be missing. She'd also be absent for the combined Fandel-Wagner St. Nicholas Day party—Carolyn's favorite celebration. She and her siblings always greatly anticipated piling into the Fandel grandparents' homestead, so crowded with relatives that people had to squeeze their way from room to room.

Carolyn reminisced about the multitude of cousins playing together all day, eating as much traditional German food as they could. She pictured her mom and aunts carrying in dishes to pass and placing them down on the long dining room table—one that stretched a mile. A mile of scrumptious German wonder. She could see the table loaded with a colossal roaster of Grandmama Wagner's famous sticky chicken, another of Ma Fandel's beer-braised kielbasa and sauerkraut, a pan stacked high with fluffy dinner rolls, and all the various salad bowls from the aunts. In her mind, Carolyn tasted the umpteen Christmas goodies baked and formed by her doting grandmothers. The German Christmas stollen fruitcake, coconut kisses, creamy peanut butter fudge, thick chocolate covered dates, soft peppermint patties, chewy butterscotch caramels, hard rock candy in all spicy flavors, popcorn balls wrapped in waxed paper, Rice Krispies treats, *Lebkuchen* gingerbread men, and the unbelievable taste of heaven itself: sour cream Christmas cookies, cut in all shapes, iced with shiny goodness, and speckled with sprinkles, colored sugar, and tiny candies. At the end of the table sat two punch bowls. One full of red HI-C mixed with Vernors for the kids; the other full of golden whiskey sours for the adults. On the stove was a pot of hot mulled Glühwein for the women, while her dad and uncles preferred icy Pabst Blue Ribbon beer. Carolyn pictured it all! Such joy to be had, yet she had to be absent.

The next morning, Carolyn sat droopy-shouldered, picking at her bacon.

"Missing your kin, dear?"

"Terribly. First, Auntie Dora's funeral, and now the huge Christmas celebration for St. Nicholas Day."

"Why don't we scare up some of those old recipes and bake ourselves silly," Aunt Hildy offered.

"That'd be great. Besides sour cream cookies, one of the sweets we can make is something a neighbor lady back in Grand Lake used to give us. I can taste the salty, marshmallow butter just thinking about them. Kristin Sherman's confections were so good."

"What are they called?"

"I'm not sure, but the recipe calls for cornflakes, green food coloring, butter, marshmallows, and cinnamon candies."

"Ooh, Holly Wreaths. I haven't had those in ages. Yes, let's make a batch." Aunt Hildy went to her recipe box and pulled out the card. "And I happen to have all the ingredients."

Carolyn gave her aunt a grateful hug. In all honesty, though, she longed for the day when the road was clear for her and her baby to go home—where they belonged. And to bake with her mom and Adeline in the kitchen she had grown up in.

CHAPTER TWENTY-FOUR

Throughout the next few weeks, Carolyn pictured her parents busily transforming Dora's room for her and her baby, and it was causing discord within herself. Forever that would be Auntie Dora's room. She had also been looking forward to gabbing with her sister in bed, but that wasn't practical. Carolyn needed space to nurse the baby, and Adeline had school. *She can't be awakened at night by my howling infant.* Yet, using Dora's room seemed intrusive.

Carolyn went outside for fresh air. She picked up the broom to sweep the snow off the porch.

"Don't you dare do those steps, Girl," Aunt Hildy warned.

"I won't," promised Carolyn. She knew she could slip on the snow, but she had to get outside and do something. She was bored with pregnancy. *I'm an immense cow and still have at least three weeks to go.* Carolyn bent over to pick up the rug, and something twinged. She straightened up and observed warm liquid running down her leg. "Aunt Hildy!" she screamed.

"My word, your water broke. Come on in here. I'll call your parents." She grabbed an old towel and handed it to Carolyn. "Here, sit on this." Then she dialed the phone. "Dana dear, it's time." Carolyn's parents must have been asking questions because then Aunt Hildy said, "Well, it makes no difference that she's not due for a few more weeks. Babies can't read calendars. Get a move on."

Pretty soon, Hildy handed the receiver to Carolyn. "I'm okay, Mom. But I'm scared. Could you and dad please come up here as soon as you can?"

Her aunt took the phone back. "Phone when you're on your way."
Aunt Hildy guided Carolyn up to her room to settle her in for labor. "Sit in the rocker while I gather some items."

Aunt Hildy whirled around in tornado fashion, assembling things for the birth. She tucked a plastic drape and thick rags under the sheets to soak up any birthing fluid. Next to the bed on the floor, she placed an arsenal of items—a warm washtub of water, a pitcher and bowl of the same, some more rags, and a stack of clean towels. On the nightstand, she meticulously arranged a bottle of rubbing alcohol, a vial of ether, a roll of cotton batting, a handkerchief, and a pair of scissors. Finally, Aunt Hildy said it was time for Carolyn to get into bed.

It seemed as though it was taking forever for her parents to arrive. Carolyn could hardly stand the waiting. It was driving her crazy. Her apprehensions flitted back and forth from the looming pain of childbirth, to wondering if her parents got in an accident, to worrying whether her baby was still alive, to crying about having to do this hard thing in the first place. It was difficult for her to remain rational. Sprinkled in were sporadic, incomplete prayers. She struggled to stay rooted in the present reality, not where her emotions wanted to take her. She felt alone, even though Hildy was right there. She needed her mom to be there. Finally, she heard their voices on the main floor.

Her mom shouted up the stairs. "We're here, Carolyn! I'm going to use the bathroom first. Your dad's unpacking the car."

Simply hearing her mom's voice gave her monumental relief. She was excited to hear her footsteps coming up the stairs. "Hi, Mom." Carolyn forced a smile, but inside she was a wreck.

"How are you doing, Doll?"

"Better, now that you're here." She held out her arms to welcome a hug.

Her mom sat down beside her daughter, stroking her hair to get it out of her eyes. "How about we put that hair in a ponytail?"

Carolyn sat up and twisted her head so that her mom could brush her hair back into a long tail, wrapping it tightly with an elastic band.

When she turned back around, her mom gave her another hug and offered to pray the Rosary to pass time and divert her from the pain. "You can pray in your head. It'll help relax you." Carolyn reached over to her nightstand and obediently grabbed her blue First Communion rosary, made the Sign of the Cross, and kissed the feet of Jesus, as her mom began the repetition of the comforting prayer. She sank into the pillows and closed her eyes. Her breathing became more regular, a sign that she was renewed in strength to see this labor through.

With the Rosary complete, her parents chatted about random stuff going on at home to kill time between contractions. Her dad stayed in the room for quite a while before excusing himself. "Hey, ladies, I'm out of my element here. Got any chores a man can do?"

Aunt Hildy rattled off a shortlist. "You could sweep off the porch again, including the steps, and shovel a clearer path in the driveway."

"I'm on it. Just call me for anything." He bent down and kissed Carolyn on her forehead and Dana on her cheek. "I'll be praying the whole time."

With him gone, Aunt Hildy performed an internal check. "She's about six; won't be too much longer," the experienced midwife told her great-niece. And then she added, "But it's going to get rougher." Mother and daughter nodded at each other in agreement that Hildy could have left out the last part.

Carolyn's mom fed her ice chips and hummed as her daughter labored. She massaged her lowered back.

"I'm scared, Mom."

"It's going to be all right, Doll."

Through gritted teeth between contractions, Carolyn managed to say, "I can't believe you've gone through this six times."

"The result is worth it," her mom assured her.

"If you say so." It was all a laboring Carolyn could utter before the next contraction hit. Carolyn cried out in pain and gripped her mother's sweater. Her mom tried to soothe her as best she could. "Breathe in through your nose and out through your mouth."

Carolyn tried.

"Good," said her mom. "That one is over. You've got about sixty seconds to rest till the next."

To pass the time, her mom picked up a box from the floor and rummaged through it. She showed Carolyn some baby items. "I brought a few neutral-colored things necessary for a newborn. Mine won't be arriving for a while." Between contractions, she held up a good stack of cloth diapers, some plastic pants, large diaper pins, two flannel receiving blankets, and a few sleeping sacks. "These will be enough to get you through till we can return to Grand Lake."

"Thank you, Mom." Carolyn winced in pain. "Oh, no, here comes another one."

"Squeeze my hand," her mom offered.

Finally, Aunt Hildy told her it was time to push. Carolyn was a champ, not allowing her emotions to get the better of her. She listened and did exactly what Hildy told her to do. There was one time near the end when Carolyn panicked from the pain and yelled, "I can't do this!"

Hildy, the midwife, took charge. "Stop talking nonsense. You can, *and* you will do this, Girl! Now put your leg up here in my hand, and when I tell you to push, you take the deepest breath you can, bear down and pretend you're having a bowel movement, and push!" Motioning with her elbow, "Dana, you grab that other foot. Now, let's get this baby out!"

Twenty minutes later, at dusk on Sunday, December 14, 1958, a new human being entered the world. "Praise be to God!" the midwife exclaimed.

"Praise be to God," Carolyn and her mother repeated, releasing several emotions: joy, relief, exhaustion, and even fear.

Her mom studied the baby closely. "It's a girl. You've got a daughter!"

At seventeen, she was *really* a mother—and, unfortunately, an unwed one—a weighty fact. Yet, she was so happy to have her baby out of her womb and into the world. She cranked her head toward Aunt Hildy, who was busy with the newborn protocol. "Hi, Wee One! I'm so happy you're finally out of there." She exclaimed as she threw her head back against the pillows, "I'm so glad that's over!"

Aunt Hildy gave the baby a whack on the fanny, causing it to cry. Then she cut the cord, took the baby down to the mat on the floor, and cleaned her up. After weighing her, she handed the infant to Carolyn, announcing, "Six pounds, eight ounces and nineteen inches long. Good and healthy!"

The new mommy counted fingers and toes and marveled that minutes before, this precious, tiny human person was inside of her. Together, the women said a prayer of thanksgiving to God for the safe delivery of this healthy, tiny life.

Hildy was already filling out the birth certificate. "Does your daughter have a name, my dear?"

"Yes. Yes, she does," Carolyn answered with motherly tenderness. "Her name is Mary Catherine. Mary for God's mother, and Catherine for my sister, Adeline Catherine, and after Saint Catherine of Siena." Carolyn smiled but then stopped short and, for the first time, worried about one detail she had failed to consider.

Aunt Hildy winked. "Mary Catherine Fandel, it is!"

Carolyn's face slackened. "Thank you, Aunt Hildy."

"That's a beautiful name for my first granddaughter!" said the grinning new grandmother. "She resembles you, Carolyn. I remember well the day you were born. I couldn't have been happier that day, and I couldn't be happier on this day!"

"Me too, Mom, but I'm glad it's over." She hugged Mary Catherine tenderly and put her to her breast for the first time with her mom's assistance. It was a struggle to get the baby to latch on because Carolyn was so nervous.

The expert midwife jumped in and took over. "If you can relax, Girl, this will go a lot better. Believe me. Now, lean back against that pillow, and I'll put the baby on her tummy with her head toward you. She'll find that teat a lot easier." Carolyn was embarrassed by the word 'teat,' but she had no choice but to try to do exactly what she was told.

Little Mary Catherine inched up and took hold of the comfort of her mommy. Carolyn's mom patted her new granddaughter's fanny. "There you go, wee one." She then praised her daughter, "You're doing well, Doll," she said, as she kissed Carolyn on her forehead. "I'm so proud of you."

The new mom and grandmother sat together and admired the intriguing new life. No matter how many times a woman gives birth, each baby holds a mystery and a joy unmatched by another.

After a while, Hildy opened the window and hollered in her big, German voice, "Hey, Robert, come meet your new granddaughter!"

CHAPTER TWENTY-FIVE

Carolyn was relieved that her mother was staying over. She did not realize how much help she was going to need nor how little she knew about taking care of a newborn. It was a steep learning curve.

And it was painful to sit. Hildy had made her an ice pack for her lower region. "It'll take you another good week or so to heal up down there," the midwife warned. "You tore a smidgen."

The amateur mom was handling fairly well the demanding nursing schedule newborns require, but she groaned when her mom woke her up in the middle of the night. Carolyn craved sleep. Not only that, it caused her extreme discomfort when the baby latched on. She was sure the baby had razor teeth hidden in that puny mouth. She tried not to dread it each time the baby took hold. She had become accustomed to drawing in a huge breath and "grinning and bearing it," as they say, until her milk let down and the searing pain subsided.

The first week flew by, and before she knew it, Carolyn was gathering her belongings. She was nervous about leaving the safe, hidden surroundings of Aunt Hildy's farm, but she was excited, as well, to return to Grand Lake. Her comrades had sent her many letters in her months away. As she reread them while packing, their unconditional support was a surety.

Her dad made his return trip on Saturday to collect the three of them. All of their things were stuffed into the maroon station wagon, including a pile of new baby gifts from the church ladies. "Very charitable of them," her dad said.

The three of them said their goodbyes and huge thank you's to Aunt Hildegard for all she had done.

"It was my pleasure." Turning to Carolyn, she said, "Girl, you put new life in these old bones."

When Carolyn went to express her gratitude, she was unable to control her sobs as the words tumbled out. "Aunt Hildy...I have no idea how... I am ever going to...thank you."

"There, there now. It's the hormones getting to you." Choking up herself, Hildy added, "Okay, now, get a move on." Kissing Carolyn on the forehead and Mary Catherine on the cheek, she added, "You are quite a woman, Carolyn Fandel. You've done well. Go now. Enjoy your wee one."

With that, the four Fandels occupied the station wagon and waved one last time. As they pulled away, they heard the familiar voice yell, "Visit when you can! God be with you!"

On the way down the drive, Carolyn's dad put his foot on the brake and the car in reverse. Backing it up, he turned the crank to roll down his window. "Say, Aunt Hildy, you're invited to our house for Christmas this year."

"Thank you, Robert. I'll think about it."

Carolyn knew she wouldn't come. She enjoyed the attention she received from her community and, at her age, she didn't enjoy traveling away from home. Aunt Hildy had a favorite saying, "When the Lord takes me, it'll be on my turf."

With waves and blown kisses, the car rolled down the snowy driveway as the farmhouse disappeared from sight. Carolyn's dad made the turn onto the two-lane road that took them back to Grand Lake.

The drive gave her time to process her circumstances, mostly that she was exhausted physically, emotionally, and spiritually. She longed to be in her own house with her people. She smiled, picturing her comrades. She imagined the expression on her youngest brother's face when he saw the baby. Frank Stephen was a sentimental guy, and he had a soft spot for babies.

Her thoughts moved from their faces to others—one in particular. He had been so gracious, even sending a few handwritten notes while she was at the farm. Carolyn had considered him often in her months away. *I wonder what our relationship might be now.* With Mary Catherine in tow, she and Paul Johns would remain forever friends, but it warmed her that he had not judged her. Not even once.

Daydreaming had passed the time on the drive. In no time at all, the car was pulling into the driveway. Ready to welcome her back and greet the newest member were Adeline and her four brothers, along with both sets of their grandparents.

Never were there more "oohs" and "aahs" and "she's so cute" ever spoken in such a short time frame. They all took their turns fawning over Mary Catherine and hugging Carolyn, continuing right into the house. It was a joyous homecoming and a tiring one for the new mom.

Her mother insisted that Carolyn and the baby should rest. So, Carolyn carried her daughter upstairs, followed by her parents. Silvester and Adeline toted up her bags.

Carolyn opened the door to her new freshly painted mint-green room, with gingham curtains made from one of Auntie Dora's bedsheets. "Oh, Mother, it's beautiful!" A photo of Auntie Dora holding Carolyn as a baby was on the dresser, which made her sad, but mostly nostalgic. She walked over to the mahogany highboy and picked up the frame. She kissed her index finger and traced the picture with it as if to kiss her great aunt goodbye. "I have always been fond of this picture of Dora and me. Thank you, Mom and Dad. Mary Catherine and I already love this room."

Her parents and Sil retreated. Carolyn spotted Adeline standing in the hall. "Get in here, silly."

"Mom said to give you space and that I wasn't to intrude."

"You're welcome any time in our new room. All I ask is that you knock first. I might be nursing the baby."

"Don't worry, I will," Adeline promised.

Carolyn sighed. "It's so good to be home. You have no idea." And then smiling, "Would you like to hold your new niece?"

CHAPTER TWENTY-SIX

Carolyn's first day back with her Fandels was rougher than she had imagined. The rambunctious brothers forgot that she needed her rest. They ran up and down the stairs and fought in their bedroom as they always had. They yelled during the day, and the baby did likewise at night. Carolyn was exhausted from lack of sleep. She cried a lot in the privacy of her room. And her breasts were sore.

"Don't worry, Doll, they'll toughen up," her mom assured her, but Carolyn could not see that day on the horizon.

Not ready to face outside people, she stuck close to home. Her parents even let her and the baby sleep in on Sunday, while they took the rest of the group to Mass.

Carolyn heard the boisterous bunch clamber into the kitchen after church. Soon, her parents were knocking on her bedroom door.

"Come in."

"Father Fedewa approached us after Mass. He offered to baptize the baby on Christmas eve morning. How does that sound?"

"Sure, let's do it. This way, we can all attend together to Midnight Mass on Christmas Eve and keep the family tradition going."

"We'll have a simple gathering. Just us and your grandparents," her mom suggested.

Low-key was better for Carolyn, anyway. She chose her parents to be Mary Catherine's godparents.

On December 24, the Fandels gathered in the vestibule of Saint Michael Church to witness the baptism of a new generation. Carolyn saw her parents radiate joy, as they proudly presented ten-day-old Mary Catherine for the Sacrament.

The baby's head and chest were anointed with oil. Then Carolyn held Mary Catherine over the baptismal font. Father Fedewa prayed the words of Christian baptism while pouring water over the baby's head three times, "Mary Catherine, I baptize thee in the Name of the Father and of the Son, and of the Holy Spirit. Amen." The infant jerked and wiggled at the first pouring but held still for the other two.

Carolyn's mom blotted her granddaughter's head with a white fingertip towel. Then a baptismal garment "to put on Christ" was placed over Mary Catherine's chest.

A baptismal candle "to keep the faith burning brightly" was lit from the large Easter candle and given to her dad. Not only her godfather but also her grandfather, a tear formed in his eye. He wiped it away. "It's always a moving ceremony to witness a new soul be cleansed from original sin and welcomed into the family of God," he said.

The Fandels clapped quietly when the rite was completed.

The benevolent priest offered a new mother's blessing over Carolyn. He added, "The Church is delighted to welcome you and your daughter home, young lady. It's where God desires you to be for now."

"Thank you so much, Father, for all of your support."

Carolyn, her baby, and her Fandels departed. They headed back home for coffee cake and punch, before they resumed decorating for Christmas.

***

Midnight Mass was glorious in Carolyn's opinion, as she held her new daughter in her arms the entire time. Mary Catherine never made a peep, even with all the music. Carolyn noticed more than a few people staring at her. She returned their curious gawks with a smile. She noted one curmudgeon who gave her a dirty look. It embarrassed her, but she took a deep breath and let it go. Many others in the parish, mostly Carolyn's friends and their families, made it a point to come over to see the baby and offer their best wishes.

There was a tall straggler at the back of the crowd. He caught Carolyn's eye, and her heart leaped. She flushed all over and became self-conscious of it. Her body's reaction took her by surprise, but she understood exactly where those emotions came from.

Soon, Paul Johns was face-to-face with her. She was delighted that he had made his way through the crowded church to see her. He admired the sleeping baby. "Congratulations, Carolyn. You have a beautiful daughter there."

"Why, thank you, Paul! You're the first person to congratulate me. I mean, people have been great and complimentary, but you're the first one to offer real congratulations. I truly appreciate that."

"Bringing a new life into the world is cause for congratulations. It's hard work! Or, at least that's what my mom has told me." He blushed.

114

Carolyn first noticed how darn cute he was, but she also marveled at his ability to see things for what they are. He wasn't clouded by all the ancillary details of the situation, and she was moved by that. They were both smiling as they said their goodbyes.

As she turned to join up with her pack, Paul inquired, "Hey, Carolyn. May I stop around some time to see the baby? I would have by now, but my mom said that I should give you more time to—you know—adjust." He blushed again.

"Anytime," Carolyn said. She hoped to the nth degree that he didn't just want to come to see the baby.

CHAPTER TWENTY-SEVEN

"Look what Santa left!" exclaimed Frankie. He and the rest of the Fandel kids were, of course, wise to the legend, but they still pretended.

"Thanks for all the food and goodies, Ma and Grandmama," Carolyn said. Now nearing her eighth month, her mom's energy was waning, so Carolyn's grandmothers had teamed up to provide a Christmas feast for the brood.

***

Toward the end of Christmas vacation, her mom asked Carolyn about school. Most districts would not sanction pregnant nor unwed mothers in their halls, so students in Carolyn's situation might never complete their educations.

"I want to go back and finish with my class, if the principal will allow it."

"Doll, be aware that getting the school to accept you back will be no easy feat."

"But I can try," Carolyn said firmly. "I understand there will not be time for any extracurricular activities, including the spring play. And I'm fine with that." Carolyn wouldn't trade being a mother to Mary Catherine for even the best role. "It'll be enough to attend classes." She was already looking forward to graduating with her friends.

"You have our full support, Carolyn. I pray it works out. In case it does, you should start practicing with the baby so she can get used to a bottle while you're in class."

This proved to be harder than Carolyn expected. Mary Catherine put up a good resistance. The trick was for her mom or Adeline to feed her. If Carolyn tried, Mary howled and flat-out refused the bottle. "It upsets me so much to hear her fuss like that." But obtaining a high school diploma was a must for any chance at a good job. "I can still nurse her when I'm not at school," she reasoned.

Her parents went to bat for her. After two unsuccessful attempts with the principal, her father made an appointment with the superintendent. He took Carolyn with him.

Her dad had his arguments lined up. He had again contacted his lawyer friend, Jerry Edmonds. The mere mention of an attorney seemed to set the superintendent on edge enough to at least consider allowing Carolyn to be the first unwed mother to return and graduate from Grand Lake High School. After exchanging pleasantries with her dad and the principal, who had also been invited to the meeting, the superintendent tilted his head down and peered over his glasses. He was stern. Glaring at Carolyn, he said, "This is not going to be trouble-free. The school is not going to grant you any leniency. Are you sure you're ready for this, young lady?"

She felt scolded, but she remained stout-hearted. "Yes, sir. I believe I am. I'm a good student, and I've got my family's full support. I'm certain I can do it." *Those men aren't going to scare me away.*

"Well, all right then, but there are some conditions, Miss Fandel."

And then the principal dropped a bomb. "You will be allowed to come to regular classes, but you must leave the school grounds promptly at the dismissal bell. You may never bring your baby into the school, nor are you to talk about the baby and distract the other students with pictures. And you may not participate in any extra-curricular activities, nor attend them as a spectator."

Carolyn sat stunned. Her head was swimming. Even though her parents had warned her that this might be the case, she did not foresee how strict the parameters might be. But she needed that diploma. Attending even one class with kids her age was better than having to do it alone. "Okay. I agree to those terms."

"And one more thing, Miss Fandel. You will not be allowed to participate in any graduation ceremonies, not even commencement."

Carolyn teared up, but she had no other choice but to sign her name to the agreement, which they had shoved across the table.

There were many afternoons in those early weeks of the new year when she paced her room, letting the endless tears flow. Although she was thankful for a healthy baby and her loving Fandels, her life had been completely upended, and she often felt trapped and crowded. Mary Catherine, small though she was, seemed to take up a lot of space. The room appeared to have shrunk. Carolyn felt constricted with no way out. She sighed loudly. *Being a mom is a lot harder than I realized.*

Not having a clear picture of when she might feel normal again, or if she could ever feel normal again, nagged at her. She often got up out of the rocking chair and paced around her room, staring for long periods out of her bedroom window. She felt like her choices had been ripped away from her, but every time she revisited her decision to keep the baby, the conclusion was always the same. Mary Catherine belonged to her. Adopting her out was never an option. Not for Carolyn anyway.

Her closer friends—Julia, Nancy, and Patricia—stopped by after school a couple of times to take a peek at the baby, but it was awkward. She didn't blame them for being standoffish. They were living their regular lives, and hers was highly irregular. *How are they supposed to handle my new motherhood?* She barely knew herself. *At least they came.*

The person that surprised her the most, however, was Phyllis. Carolyn had daydreamed about picking back up with her freckled-faced, dimpled friend and maybe even disclosing the awful details of how it happened. Her friend, though, visited only one time, and the air was stiff. Carolyn tried to break the ice and make small talk, but Phyllis didn't seem all that interested in Carolyn, the baby, or the friendship. She just kept talking about how her senior year was going—the play, the yearbook, the teachers, the boys—all the things Carolyn had given up in becoming Mary Catherine's mom. Phyllis didn't seem to have an ounce of empathy. She was oblivious to the hardship, and she had no interest whatsoever in holding the baby. It devastated Carolyn that her best friend was slipping away as they spoke, but she had no way to control that. She was a mom now, and that had become her priority. And rightly so. She tried to call Phyllis various times after that, but the friend was always too busy.

***

By the time spring unfolded, Carolyn was used to her restricted school routine and quite content. She was happy to be home and share her sister's joy about the Spring Formal for Adeline's junior year, despite bad memories from her own.

It was quite the task to get their father to agree to let Adeline attend. He imposed conditions, one of which was that under no circumstances was Adeline allowed to attend any post-party. Intellectually, her sister got it. Emotionally, she did not.

At bedtime, a guilty Carolyn followed her little sister up the stairs and into her old room. "I'm so sorry, Adeline. Maybe Mom and Dad will allow you to go to the post-party next year after some more time has passed."

"I hope so."

Carolyn now felt even worse. "I am so sorry, Adeline."

"Oh, Carolyn, there's nothing for you to be sorry about. It's not your fault."

"Yes, it is."

Her sister snapped, "No, it isn't! Get over it! Your ridiculous guilt doesn't make it any better."

Carolyn looked down at the carpet, and her eyes filled with tears.

"I'm sorry, Carolyn. I know it's been hard on you. It's been hard on all of us. But it isn't your fault. No one thinks it is. Geesh! You have nothing to apologize for." Her sister paused to breathe and continued in a nicer tone, "Believe me. We wouldn't trade you or Mary Catherine for anything!"

"I wouldn't trade Mary Catherine either. I just wish it hadn't happened—you know—that way."

A teary-eyed Adeline embraced her sister. "I can't imagine how awful it was. I'm so glad you're home, though."

Carolyn exhaled, "Me, too!"

"Besides, I wouldn't want anyone else to be here when I take off with my date on Friday."

There were, of course, no spring formal events for Carolyn that year, as part of her parameters set by the school, which was completely fine with her. The details of last year were still too fresh. Besides, she had more important things to do with her evening. Foremost was being a mom.

Earlier that spring, Paul offered to come over to play cards on the night of the formal. Carolyn insisted he go to the dance. "There's no reason your senior dance is ruined. You should go, Paul." He had said he'd think about it, but he said he wasn't going to take a date.

After the dance, he called the Fandel home. Carolyn was delighted when her mother told her who was on the other end of the line. "All right if I come over, and we overthrow Gus and Wally in Euchre?"

Paul was knocking on the door in no time. Gus answered with typical guy sarcasm, "Come on in, Johns. Get ready. Tonight is not your night." He was right. Paul and Carolyn could not keep pace with the brothers, who had five loner hands in the three games played. No matter, though. Carolyn was happy just to be with Paul. He took turns holding Mary Catherine, pretending the baby was dealing the cards.

Around eleven, he jumped up. "Time for me to go. You need your rest." He gave her a hurried hug at the door and left.

She retired to her room, which held her sleeping child. As she leaned over to kiss Mary on her head, she pondered that Paul preferred to come over and play cards with her, rather than take a date to the post-formal party. His visit made her feel validated and appreciated. *Whatever his reasons, I'm lucky to have him in my life.*

CHAPTER TWENTY-EIGHT

1959

Graduation came and went for both Silvester from college with his associate's degree and for Carolyn from high school. Carolyn had long accepted that she wasn't going to be able to walk across the platform with her classmates to receive her diploma. She took pride that she was still given the honors' recognition bestowed on all seniors in the top ten percent of the class, but it didn't matter that much. "Quite frankly, at this point, I'm just satisfied to have a diploma," she told her parents.

School had been socially burdensome anyway. The girls were polite enough, and small talk could be managed, but the deep friendships Carolyn had previously never rekindled. She had been invited to a party or two, but she couldn't go because she didn't have a babysitter. Adeline, the one who usually offered, had been invited to the same parties. Her parents had made it clear that they were going to focus on being grandparents and, besides, they had enough on their plates, especially with their newest addition.

***

Her mom had given birth four months ago, right on time, the afternoon of February fifth to her seventh child, a third daughter with dark hair like Adeline and green eyes like Carolyn's. The chosen name delighted Aunt Hildy, who *did* travel to the Fandels' church for Anne Hildegard's baptism. Carolyn and Silvester were the godparents.

***

During the warm summer days after the chores were completed, the two moms sat under the maple tree with iced tea, while their infants lay together in the playpen. Carolyn's mom put up a netting to fend off biting insects. If the babies drifted off to sleep, the tired mothers shut their eyes. Her mom had dubbed her brief naps as "watching the inside of my eyelids." Now Carolyn understood the value of brief rest on long days.

Paul had been coming around frequently to "see the baby," as her dad would say in a sarcastic tone. In mid-July, he phoned Carolyn's dad asking for a private meeting. Finding Carolyn in the kitchen feeding Mary some applesauce, he said, "Your young man called."

"He's not my young man, Dad. He's a good friend." Carolyn used an annoyed tone of voice, but secretly she was pleased. She loved it when Paul visited and always anticipated the next time.

"Well, then," her dad smirked, "I invited your 'good friend' to meet me at All-Star Lanes to bowl. I'll fill you in on how it goes."

"Okay, Dad, but—" Hesitating, she said, "Dad, go easy on him."

He chuckled as he headed out the door with his bowling bag. The whole time he was gone, Carolyn was on pins and needles, trying to imagine the conversation they were having. She had to do something to detract from it. She decided to put Mary Catherine in the stroller and go for a walk. "Adeline, wanna come with us?"

"Sure! Let me ask Mom if I can take Anne along."

***

Back from bowling, Carolyn's dad hunted her down in her room. "May I come in?" She could tell by the Cheshire cat grin on her dad's face that he had big news. "Well, that Johns boy is direct if he's nothing. He wasted no time in getting to the point. The short story is he wants to marry you."

Carolyn's eyes popped out of her head. She was at a loss for words. She wasn't sure how to react. In recent months, Paul had never as much as hinted about taking this step. "I don't know what to say. Tell me more, Dad. What do his parents think? Oh, my gosh—"

"Exactly. That boy has had eyes for you for a long time, Doll. Only a fool hasn't been able to see it. But, marriage? That's serious. And I told him so."

"And?"

"He appears to have sorted this all out. He said his parents were shocked at first, but they support him. And they admire you, Carolyn, so it isn't that. They maintain, as your mother and I do, that it is all rather sudden. And you both are pretty young to be married."

"You're telling me! I had no idea!"

"He's got plans to support you. Although his dad offered to help get him a job at Fuller Brick, Paul is more interested in the insurance business. He's been talking to his Uncle Scott, who works for the Insurance Company of North America. Paul was quite animated while explaining it and has already enrolled at the community college in the basic courses to get him started."

"Wow! I had no idea about that either." She realized there was a lot to Paul Johns she didn't know, such as why he hadn't talked to her about any of this. She was miffed. He had deliberated everything for both of them. "So, what did you tell him, Dad?"

"I told him that I would apprise you of our conversation and talk it over with your mother. I also told him that this would ultimately be your decision."

"Thank you. That means a lot. I'll certainly consider it."

***

For the next couple of weeks, Adeline offered to babysit Mary Catherine more, so that Carolyn and Paul could be alone. She was hesitant to confront him about the meeting with her dad. She hoped he would bring it up. Instead, they talked about what was important in life and where they saw themselves in the next few years. The affection was real on both sides; that was a no-brainer. Most days, it all seemed an inimitable fit to Carolyn. But although Paul did not share a specific plan, he seemed in a bigger hurry to get it all done. Carolyn, not so much. There were things to figure out on her own. After all, she was still only seventeen.

CHAPTER TWENTY-NINE

On a muggy, late-July night under the stars at the beach, two months before she turned eighteen, Paul took Carolyn's hands and gazed deep into her eyes. She found herself mesmerized by how warm and brown his eyes were, and she melted inside.

"Carolyn Joanna Fandel, I love you. I love you deeply. Will you marry me?"

Carolyn drew in a long breath. Her heart skipped at least two beats. One because she knew it was coming. The other because she was shocked it came so soon. She wasn't ready. Half of her wanted to shout YES at the tops of her lungs. The other half was unsure if it was the right thing to do. A tear rolled down her cheek, and she dropped her face to stare at the ground.

When she hesitated and avoided eye contact, it was as if she could hear Paul's heart sink. "Wow," he said, deflated. "I guess the answer is 'no.'" She said nothing because she wasn't sure what to say. His impatience tumbled out in a frustrated tone. "Could you please look at me, Carolyn? What is it? Don't you love me?"

She found the courage to lift her head, tears trickling down her face. "Oh, Paul, it isn't that! I do love you! But I'm worried that I'm too much of a burden for you to take on. You don't need to marry me and take on my responsibility."

"Burden?!" He asked it as if she were crazy. "I don't see it that way. I love you. And I love Mary Catherine as if she were my flesh and blood. I desire to be your husband and her father. I want to do this, Carolyn." Paul sounded as if he were pleading.

"Paul, you are so good! You have been a superlative friend through all of this, never once judging me. I can't tell you what that means to me."

"Friend? Is that all I am to you? Gosh, I feel so stupid."

She could tell by the tone in his voice and the look on his face that she had kicked him in the gut. "I'm so sorry, Paul. I really do appreciate your offer of marriage." She paused and forced a smile, even though she, too, was hurting. She comprehended the magnitude of his offer. She had dreamt of it on many occasions, but she was torn. On the one hand, hearing his proposal was balm to her soul. On the other, she had an unmistakable, interior nudging toward independence.

She hugged him, but when he didn't hug back, she pulled away and lifted her eyes to meet his. "You are not stupid. My behavior has nothing to do with you. It has to do with me." He cocked his head, waiting for more, so she continued, "I've decided that after Labor Day, I am going to move back up north. Aunt Hildy said I could stay with her until I saved enough money for a place of my own. I'm going to seek work at a bank or something." She could tell that this was not what he expected to hear.

His brown eyes widened, and he blanched. "You're moving back up north?! But, why?"

The tone he used caused Carolyn to question her decision herself. Carolyn refrained from answering as she tried to process her 'why' and form her next words. "I can't explain it other than to say God has put it on my conscience that I need to gain some independence. I need to handle this parenting thing on my own. I know it sounds ridiculous since I have my family so willing to take us in and subsidize us. And here you are with this breathtaking proposal. I've surprised myself with my decision, I think."

She expected him to say something. He didn't utter one syllable. She had no idea how to read his silence, so she started rambling on in further explanation of why her plan was a good idea. "Aunt Hildy found some mother's helpers who have offered to babysit while I work. She's not able to bear the full brunt at her age. Her friends at the neighboring farm have two homeschooled preteens willing to donate their time for Mary Catherine's care." She searched his face for understanding and empathy yet found neither.

"I see," said Paul flatly, "sounds as though you've figured it all out. Without me."

Sudden anger rose in Carolyn, and it was biting. "Without *you*?! How dare you, Paul? You never so much as hinted all those times we spent together this summer that you were thinking of proposing." She clenched her fists and huffed. "And then *you* go and call *my* dad and talk to him about it? It seems you are the one who decided on our life together without me! I, on the other hand, have made decisions for my own life and the life of *my* daughter!" Her pulse quickened, her brain was fuzzy, and she was within seconds of screaming. She was so infuriated with him.

"Whoa, there, Carolyn! That's unfair!"

He's ticked. She had struck a nerve.

With his lips tight, Paul continued, "I have been there for you. I have never judged you. I'm sorry if this pledge of undying commitment has inconvenienced you." He turned from her and started to walk away along the water, picking up pace as he went.

His words stung. He was right. He did not deserve to be unleashed upon. After all, she hadn't shared with him that she was moving back to Kalkaska. Calling after him, "Paul, wait! I'm sorry. Please, can we talk this through?"

He turned around. He stood about thirty yards away with his arms crossed and shouted. "Maybe. What else have you to say?"

"That I realize I didn't share my plans with you either."

Paul's walk back to her turned into a trot. Carolyn ran toward him until they were embracing like lost lovers. They held one another for a long time. Carolyn felt right in his arms. She just wasn't ready.

"So, that's it, Carolyn? You've decided that, for sure, you won't marry me?"

She answered with a heavy sigh. "Yes, Paul, I believe I have." She wasn't sure if it was a sigh of relief or terror. Time would tell but, for now, she was committed to sticking to this agenda of making it on her own. Somehow. Somehow, she had to do it.

She had broken his heart, and she knew it. That night, she lay in bed awake until well after midnight, replaying the proposal and the conversation. *Have I made the right decision?* Verbalizing her plans to Paul had been tough. When she had said them out loud, she hoped they made sense—especially to herself. She did love him, after all. And she was going to miss him. It made her sad, but moving away was a chance to prove to herself that she could fly as an adult and take care of her baby.

Telling her parents and siblings was going to be tougher still because she had learned to depend on them to a great extent in recent months. They had been indefectible.

Unequivocally, her parents were dumbfounded upon hearing her announcement. Their eyes glossed over as their mouths hung open. When they got their bearings, they peppered her with a hundred questions and "what ifs." They utilized any logical angle they could to get their daughter to reconsider.

Sil tried to talk her out of it with his brand of logic. "You're a fool for thinking you can go it alone when you have all of us to help you *and* a marriage proposal." He shook his head in disgust. That stung to the point that she did not retort.

Even the younger boys viewed Carolyn as crazy for turning down Paul Johns. They followed Sil's lead, holding nothing back in telling her as much. One after another, they had their say—even her little buddy Frankie.

Adeline sobbed, which was no surprise. Her tears of anguish were real, though. She pleaded with her sister not to leave. "It's our last year together, Carolyn, in mom and dad's house because I'm going to head to college after I've graduated."

"I'm sorry."

"And Paul proposed! I could rattle off a million gals who would give anything to marry him. Sil's right. You are a fool."

Carolyn got kicked around pretty well by those who resided in the Fandel home. Yet, not a pile of reasoning, name-calling, nor begging could sway the young mother. Not even crushing the hopes of the guy she loved. Carolyn cared about them, but she could not let their feelings dictate her life. She was unfaltering, no matter how hard it was—even amid the strong arguments of her loving comrades.

CHAPTER THIRTY

Carolyn was sure she was doing the right thing—most of the time. When the doubts came, though, they hit her full force. Moving day was fast approaching. There remained many unknown details. Her head swirled. *Is this why I was always afraid? Were my childhood fears a precursor to this whole wretched thing? Should I stay here in the safety of home?* A quiet atmosphere was needed to gain clarity. She asked Adeline to babysit and then headed to the best place she knew.

She dipped her fingers into the holy water font and made the Sign of the Cross. Making her way to the pew closest to the tabernacle, she genuflected, acknowledging the true presence of her God. She took her place on the slick wooden bench and pulled down the kneeler. On her knees, she rested her elbows on the seatback in front of her and clasped her hands in fervent prayer. In the quiet, she poured out her concerns to the Lord. *Please, God, I beg you. Send me a sign I've made the right decision.* After a short while, she sat back, feeling more at ease. She grabbed a songbook and opened it to her favorite hymn, "The King of Love."

God had always spoken to her through church music. The light streaming into the church through the stained glass windows obscured the words. She squinted at the page until she had the tune in her head. Soon she was singing as quietly as she could so as not to disturb anyone else who might have come into the dark church. "The King of Love, my shepherd is, His goodness fails me never. I nothing lack for I am His, and He is mine forever." She finished all six verses and peeked at her wristwatch. Her holy hour had passed. She sidled into the aisle, genuflected, and turned to depart. Her breath caught. She had not been alone.

Paul was on the other side of the church near the opposite door through which she had entered. She had no idea how long he had been there. She wondered if it had anything to do with her. They had not seen one another for almost a month. Not since that time on the beach when Carolyn rejected his proposal.

She stood watching him, admiring him. Seeing Paul alone in the church made him even more attractive. Tall and lanky, masculine. His head was bowed down, deep in prayer. She noticed just how thick and dark and curly his hair was. She stared at him for a long time. A tear ran down her cheek. He had her heart, but she must keep that to herself. She had no idea what her future held, but she had to stay focused. She must stick to her plan. She softly wended her way toward the door to exit, hoping she had escaped without being noticed.

A week later—Mary Catherine on her hip—Carolyn opened the front door to go get the mail. Paul was standing on the porch, hand up, and ready to knock. Both were surprised.

"I came to say goodbye."

"What?! Where are you going?"

"I've spent the last month discerning—ever since you turned me down. God might be calling me to religious life."

"That does not surprise me."

"It doesn't?"

"You have all the makings of an incredible priest, Paul." She kept hidden the fact she had seen him praying. It seemed intrusive. There was no point in his knowing she had been spying.

"Thank you. That means a lot. I know you've been praying, too."

Her eyes expanded. "You do?"

He winked. "I saw you, Carolyn. I came in after you and saw you close to the tabernacle. That's why I took the far back corner."

She grew warm with embarrassment, averting her eyes. "Well, I feel stupid."

"Why should you? There's no crime in two people praying in the same church," Paul reasoned.

"True."

"I wasn't just praying for myself. My decision had already been made. I was praying that God would send you someone to cherish. I was praying for him to send you a Joseph."

Quick tears stung her eyes. It was precisely what her father had said. She was touched. She was in awe of this tall, handsome guy in front of her offering true and pure charity. And he was giving it to her after what she had put him through. She refrained from throwing herself into his arms, although she wanted to at that moment. "Oh, Paul. You are a gift! There's no doubt that you will bless anyone in your life."

"That's good to hear because I'm leaving tomorrow to go with my Uncle Mark, the Maronite priest. He's taking me to Lebanon for some missionary work."

"Lebanon?!" She was astounded. "That's a world away. How long will you be gone?"

"At least eighteen months, maybe more. That's why I came over. I can't say when I'll see you again. Is your family around so I can bid my farewells to them?"

Carolyn beckoned all the Fandels to the porch. "Mom, Dad, everybody. Paul is leaving for Lebanon tomorrow."

"Lebanon?!" Her mom inquired in the same way Carolyn had.

"Yes, Mrs. Fandel. As you know, my mom is Lebanese, and her brother—my Uncle Mark—is a Maronite missionary. Since I am now discerning the priesthood, this will be a great opportunity to see if I am cut out for it. I'm also going to take some classes at the American University of Beirut."

Her mom's face looked blank, revealing her disbelief.

Her dad came to the rescue. "What a great opportunity, Paul! What category of work will you be doing?"

"Mostly meeting people where they're at, my uncle said. If they're hungry, we'll feed them. If they're lonely, we'll sit with them. Fr. Mark calls it the 'nitty and gritty of life.' I am sure I'll learn a lot."

Carolyn's mom had gotten her voice back. "That's wonderful. Meet their pressing essentials first, then preach."

"That's the idea, Mrs. Fandel," Paul confirmed. "Well, I just came to say goodbye to you all."

"See ya' later, Johns," Silvester said, slapping Paul on the back.

"Good luck, son," Carolyn's dad offered, shaking his hand.

"God be with you, Paul," said her mom. As she hugged him goodbye, she whispered in his ear, "Be patient and keep praying."

Carolyn wasn't sure what to make of that statement. Paul's face was quizzical. Carolyn shrugged her shoulders. She was in the dark as much as he was.

Gus, Wally, and Frankie took turns slapping Paul in various places on his body as Sil had. Paul playfully slapped them all back.

Adeline cried, of course. She had begged and begged Carolyn to accept his proposal. Through tears, she managed, "Take care, Paul. It's been great having you hang around this summer. See you when you're back in town." She hugged him extra tight.

Carolyn accompanied him off the porch and to his car with the baby on her hip.

"Last chance," said Paul with a wink.

Carolyn knew he had long given up. "I will never, ever forget all our special time together, Paul. You're going to do great things in the mission field and with your life."

"Thank you." He took hold of her and the baby in one giant hug.

Carolyn breathed his scent. *He even smells good!* "God be with you, Paul."

"And with you. Take good care of your mommy, Wee One," he said to Mary Catherine as he kissed her tiny hand. He made a swift sign of the cross on their foreheads with his thumb, and that was that. Paul Joseph Johns hopped in his car, waved goodbye to the crowd of Fandels, and drove away.

Carolyn stared down the road for quite a while, praying. *Please, Lord, shelter him. Reveal to Paul the vocation he is meant to have for a lifetime.*

She couldn't pinpoint where he would serve, but at least she knew he would be in Lebanon for most of his time. She was pleased with how excited he had sounded about heading out into the mission field. She had worried about him since she turned down his offer that evening on the beach, but now she knew she no longer needed to.

CHAPTER THIRTY-ONE

Carolyn spent her final weeks of summer making the most of it with her Fandels. She worked at staying positive and joyful. She hid any reservations she might still have about moving. Or about Paul. She was avoiding him as a topic altogether and, apparently, they had decided to do the same. Opinions the mob had expressed about her turning down his proposal were no longer discussed. Emotions had settled. It appeared they were on board with helping her make a smooth transition. She focused her time organizing her belongings and assisting her mom as much as she could around the house. She even took up some of Adeline's chores, since her sister would be left with a growing list once she was gone.

The remaining days of summer sped by faster than she had anticipated. Soon, Labor Day morning was upon her. Silvester and Adeline crammed the last of their sister's and niece's belongings into the station wagon. Their parents had concluded that the two were mature enough for the task of moving Carolyn and Mary back to the farm. Carolyn hugged the rest of her fellow Fandels goodbye.

A few hours later, most of her things had been unpacked and put away, and the three oldest Fandel kids were on their great-aunt's driveway for another round of goodbyes. Carolyn reached out, and the trio of comrades hugged. "Thanks again, you two."

Adeline had carried the baby on her hip out to the car. "I don't know what I'm going to do without you, Sis." With sweet affection, Adeline Catherine said to her tiny namesake, "Nor without you, Mary Catherine." She passed the baby back to Carolyn and broke into tears. Again.

"I promise to come to visit when I can. And you're always welcome here," Carolyn offered. However, their trips would be limited. Adeline would be busy with her senior year, and Silvester was entering the adult world of holding down full-time employment.

The Chevy station wagon got smaller and smaller departing down the driveway. There were tears in her eyes, for sure, but with positive determination. She felt good about her decision, even though she would miss her Fandels.

She entered the farmhouse and retreated upstairs to the bedroom where she had given birth almost ten months ago. She opened the lid of the last box of her belongings to reveal her winter outdoor gear. She pulled out her blades and instantly envisioned the annual New Year's skate, a big deal for Grand Lake. For a moment, she was sure she could taste the fruity snow cones made from real snow and flavored syrup in a variety of colors.

Carolyn recalled the scores of people donning their ice skates on New Year's Eve to glide along the stream that led to the big lake. It was a merry winter event the whole town embraced. Vendors sold hot dogs and hot chocolate. There was an ice sculpture contest that her father and brothers always entered. She pictured herself there, even though it wasn't to be. *Not this year.* She sighed.

With a heap of regret in her spirit, she tromped down the creaky stairs and across the kitchen to turn on the gas burner. It wouldn't be long before the familiar chirp signaled to Carolyn that a warm cup of comfort was coming her way.

She smiled as she collected Mary Catherine from Aunt Hildy's arms. She took her baby and her tea out to the porch swing, where she could gather her sensibilities in preparation for her job search the next day. She cuddled her daughter close and hummed lullabies. The two swung back and forth in the early fall sunshine until Mary was fast asleep in her arms. Aunt Hildy offered to take the baby up to the crib, and Carolyn let her. She was wiped out from putting on her happy face for her family's sake. Striking out in independence was emotional and exhausting.

Adolescent Carolyn—still six weeks shy of her eighteenth birthday—bent her knees and drew her feet onto the swing and sipped warmth as she swayed. She relaxed a little. She willed her mind to do likewise. She surprised herself to find that she was crying. Without warning, sobs throttled inside her. She tried to control them, but they tumbled out in a torrent. She wailed and wailed. It was all coming down on her now. She was, for all intents and purposes, alone. Alone in her new life as a single mom. And worse, alone in the awful memories.

The encompassing nightmare of that post-formal party came into focus. She threw her head back, trying to toss it to the back of her brain. To no avail. She shuddered so much that the chains on the porch swing tremored. Carolyn berated herself. "I was SO stupid!" she shouted to no one. She revisited all the what-ifs. Through images of doom, she replayed the drastic events that had altered the course of her life. As they became clearer and clearer, her anger increased. She sat there and indicted herself. Over and over and over. "Stupid, stupid, stupid!"

The rising from within her was unplumbed. She felt it in the depths of her being—where she wasn't even aware existed—and she did not stuff it down. It grew and grew until it spewed out of her into the country air. She was incredibly angry. Angrier than she had ever been. What had begun deep down now rose inside of her, and it was a clambering, agitated bear. She was furious—with herself and at *him*! She bellowed his name with spite. "SKIP JERGEN, you are scum!" With every fiber of her being, she hated him. She had been taught it was wrong to hate anyone, but she could not stop herself.

She imagined herself facing him and letting him have her rage. She even prayed for the opportunity. She wailed out loud, "Oh, God, grant me justice!" She howled as if Skip were standing in front of her. "You monster! You wrecked my life!"

She pictured herself flailing him with her fists as she yelled, "You took away all the things I dreamed about for my future! You stole my chance at a great senior year! You stole my chance to go to college right after high school! You stole my visions of how intimacy should be! You stole my virginity! MY gift to give to MY future husband! You stole my chance to marry PAUL JOHNS!"

Her fists were clenched as she sat on the porch swing, pounding its seat. She imagined pummeling him as hard as she could. Her hands stung and throbbed from the thwacking. She had bruised herself, but she didn't care. Nothing was as bruised as her body and spirit had been on that disgusting night. And every night since.

She played out this scenario several times with similar words, crying, and using up all the handkerchiefs she had tucked into her jacket pocket on the way out of the house. When they could absorb no more, Carolyn used her jacket sleeves.

By the end of it, her hot tea had spilled down her legs and onto the porch. Her pants were drenched. She stared at the teacup and then kicked it as hard as she could across the planks. It shattered, and she couldn't have cared less. She shrieked, "What's a STUPID CUP compared to my SHATTERED LIFE?!"

Her voice was hoarse. A faint buzzing vibrated within her from head to toe. Her nervous system was overloaded. She had no idea how much time had passed, but sheer exhaustion had enveloped her. She was wiped-out, depleted. She closed her eyes and fell into a deep sleep right there on the swing.

She awoke hours later with swollen eyes to discover the broken teacup across the porch, the soggy handkerchiefs next to her, and snot dried on her sleeves.

And Carolyn noticed something else—a refreshing sense of calm and space inside herself. The young mother felt strong, capable, and ready to tackle what lay ahead. Her first task would be landing a job.

CHAPTER THIRTY-TWO

Anticipating the baby's wake-up time of seven, Carolyn set her alarm for six. After washing her face and applying some light make-up, she pulled out the pink stickpins from the prickly rollers and let her blonde curls drape around her shoulders. She was hoping the extra effort made her appear more mature than her years. She chose her slightly-below-the-knee emerald green skirt and white button-down blouse. She tied a multi-colored pastel scarf around her neck for extra flair and put on her best nylons, followed by low-heeled black pumps.

After giving Mary Catherine a bottle and offering her a bit of finger food breakfast, she turned her over to Aunt Hildy for the rest of the morning. Given her aunt's age, it wasn't fair to saddle her with the demands of a baby for more than a few hours. Factoring in time to fill out applications and being granted potential interviews, Carolyn calculated she could manage two or three places per day.

An energetic Carolyn Fandel set about her job search at the small bank in town—her first choice. She meticulously filled out the application, making sure to proofread it before turning it in. She then took the required math test. Although math was Adeline's forte and not Carolyn's, she was certain she had done well. When it came time for the actual interview with the bank manager, he smiled and shook her hand. She recognized him as someone who attended Hildy's church. This gave her comfort, but she soon realized it shouldn't have.

"Your application and test are impressive. But I'm sorry, Miss Fandel. We have a certain reputation to maintain here at Bank of Michigan." This was all he said, but Carolyn got the message. Loud and clear. And it stung. He wasn't going to hire a tainted woman and let hers be the face his customers saw behind the counter. Getting someone to employ her might prove to be more difficult than she had considered.

"Thank you, Mr. Snider. I understand," said Carolyn, even though she didn't.

She met the same fate with the pharmacist and the editor of the newspaper. She returned to the farm, ashamed, with sore feet and a wounded spirit.

"Don't worry, Girl. Something will come your way. God will open a door." Hildy strode into the kitchen to start dinner. Carolyn couldn't help but overhear her aunt muttering. "For crying out loud, I've endured wailing mothers and impatient fathers and meddling grandparents while delivering all of their children! They're going to get a piece of my mind next time I see them." Carolyn broke out in a grin. She felt fortified, knowing Hildy had her back.

Over the next two days, Carolyn tried the hardware store, the dress shop, the gift boutique, the veterinary clinic, and the library with the same empty results. It appeared that her plan to be independent wasn't going to happen after all. She dreaded returning to Aunt Hildy's on that third day, fearing her aunt's disappointment. Carolyn berated herself as she turned off the road to walk up the long drive, murmuring to herself, "Stupid girl. Who's going to hire you now? No one is going to hire a dumb broad strapped with a kid."

She plodded up the gravel lane with slumped shoulders toward the farmhouse and saw Hildy stepping onto the porch with her arms extended, offering one of her big German hugs. "I'm sorry, dear one. You'll find something." Her aunt paused and then suggested, "Tell you what. Why don't we head on down to the Log Slide for dinner tonight? My treat!"

Carolyn returned the offer with a big smile. She knew what a frugal person her aunt was. The gift of dinner out was a magnanimous gesture, and the niece was touched.

The Log Slide was sprinkled with a few regular diners, most of whom Aunt Hildy recognized. At one table sat Mr. Snider from the bank with his wife and three young children. Carolyn was embarrassed enough, but even more so when Hildy ventured over to let her presence be known. "Hello, Mr. Snider. Mrs. Snider. I hope you are enjoying your dinner this evening. My, how your trio of young lads have grown since the day I was there to assist each of their entries into the world!" Carolyn cringed and backed up, fearful of what might come next, but that was all Hildy offered.

It was satisfaction enough to have the bank manager blush. He returned a mumbled, polite response to Hildy. Carolyn saw him catch a glimpse of her and the baby. The man's face reddened even more. He pulled up his collar and winced as he turned back to his wife.

Aunt Hildy led her niece and great-niece to a booth on the opposite side of the restaurant, much to Carolyn's relief. Once seated, Carolyn relaxed and perused the menu. Going out to eat was a foreign concept for her. Being raised in a household full of kids and on a scant budget, she could remember going out to eat only one other time. She settled on the meatloaf dinner after Aunt Hildy ordered the same. She shared her mashed potatoes with her baby.

As they were leaving, Carolyn ignored the "Help Wanted" sign near the cash register. But Hildy didn't. She pointed to it. Carolyn was skeptical. She could not take one more rejection. But her aunt nudged her forward—pushed was more like it—winking at the gal behind the counter, who winked back. *Gosh, the whole town knows Hildy.* With her baby on her hip, Carolyn had no other option but to say, "I see you're hiring."

"Yes, we are. Are you interested?" A slight woman with salt and pepper hair noticed Mary Catherine in Carolyn's arms. "Darling baby you have there." Then she added in a perky voice as she stuck out her hand, "Hi, I'm Elaine!"

Carolyn reached out and shook. "Hello. Thank you, and yes, ma'am. I am looking for a job. I'm Carolyn, and this is Mary Catherine. I'd be humbled to fill out an application, please." She smiled and breathed a sigh in Hildy's direction, releasing the trepidation she had been carrying. Aunt Hildy winked again.

"The application is standard protocol, but I can tell you that you're already hired!"

Carolyn couldn't believe it. "I am? Honestly? Oh, thank you! This job is an answer to my prayers." She was curious why getting hired here had been straightforward yet onerous everywhere else. *Thank you, Jesus, for opening this door.* Her faith told her this must be the place God planned for her to work.

CHAPTER THIRTY-THREE

Landing the job at the Log Slide gave Carolyn's suffering confidence a colossal boost. Scheduled to start on Monday, she had the better part of three days to settle into her new life. She picked up her uniform from the diner and met the owner. Mr. Maloney seemed friendly, too, like Elaine. The mother's helpers came over on Saturday to meet Mary Catherine. Carolyn assessed how the baby interacted with them and decided they were up to the task. She discussed the household expectations with Aunt Hildy. Accomplishing the list of to-dos invigorated her, and she looked forward to making money.

On her first day of work, Carolyn donned the ugliest gold waitress uniform she had ever seen, along with a pair of rolled white anklets and saddle shoes. She tied her hair up with a ribbon to keep it out of her eyes. *Maybe lipstick will give this hideous ensemble some class.* She skimmed on a coral color as she trotted down the stairs, kissed Mary on the forehead, and dashed out the door.

She borrowed Aunt Hildy's old bicycle and rode the two miles to the near edge of town. Parking out back, she opened the door to the Log Slide's service entrance. Elaine was there to train her.

Carolyn dove right in and was a natural with the customers. She was punctual, pleasant, and self-initiating. If it was slow, Carolyn kept herself occupied by various other chores. She put her nose to the plow and worked. Hard. The other waitresses seemed standoffish, which surprised her. They didn't seem congenial at all. She tried not to let it bother her. Her focus was on keeping this job. And she had no idea what she was doing to make them dislike her.

She learned later that they were taken aback by her. Elaine had said, "They don't know what to do with you. You're young, beautiful, and a hard worker. They've been here a long time, and some of their customers seem to prefer you now."

While hearing that left a sting, Carolyn understood. It was similar to all the times Sil had called her "Miss Perfect." From then on, she made a genuine effort to chat with the other ladies before diving into work.

Animosity settled down, and she was on her way to making friends with her fellow waitresses. The other servers—mostly middle-aged or widowed—began sitting potential eligible bachelors in her section.

"You're missing a lot of opportunities," said forty-something Rae.

"I have a bigger task ahead of me," Carolyn explained.

Several months went by, and Carolyn was diligent in saving her money. She got paid one dollar per hour as a base salary. She could keep an additional thirty-five cents from each customer bill and a share of the tips. Net pay was somewhere around thirty-five dollars a week. She turned over five dollars to her aunt, spent another five on things for Mary Catherine, and an occasional treat for herself. She stashed away the rest, increasing the fund she had rolled over to her new bank in Kalkaska. Always a good saver, by Thanksgiving, she had squirreled away an additional four hundred dollars and was ecstatic to see that she was closing in on eight hundred. Carolyn grinned, proud of providing for her baby and making her way as a responsible adult.

She conversed weekly with her clan on the phone. Her parents wondered aloud why she couldn't accomplish the same goals living under their roof. She kept her patience and explained each time, "God is calling me to be independent, live here, and focus on being the best mother possible." They could not argue with logic, and Carolyn was relieved when that no longer had to be a part of every conversation.

CHAPTER THIRTY-FOUR

By the time the end of November rolled around, the weather had grown familiarly cold in northern West Michigan. When it was too snowy for Carolyn to ride the bike to work, she walked, boots on her feet and shoe bag in hand. It took her under an hour, so that wasn't bad, but there were times the breeze and lake effect snow about knocked her down. If one of Aunt Hildy's friendly neighbors saw her, they picked her up in their vehicle. Or one of her co-workers would offer her a ride if they were passing the same way. She was always grateful because her day was far from over. Mary Catherine was cutting more teeth and awakened throughout the night. Most days, Carolyn found herself exhausted.

***

The calendar flipped to December, and with Christmas festivities in full swing, she and Mary Catherine spent as much time as they could in Grand Lake. Carolyn's co-workers were understanding and even took extra shifts to fill her hours, allowing Carolyn to go home for a few holiday events. The cutest thing ever was to watch Mary Catherine and Anne Hildegard, six weeks apart, attempt to play together. Carolyn loved snuggling with baby Anne, too, who was not only her little sister but also her godchild.

Thrown into the busy Christmas mix was a birthday party for Mary Catherine, who turned one on December fourteenth. It had been a while since the Fandels had celebrated a baby's first birthday, but they were determined to make the family secret recipe. It was then that Carolyn discovered sour cream was responsible for the lusciousness of the three-layer chocolate cake. "No wonder!"

Even Adeline jumped in to decorate. "There's no way I'm missing out on any part of my niece's first birthday details," she said, as she tried her hand at squeezing out pink frosting flowers around the base of the fudgy-brown tower.

Carolyn tried to reconnect with Phyllis, for old times' sake. She deliberated inviting Phyllis for cake to try to smooth things over, but Carolyn's phone calls went unreturned. *Why did I expect something different?*

141

She's been ignoring me for a year.

The friendship had gone cold for a reason Carolyn could not detect. She had tried in vain numerous times to keep the friendship intact, to no avail. She finally accepted it, figuring Phyllis's parents were no longer allowing their precious daughter to be influenced by Carolyn. She let that roll off since there was no use in trying to defend herself. According to rumors, Phyllis was off at beauty school and involved in Civic Community Theater. Carolyn, busy with the baby and her job at the Log Slide, had neither the time nor the energy to track her down.

Placing a solitary candle in the center on the top, the young mom smiled. She relished being home and celebrating her daughter's first year of life with the people she loved most. As she was about to strike the match to light the candle, the front doorbell rang.

It was Paul Johns, home from Lebanon for a short break, with a bouquet in one hand and a stuffed toy poodle in the other. "I couldn't let this important day go by without a gift for the cutest one-year-old in the whole world and the best mother to match."

Carolyn's face grew warm at the compliments. She was conscious that her cheeks were blushing and reached up to touch them. "Thank you, Paul, for remembering Mary Catherine. For thinking of the both of us. Come on in!"

"No, I didn't mean to intrude. I'm due back at our house for a big Christmas gathering. I have to leave tomorrow, so my family decided to celebrate early. It was important to me for you to know that I remembered."

Carolyn was touched and beamed at him. "You've been an extraordinary friend, Paul."

"That's what friends are for." He forced a smile. Nothing had changed. "You take care. Happy Birthday, Mary Catherine!" He turned and headed back down the porch stairs to his car.

She leaned against the doorway and watched until his car was out of sight. She found herself wishing his visit could have been extended for a longer interval, but she was aware of how blessed she was. He had been a steady anchor for her in the biggest storm of her life. And she was delighted that he had remembered her daughter's birthday.

***

Carolyn was back at Hildy's in time to fulfill her three-to-midnight on New Year's Eve. It was going to be a long, hard day, but she was looking forward to it. Working would take most of her attention, leaving her little time to sulk over missing Grand Lake's big community skate. She could visualize the mob crowded in the laundry room by the back door, bundled up for the day of fun. No doubt, Adeline had taken over Carolyn's job of hunting for mittens that matched. They would pile out the door, blades tied together with the long laces draped over their shoulders, and walk the few blocks to Lake Michigan. She could almost feel the excitement of arriving at the channel by the marina. How Carolyn longed to be there!

Upon entering the restaurant, she noted the Log Slide workers—including the cooks—all wearing festive hats. She grabbed a red, white, and blue cone-shaped one and plopped it on her head, snapping the elastic under her chin. An air of joy was afloat as holiday music played over the loudspeaker. The dinner guests were singing along to Mitch Miller's "Deck the Halls."

Carolyn waited on one couple who were in town celebrating their fifty-first wedding anniversary. Watching them interact made Carolyn picture her grandparents and even her parents. Her notions about marriage connected immediately to fond images of Paul Johns. She shook her head, surprised at herself. She knew full well she had sent that ship sailing when she didn't accept his proposal.

Her elderly patrons couldn't have been more charming. Carolyn learned they had six living children and four deceased ones. They were married at Aunt Hildy's church and were acquainted with her because Hildy had been at the ready for that woman's multitude of births. They had thirty-eight grandchildren, twelve greats, and two great-greats. Last year, their family had thrown them a huge party on their golden anniversary.

She found herself searching for reasons to return to their table just to hear another story. They were in the diner way longer than anyone expected and left an extra-large tip. On the bill, they wrote, "This tip is for our waitress. It's our anniversary. Please respect our wishes." To Carolyn's delight, Mr. Maloney allowed her to keep it all. She was full of gratitude upon leaving work that evening, and her pockets fuller with the three-dollar tip!

Happy thoughts led to home. No doubt the rosy-cheeked comrades were back by now from the Skate. Carolyn imagined them laughing around the fireplace, drinking hot cocoa, and settling in for night prayers.

She hadn't had much time lately to pray. She vowed to say a Rosary tonight.

Elaine offered to give Carolyn a ride. "Too many drinkers on the road."

"Thank you! Walking home in the dark is the least favorite part of my job." As she climbed into Elaine's car, she smiled to herself. *I wonder if Daddy and the boys won a prize for their ice sculpture.*

CHAPTER THIRTY-FIVE

Carolyn opened the passenger door at the edge of Hildy's driveway. "Thanks so much, Elaine. Happy New Year!"

"Same to you and Aunt Hildy. I'll drop you off here if you don't mind. That driveway is long and full of snow."

"Not at all. You got me this far!" She closed Elaine's door, waved goodbye, and started trekking up the long, wintery path.

As she lifted her knees high over the snow, she made the Sign of the Cross. Although separated by almost two hundred miles, praying in unison with her Fandels made her feel warmer despite the frigid temperature outside. "I believe in God, the Father the Almighty, maker of heaven and earth—"

Her prayerful and peaceful trudge was cut short as she made the final turn. A lot of lights were on in the house, which was odd. Hildy had the habit of leaving only the solitary porch light for Carolyn, as more were wasteful. She could make out the familiar figure standing in the living room window, and it surprised her. Her aunt had long abandoned the practice of waiting up. She recalled the slight admonishment: "I can't be waiting up for you till all hours. This old aunt of yours is plumb tired out at the end of the day."

Yet, despite it being the eve of January first, a Holy Day of Obligation for Catholics, which meant an early morning Mass, Hildy peered down her driveway, waiting for her niece's return. Carolyn's pulse quickened, and she picked up her pace, abandoning the prayer. "Something's wrong! Oh, no! Oh, my good and gracious God!" She tried in vain not to panic, as she attempted to run through the deep snow. She tripped and fell. Bolting upright and dusted with snow, she continued her hurried pace to the porch. She reached the first step, panting from her knee-high jog and fear. She saw that her aunt had tears in her eyes. It was then that Carolyn knew it wasn't bad news; it was horrible news.

Her heart was pounding. Her throat was tight. Her voice came out in a nervous pitch. "Whatever is the matter, Aunt Hildy? Is it Mary Catherine? Is she okay?"

"Oh, dear heavens, no, it's not the baby, but something terrible has happened."

"What then? Aunt Hildy, tell me! Who is it?!" She conjured up images of her father and her brothers, who were out in the cold using power tools. "Was there an accident involving my dad or one of the boys?"

"It's Frankie." The old woman's voice shook.

"Oh, no!" Carolyn's eyes were filling with tears. "What happened? Did he injure himself with the chain saw?"

"No," said the aunt shaking her head. "It's more serious than that."

Carolyn pleaded, "Please, Aunt Hildy, tell me!" She was growing impatient, fearing the worst.

Hildy led Carolyn inside. "Your family was enjoying their tradition on the shores of the lake in the channel. Little Frankie went too far and, before anyone could catch him, he fell through the ice." Hildy's face was paler than usual. Carolyn had never seen her so shaken.

"Lord, have mercy!" Stunned, she put her hand over her mouth. "Is he...is he...?" Carolyn couldn't bring herself to finish the question.

"He's at the hospital. In Grand Rapids. He had to be taken there by ambulance."

"Is he going to be okay?"

"They don't know yet."

"They don't?!" Carolyn screeched. She listened for Mary Catherine to see if she had woken her up, but the baby had slept straight through it.

"Sil got to him first and held on to the hood of his coat for his life, but he lost his grip. Frankie's arms slipped right out of his coat. Your father was there by then and, between the two of them, they were able to reach down into the water and grab his arm. The current was strong, fighting against them. Frankie's head had gone under, but your father got hold of one of his armpits, and, together, he and Sil were able to keep his head above the water."

"Oh, my word!" Carolyn lowered herself to the sofa and buried her head in her hands, rocking back and forth. "Poor Frankie." A horrifying scene played in her head. "Where was the rescue team?"

"They were there, but it took them some time to wend their way through the crowd with their gear. When they hauled him out, he wasn't breathing."

"Oh, my good God, have mercy." Frenzied images whizzed through her mind. She kept picturing poor little Frankie's petrified face as he was falling through the ice. She imagined him thrashing to save his own life. She could see her dad and Sil working together to save him. She could see Frankie's purple body being dragged from the water and onto thicker ice. She envisioned the crew administering CPR watched by the helpless, horrified faces of those she cherished the most. She swore she could even hear Adeline, Gus, and Wally crying at the sight of their limp baby brother. All their faces flashed in vivid, terrifying colors. Carolyn felt a pang of guilt that she wasn't there with them. She pushed all that aside to focus on any other information Aunt Hildy might be providing.

"They worked on him for quite a while, from what I could get from your dad. The paramedics got Frankie breathing again on his own and then put him in the ambulance. Dr. Imthum was there. He rode in the ambulance with Frankie and your father. He's in critical care at Saint Mary's."

"Oh, my word." Carolyn shook her head. "Where was Mother?"

"She had already departed to put Baby Anne to bed."

"Of course." Carolyn sat quietly for a second. "I'm glad my mom didn't have to see that."

"Your grandparents are at the house to stay with the other kids. Your mom and dad are at the hospital with Father Fedewa. They said they would call with updates."

"I wish I could get there." But she could not. She was expected to work the day after New Year's Day. The ladies at the restaurant had already been generous with giving Carolyn extra holiday time with her Fandels. It was her turn to cover for them. She felt stuck, and she was. She sat, staring off into space, not saying a word.

"Your parents realize that you want to be there. They understand. Work will keep you occupied, dear."

Glancing at the phone on the end table, "If you don't have a preference, I'll make myself up a bed near the phone here. How was the baby tonight?"

"Good as gold, child. Little Mary is secure. When her two homeschooled buddies left, she came right to me, took her bottle, and went into her crib without fussing. She should sleep till it's time to go to Mass in the morning."

"We must pray for Frankie, Aunt Hildy!" Carolyn choked back sobs.

The phone rang. Carolyn answered and heard her father's voice on the other end. "Oh, Daddy! How bad is it?"

"It's pretty bad. He wasn't in there for that long, but he's so young. His body temperature is a concern. For now, he's stable."

"Stable? Is that good?"

"It means he's holding his own with no assistance from any ventilator or anything. He's in a coma, but the doctor said that means he is trying to heal. I guess that's a good thing."

"Oh, Dad! I'm so sorry that I can't be there. How's Mom?" Being a mom herself now, she could empathize with her mother's worry. "I can only imagine what she's going through."

"She's doing okay. You know your mom. She's had her rosary in her hand the whole time, naturally, and she won't leave his side. Father Fedewa is still here with us. He anointed your brother. He intends to stay until we received more definite news. In fact, I'd better get back to the room, Doll."

"Please, please call me with any updates."

"I will. For now, pray. Frankie could use lots of prayers."

Hildy shouted into the phone, "Tell Dana that we're about to start a Rosary, Robert."

She and her aunt made good on their promise. It was two-thirty when they finally said their 'goodnights'. Carolyn ended up in her room with Mary Catherine. She watched her daughter sleep, resisting the urge to pick her up, and thanked God for her health and safety. "God, bless Frankie. Watch over him, Lord. Restore him to health, O Jesus Divine Physician," was her last prayer of the night as she drifted off to sleep.

Carolyn roused on New Year's Day before the winter sun even had a chance to brighten the horizon. Mary Catherine's fussing demanded both a diaper change and a bottle. She held her daughter close as she fed her Aunt Hildy's homemade formula. Something with Hildy's endorsement was going to be better for the baby and more cost-effective than store-bought formula. Each day, Carolyn mixed up a pitcher consisting of evaporated milk, water, and a small amount of light corn syrup, enough for three bottles spaced throughout the day. Now that the baby was a year old, the milky goodness supplemented the softer finger food. Her daughter's dimpled hands and general chubbiness were signs that Mary Catherine was thriving.

Carolyn relished the dawn when things were still quiet in the sleeping countryside before the nearby farms became alive with chores. She marveled at her child's newfound independence, as Mary Catherine had ventured into the world of walking.

For Carolyn, the hardest year of her life had crept along slowly and, yet, passed swiftly too. For a brief moment, she was tossed back to that fateful night at Starrett Farms, and she choked back sobs. The memories of it had come and gone multiple times since it happened. Holding her snuggly warm babe juxtaposed both comfort and sadness. By examining the beauty and wonder of her precious child, Carolyn wouldn't change the outcome of Skip's violation, even if she had the chance, because that would mean she wouldn't have her daughter. So, she did what she always did in these moments of revelation; she prayed: *Thank you, Lord, for blessing me with this precious baby. In your power, you triumphed over evil and created a new soul created in your image. I pray to be worthy as her mother.*

She switched back to the present and her little brother's plight. She was consumed with images of Frankie's cold, lifeless body. He must have been terrified! She shuddered and gathered Mary Catherine even closer to gain the warm reassurance her baby always rendered. Somehow, holding her made Carolyn more confident that Frankie was going to be okay. At least she prayed that would be the case. *Dear Heavenly Father, come to Frankie's aid and send Your Holy Spirit to my worried parents.*

She dressed Mary Catherine and herself for church. "This is one of your feast days, Mary Catherine," the young mother whispered to her little daughter once they were in the pew. "It's a great day to honor Mary, the Mother of God. She was the first who said, 'Yes!' to God, making her the first Christian." Of course, her baby couldn't possibly understand the theology of that, but it was fun for Carolyn to share the Catholic faith with her daughter, and it took her mind off her brother.

The ladies returned to the farm and heard the ringing telephone from the driveway. Carolyn rushed up the steps, through the front door, and to the side table to answer.

"Oh, Mom, it's good to hear your voice. How is Frankie?"

"He's going to be fine, we think," she said with reserved excitement. "Our prayers have been answered for now. Frankie woke up early this morning. The doctor is confident he's out of the woods."

"Praise be to God!" exhaled a smiling Carolyn. Instantaneously, Mary Catherine babbled and clapped her chubby hands together. She swore the baby must have understood the sound of happiness in her voice.

Her mom continued. "There won't be any long-term ill effects, the doctor told us, but they are going to keep him overnight again, to be positive."

"Tell him I love him, Mom. And that I'll come for a visit as soon as I can."

"I sure will. Please thank Aunt Hildy for her prayers."

When Carolyn passed on that message, Hildy's response was, "Praise be to God; crisis averted!"

CHAPTER THIRTY-SIX

By the end of January 1960, Carolyn had saved another eighty dollars and was ready to make the next transition. Elaine had a small apartment over her garage. It wasn't anything special, but it had a kitchen, bathroom, and bedroom, along with a small living space. It was already furnished, too. One of the other waitresses used to live there until she remarried. Elaine had kept it vacant "in case someone exceptional needed it," she had said. She offered it to Carolyn, who humbly accepted.

"Rent will be twelve dollars a week."

"Thank you so much, Elaine." It was about a third of her paycheck. The young mom had prepared, emotionally and fiscally, to go out on her own. It was time to give her old aunt a break. The woman never complained about the cranky child in the middle of the night or all the toys strewn about the house, but Hildy wasn't used to toddler commotion either.

Carolyn decided to keep saving until her total was closer to a thousand dollars, and the weather was closer to spring warmth. By the end of March, she and Mary Catherine had moved into the tiny garage apartment and couldn't have been more content. There was one small bedroom, which she gave to her daughter. Carolyn's sleeping quarters were in the living room on a pull-out sofa. An end table was on one side of it. There was a small dining table with two chairs. The kitchen consisted of a few cupboards, which contained all the essentials. There were a tiny sink and an apartment-sized stove, yet a decent-sized refrigerator. The bathroom was big enough for a stand-up shower but no tub. *I don't have time for baths anyway.* If the bedroom door was open, Carolyn could stand at the sole door and see her entire new home. She loved it.

She now had a place to call her own and was up for this next step of independence. She was taking care of herself and her daughter without feeling that, somehow, her great-aunt had been acting as the mother of both of them.

The apartment was near the Log Slide, which saved Carolyn from having to buy a car. She could walk the six blocks no matter the weather.

The trouble with not having a car was that she was unable to get herself back and forth to Grand Lake for special events like Gus' Confirmation and Frankie's First Communion. She also had to miss seeing Adeline off to her senior spring formal.

Via several phone conversations, Carolyn learned Adeline had settled on a hand-me-down from one of her older female cousins—a canary yellow, crisscrossed bodice dress with the same color tulle streaming from the waist around the skirt. Carolyn could picture how fabulous that color was for her brunette, blue-eyed sister.

Carolyn had also heard from Adeline that once again that she had to trudge through quicksand to talk their parents into letting her go to the post-party. These were the times that caused her guilt to return. *If only I hadn't been such a stupid girl, Adeline wouldn't have been put through the Papa Protection Program—TWICE— and I wouldn't be missing all these family milestones.*

"Oh, Adeline, you had to be put through the wringer two years in a row because of me."

"Don't be ridiculous. Dad wasn't that bad." She paused about two jiffs and admitted, "Okay, he was that bad, but I get it. And I lived through it, and so did my poor dates." Both of them laughed. Adeline continued, "Carolyn, can we agree to let this pass? I mean, can you please stop apologizing for something you don't need to?"

"Okay, sister, I hear you. Agreed. Never again."

The call ended with Carolyn struggling to stay positive.

CHAPTER THIRTY-SEVEN

Deep down, Carolyn realized what caused her negative self-talk. Rape is a horrible violation of the human person. With lots of encouragement from a multitude—along with bulldog diligence—she was getting better about quieting her bad thoughts.

The pain of the past had waxed and waned multiple times, but now she couldn't help but smile each time she gazed at her daughter. She could observe her for long periods and see only her beauty, rather than the ugly incident surrounding her child's beginning. Mary Catherine was evidence of the dignity that God bestows on all human persons, no matter the circumstances of their conception. Carolyn smiled. She was finally finding true healing.

It was Father Morrow, the pastor at Aunt Hildy's parish, who had counseled Carolyn to see her daughter for who she is: a beautiful child of God and a manifestation of His love. He had spent many hours working through the whole incident with her, often offering her the wisdom that Mary Catherine had nothing to do with the sins of her father. He had told Carolyn, "Your little daughter deserves every happiness and comfort a child should receive." Carolyn worked at making sure that was the case, no matter how she was feeling on a day-to-day basis. With the pastoral guidance of the good Father, she was transforming into a selfless mother.

All in all, her life was fulfilling, and she was proud of the choice to forge her path as a single mom. It was the right decision. She certainly could not have done so without the unwavering loyalty of her parents, Aunt Hildy's generosity, the friendship she enjoyed with Paul, and her family's support.

Elaine, too, had become a life-saving friend and instrumental in her healing. She had even given Carolyn a gift of encouragement. It was a small pewter dragonfly with the words, "You are beautiful and strong." Elaine explained that her mentor had given it to her at a turning point. She had told Carolyn to pass it on to another woman when the time felt right.

"Thank you, Elaine. You've been such a godsend."

On many occasions, Carolyn bared her soul to Elaine, who never judged. She had never met any of the people in Grand Lake, which was a plus. Even though she was not of the Catholic faith, Carolyn had come to regard Elaine as more than a landlord and fellow waitress. The older woman had become a confidant and true friend. Carolyn was appreciative to have a woman with life experience nearby. She could count on Elaine to give sound advice about parenting, children's illnesses, or just listen when the young mother was exhausted by her responsibilities. She encouraged Carolyn to strive to maintain confidence in herself and keep a positive outlook on life.

She spurred Carolyn's commitment to stay on track with budgeting, too. Elaine understood the desire to make the apartment more personal, but she had mentioned that extra things weren't necessary. "Denying ourselves material pleasures is the fastest way to save money." The statement reassured Carolyn that if she continued to live simply, she could afford to provide amply for her daughter.

During the three years that she and her daughter lived over the garage in the tiny apartment, the good woman never raised her rent. She even left a bag of groceries at the apartment door occasionally, which often included something for the baby.

Elaine was intuitive about how laborious it was to be a single mom, and Carolyn never forgot to include her landlord in her nighttime prayers. She would never be in the position to repay her confidant, her mentor, and her friend for all she had done.

CHAPTER THIRTY-EIGHT

1963

Carolyn was no longer the scared young woman who had first arrived on Hildy's doorstep. She had come into her own, obviously more and more adept at socializing at church and work. Her fellow waitresses were now regarded as a bunch of big sisters. She had become a favorite not only with them but also with certain patrons, who often requested to sit in her section.

There was one customer, Ward Hamilton, who frequented the Log Slide whenever he was traveling through Kalkaska to a farm more north, where he bought his meat and seasonal produce for his restaurant. He left excellent gratuities, gaining the appreciation of those who worked there. Mr. Hamilton was always smartly dressed in a tweed suit, white shirt, and tie. He wore a brown suede fedora, similar to Carolyn's father's, and tipped it to the ladies when he entered. In inclement weather, he wore a long black coat that doubled for cold or rain. The older waitresses swooned whenever he walked through the doorway. He was happily married but so handsome and friendly that they couldn't resist admiring him.

He had taken a liking to Carolyn and told her what a fine waitress she was. He even tried to confuse her at times to see how she handled herself. Carolyn was always gracious, hiding any frustration. She kept herself organized, waiting on patrons in a timely manner. One day in late June, Mr. Hamilton invited her to sit down and have a chat.

"I'm sorry, Mr. Hamilton, I can't tonight. I have to get home for my daughter's bedtime. I made a promise to be there to give her a bath and read bedtime stories."

"That's commendable, Carolyn," he said. Without delay, he proposed accompanying her the six blocks back to her apartment.

She hardly knew the man, and his ambiguity was causing her to be suspicious, but she was worried about offending him. "I guess that would be all right, Mr. Hamilton." Not seeing what direction this conversation would take caused her heart to start racing. She had started to panic, but he couldn't know it.

"I promise it won't take long for me to say what's on my mind," the businessman said.

As they left the diner, Mr. Hamilton began, "Carolyn, I have a confession to make. I've been coming to the Log Slide all these months to see if what I saw in you was genuine."

Confused and also flattered, Carolyn's cheeks got hot. Her throat tightened. "I'm sorry…I…I'm not sure what you mean," she said in an audible whisper. It was all she could manage, pulling back and stepping closer to the edge of the curb. Old recurrences of fear surfaced within her.

"I beg your pardon, Carolyn. I didn't intend to be ambiguous. What I mean to say is that I am offering you a job at my restaurant in Grand Rapids. I've taken over the Water's Edge on the banks of the river. I'm proposing that you would be the head waitress during the breakfast and lunch bustle. You'd be more of a manager, in actuality. I'd pay you $1.75 per hour."

Carolyn stopped walking. She had gone from being afraid to confused to overwhelmed in ten short minutes. "Well, Mr. Hamilton, this comes as quite a surprise. I appreciate your outstanding offer, but I'm happy at the Log Slide. I have friends here. Mainly, I am not sure what this move means for my daughter. She's excited to start kindergarten in the fall. This would be a huge change for both of us. May I take a while to think about it?"

Having halted himself, Mr. Hamilton asked, "How's a week? Think you can decide by then?"

"May I have two weeks?" Carolyn ventured, proud of her boldness.

"A fortnight, it is! I'll be back in two weeks for your answer."

After Carolyn got Mary Catherine tucked into bed, she called her parents.

"Carolyn, hello! Your dad is upstairs repairing a broken window, compliments of a well-hit baseball from Wally. Hang on. I'll holler for him." She yelled, "Robert, it's Carolyn!"

Carolyn's father picked up the recently installed extension. "Hi, Doll! How's our wee doll?"

"She's great, Dad. She keeps asking when she can make her next trip to the dump with you. I had presumed moving out would rid me of all of Adeline's treasures, but nope. Mary Catherine has taken after her aunt with her own special box under her bed." Exasperated and sarcastic, she laughed, "Thanks a million, Dad."

"That's our girl! I'll be sure to tell your sister."

"Oh, you two!" her mom jested. "Is there a special reason you're calling, Carolyn?"

"I'm glad you're both on the phone. There's something I need to talk to you about."

Her dad was concerned. "What's wrong?"

"Nothing's wrong. In fact, something could be very right, but I'm in a quandary. A gentleman by the name of Ward Hamilton has taken over the Water's Edge in Grand Rapids, and he has slated me to be the breakfast and lunch manager. He's going to pay me $1.75 per hour! It's a lot more than I make now, but it is a huge change."

"That's a generous offer," her mom said. "Have you made a list of pros and cons?"

"I have. Pros are the obvious financial benefits and being closer to home. I'd be a manager, which is a step up and a pretty good job for someone my age."

"All that's true," Robert agreed. "What are the cons?"

"Well, Mary Catherine and I would have to move. She'd have to get used to new surroundings and new people to care for her. She's familiar with her babysitters here."

"She'll be going off to school in the fall, which means she won't need someone for as many hours in the day," her mother chimed in. "Grand Rapids has solid parishes and schools."

"That's true, but I'm not sure I can afford Catholic tuition yet. I still have to work out the financials."

"You have a lot to think about," said her father.

"Yes, I do. Please pray I make the right decision."

Her mother replied, "We will. You'll have our prayers always."

She knew this, but it was good to hear it. "Thanks, Mom and Dad, for always supporting me—even when my decisions have surprised you."

"That they have," said her father, "but we couldn't be prouder of the way you've handled things."

"That means the world to me!"

The future seemed bright and full of promise as she ended the call. She got on her knees and gazed up to the crucifix she had hung above the couch when she moved in. She closed her eyes and prayed aloud, "Dear Lord, grant me clarity and the fortitude to make the decision that provides best for my daughter and one that glorifies You. Amen."

She played out the different scenarios in her head as she drifted off to sleep. When the sunrise awakened Carolyn, she was ready to accept Ward Hamilton's offer and relocate with her little girl to the big city. Moving nearer to home and advancing her career was the way to go, she was sure. *I guess I didn't need two weeks, after all.*

CHAPTER THIRTY-NINE

The next afternoon, Carolyn's dad phoned. She was worried to be talking with her father again so soon. There was a note of concern in his voice. Her mom was on the phone, too. "What's going on?"

"Well, I'm afraid we have news to share. Your brother Augustine told us this morning that he's going into the army."

"What? Why?"

"He desires to serve. Things in Vietnam are stirring up. His opinion is that since he didn't get his act together for college nor find a job that will lead to a career, he should do something. A lot of guys his age are already there. America, unfortunately, has its hands dirty in this conflict."

"Is there a chance that he could be sent to Vietnam?"

"Yes."

"Lord, have mercy!" Carolyn gasped.

"But not for a while. He'll go to basic training first for six weeks of boot camp and then be assigned here or in Europe."

Carolyn said nothing for a while, and neither did her parents. It was as if they were all pausing to absorb the news.

"There's more," her mom cried into the phone but then said nothing.

Carolyn could no longer stand it. "Mom, please tell me."

Her dad spoke, "Wallace informed us he's going to enlist as soon as he graduates."

"I see. Seems they've made their choices."

"Yes, Doll, it appears so," said her dad.

"Please pray," her mom whispered.

"I absolutely will," Carolyn promised. "Say, is Gus around?"

"Sure, we'll go get him."

Soon Augustine was on the phone. "Hey, Sis!"

"Hey, Gus. Mom and Dad told me. How are you?"

"I'm good. I'm ready. I'm gonna be fine."

"Yeah, that's what Dad said you'd say. Have they told you when you have to report?"

"Thirteen days. I'm going to make the most of my limited freedom

159

roughhousing with Wally and Frankie and living it up with my buddies, that's for sure!" Carolyn smiled. Of all her brothers, Gus was a man's man. He partied with his guy friends, hot-rodded around with them, and hung out at the beach. She had no doubt he'd make the most of his remaining days in Grand Lake.

"I don't blame you," Carolyn agreed. "I'll try to make a trip down to say goodbye. I'm sure Elaine will let me borrow her car.'"

"That'd be great, Sis! I can use all the hugs I can get. And, please pray for me."

"You've got it, brother. And I'll put Mary Catherine on it, too."

"Nothing any purer than a child's prayer," the soldier-in-waiting said.

The two said their "goodbyes," and Carolyn hung up the phone. Her brother was on her mind the rest of the day.

Gus could have chosen to enlist in the National Guard or the Army Reserves. This would have given Carolyn's parents some assurance that he might not be sent into a war zone. But he had opted to outright enlist, which meant he had a good chance of being called up.

Carolyn wished that Gus had gone to college. Or that he had found a girl to marry, but her brother had never had any intention of marrying to avoid military service. He had said that it would be using another human person, something in which he had zero interest. She had to accept that he hadn't chosen either of those options. The past could not be changed, and Gus was not the kind of guy to take the easy way out. After giving it more consideration, she was not surprised that he had enlisted, especially since many of his buddies were already in the military.

He opted for a minimum of four years, maybe more if he decided to make it a career. Soon, he would endure six weeks at Fort Knox, Kentucky, and then be assigned from there. After basic, he would get a brief furlough to say his goodbyes, then be shipped off to God knows where and having to do God knows what. The thought made Carolyn shudder.

She made good on her word to get Mary Catherine to pray for her Uncle Gus. Each night, Carolyn led her daughter in their nightly prayer ritual—the Lord's Prayer, a Hail Mary, a Glory Be, and the Guardian Angel prayer. At the end, they mentioned special intentions, such as "Dear Lord, bless my Uncle Gus. Keep him safe in the army, and, God, please try not to ship him to Be-It-Nam." Carolyn smiled at her little girl's sincere innocence and trust.

CHAPTER FORTY

By mid-August, Carolyn and Mary Catherine had settled into their new apartment on Broadway Street, a block from Saint Mary's Catholic Church in one direction and eight blocks from the Water's Edge in another. The pair lived in the back two-bedroom, first-floor apartment of a two-unit house the Hamiltons owned. "We reserve renting our apartments to special people," Mrs. Hamilton had said, which made Carolyn feel welcome.

The other apartment was larger and faced the street. It was occupied by four religious sisters who taught at the Catholic school connected to St. Mary's. The Hamiltons let the sisters reside there until a convent closer to the parish could be procured. Mrs. Hamilton, with her toffee-colored hair pulled back in a bun and an apron tied around her waist, was constantly running food back and forth to the temporary convent. Sister John Patrice, Sister Clare Benedict, Sister Peter Grace, and Sister Mary Fiat were always appreciative of the meals provided by their landlady.

Extroverted Theresa Hamilton was a pillar in her church and the community. The Hamiltons and their eight children were also members of St. Mary's. Fifteen-year-old twins, Karlene and Karenna, traded babysitting Mary Catherine.

The Hamilton Family were backyard neighbors with their rental house, an optimal situation for Carolyn, who occasionally still struggled with anxiety. Their near presence facilitated Carolyn's being able to settle easily into her new life. It brought her peace, knowing that she and Mary were being looked after by such great people.

Carolyn loved having the religious sisters nearby, and Mary Catherine always had a story to tell them. The sisters, who taught elementary school, always acted as if the tales were the most delightful things they had ever heard. Mary Catherine was thrilled to have such an eager audience at hand.

It didn't take long for Carolyn to regard Grand Rapids as home, and she was enthusiastic about her new role. Everything about the new place of employment said 'rich.' The upholstered fabrics, natural woods, and carefully selected antiques in the Water's Edge were stark contrasts to the shiny red vinyl and metal décor of the Log Slide. Gone were the farming patrons in overalls, replaced with ladies in hats and city clientele of smartly clad businessmen.

Many times, Carolyn was thankful for her fine Catholic education, which had taught a course in etiquette. The young twenty-something seemed to be a natural fit for such an establishment. The restaurant had started to bring in more revenue with its uptick of a younger crowd. No longer were the lunch counter stools and booths filled with just middle-aged men in suits and an occasional woman. More and more young businessmen began to patronize it. Several of them flirted with Carolyn, who doubled as a hostess during the busy lunch hours.

They didn't get far, though. The young manager was resolved to do well at this job and save as much money as she could. In another month, she had her second tuition payment due at the parish school where Mary Catherine had started kindergarten. She also desired to buy a car. With those goals written on a card and displayed on her fridge, Carolyn made a vibrant effort to appreciate the opportunity for good, hard work. She fondly regarded the customers who patronized the Water's Edge. For they, in essence, made her financial goals attainable.

One surly patron, however, would not stop hitting on Carolyn. He tried a new pick-up line each day at lunch. At first, Carolyn was flattered. She had begun to wonder about being asked out on a date again. Maybe not with him but with someone. She had noted his rugged good looks and was attracted, but the chiseled face could not mask his abrasive personality. He was arrogant and thought anything he said was worth noting. To avoid being rude, she smiled and found a way to excuse herself. He cropped up again for the dinner hour, which Carolyn worked on occasion.

One night, per usual, he insisted on sitting in her section. She made up a reason she should change tables with another waitress, but he found an excuse to switch also, bringing his double shot of Jim Beam with him. Carolyn gritted her teeth and plastered on a fake smile. "Good evening. How may I serve you, sir?" She waited on him like any customer, but she took note that he was not as friendly as he had been. *Maybe he gave up.* He paid his bill, including a large tip, and left. Her relief couldn't have been greater watching him swagger down the street and disappear. Still a bit flustered as she pocketed the tip, she tried to cast out the unnerving experience.

It took her about another half-hour to cash out. Then she said her goodbyes to the remaining staff and Mr. Hamilton. He was still in his office, balancing the books. He waved. Carolyn started off, rounding the corner out of view.

Completely at peace, she ambled along the city blocks trying to get in a few prayers in anticipation of being tackled by her waiting little girl who would demand all of Carolyn's attention. She wondered what stories Mary would require for the bedtime ritual. Carolyn guessed that *Goldilocks and the Three Bears* would be opened and ready to be read—again. It made her grin. She sighed a happy sigh, content with the relationship she had nurtured with her daughter. This move and this job had been good for them.

Even though Grand Rapids was much bigger than Grand Lake or Aunt Hildy's farm community, still, it felt small. Immigrants from several ethnicities had settled in and coincidentally divided up into burbs. Carolyn found it charming. There were the Lithuanians on the north end, the Poles to the east, the Hispanics to the south, the Dutch to the west, and the Germans and Italians right smack dab in the center. Her new city was exhilarating, and she became immersed in a moment of real gratitude.

Suddenly, she was being pulled from behind. Someone had grabbed her by the elbow with a powerful tug. Hearing the familiar voice of the creepy customer sent her skin crawling. She was catapulted back to more than six years ago. Instantly her throat went dry, and she was unable to make any sound at all. *Think, Carolyn, think!*

He spun her around and starting hissing. His dark eyes terrified her. She had seen that look just one other time in her life. "You owe me!" he yelled into her face. He was sweaty, and his breath reeked of whiskey. The realization he was drunk allowed her to start screaming while trying to pull away from him. "Shut up, you tramp!" he slurred.

Carolyn despaired as she struggled in vain with all her might to break free. She twisted as hard as she could, but she could not free herself. His grip was too strong. Panic froze her. She was no longer under her own power as he dragged her by the crook of her arm across the street to the darkened park. He held her tight as he undid his belt buckle. Carolyn could neither breathe nor move. Horrific images pervaded. She was transported back to the Starrett farm field. She imagined herself being thrown into the nearby hedges and being raped again. Her chest was pounding. Her legs went limp.

"Let go of her, I say!" a man's voice shouted. Her captor paused long enough for Carolyn to spin around out of his clutches. She collapsed to the ground and saw Ward Hamilton racing toward them. He grabbed the creep and threw him down on the sidewalk. "How dare you?! How dare you touch her?!"

The jerk didn't comprehend what had hit him, but Carolyn could see he was at a profound disadvantage. She whimpered and shuddered with her arms wrapped tightly around herself.

She watched in horror as Mr. Hamilton planted his foot down hard on the guy's chest. The furious fatherly figure bent over close to the intoxicated face. "Let me tell you one thing, mister. Don't you ever, ever touch any of my waitresses again! And if you dare come within a mile of my restaurant, you're going to have hell to pay! Do I make myself clear?"

The person on the ground trembled under the weight of Ward Hamilton and his threat. He gave an emphatic nod, sobering up posthaste.

"Now stand up, you coward!"

"Yes, sir," mumbled the drunk lying on the cement.

"I said, 'Stand up!'" Ward bellowed, yanking the guy right off the ground and onto both feet.

Carolyn trembled and inched back, wide-eyed. She had never seen a hint of annoyance or anger in her boss, but at this moment, one thing was clear: Ward Hamilton was furious.

The ruckus drew the attention of a passerby, who ran to the police station, summoning them to the scene. Soon a squad car screeched to the curb, and Mr. Hamilton gave the officer a play-by-play. Cuffs were slapped on the man. He was pushed headfirst into the back seat of the police cruiser.

Once the officer drove away with the felon, Ward turned his attention to his waitress and his neighbor, cowering by an elm tree. He crouched to her level. "Carolyn, are you okay?"

"Yes, just shaken up."

"I can see why. I had a notion about that scoundrel. I should have done something. I let my bookwork get in the way. Please, forgive me."

"But, Mr. Hamilton, how could you have known? Truly, I'm okay."

"Well, we're going to make sure it stays that way. From now on, one of the busboys or I will escort you home when you work a night shift.

And don't worry about that lame excuse for a man. I'll contact my lawyer and get a restraining order on him. He won't be able to come within five miles of us." He drew her up from the sidewalk, taking her to the safety of her apartment door.

"Thank you so much, Mr. Hamilton. It's so kind of you to keep an eye on me this way. I can't tell you how much I appreciate it."

For that was true. Carolyn could not tell her boss how much she appreciated his providential rescue. Or why. She had kept the ugliness of her past tucked close to her soul, where it belonged. There was no reason the Hamiltons had to know about the rape. It was over and done. She was confident that, with escorts always to accompany her the eight blocks, she would be fine. At least, that was her hope.

Yet, Carolyn startled easily. Any out-of-the-ordinary sound made her uneasy. Like three weeks later, when the good sisters came calling with fresh cookies. The knock on the kitchen door made her jump. She cautiously walked to the door and furtively peeked out. She was so relieved to see her religious friends. She threw open the door and erupted in tears.

"Tell us, child, what's wrong," said Sister John Patrice. It was then that Carolyn relayed what had happened and how Mr. Hamilton rescued her. The sisters didn't quite understand why she was still on edge over the situation.

"Can you tell us, dear one, why you are still so frightened?" solicited Sister Clare Benedict.

With her emotions getting the better of her, Carolyn confided in the good sisters about her tragic night. They listened with non-judgmental expressions and waited for her to finish. Then they held her one by one and prayed blessings over her. From then on, Carolyn grasped the real meaning of the term "spiritual mother" as it applies to religious women. They had both her physical and her spiritual welfare at hand. Because of them, she was able to give all her burdens over to the Blessed Mother. In the coming weeks, she gained the assurance to go forward without peeking over her shoulder, at least not as often. She made great strides in becoming the positive and secure woman God meant her to be. She became more self-reliant, too, as if almost nothing could throw her off base.

CHAPTER FORTY-ONE

The end of September brought astonishing news delivered via Adeline. Paul Johns had completed his missionary work, which he had stretched over a four-year time frame, and was in the insurance business with his Uncle Scott. "Paul is living in the Upper Peninsula. And—" Adeline abruptly stopped.

Carolyn became nervous. "And what?"

"And," Adeline hesitated, "he's married!"

Carolyn went blank. The news took her breath away. Last she had heard, Paul was still discerning his vocation to the priesthood. She had no idea that he had ended up choosing insurance as a career and marriage as a vocation. However, these details did not stun her as much as the name of the bride.

"To Phyllis Norton!"

"W…what?" was all she could say.

It took Carolyn a while to get over that. She was happy for Paul but more than slightly conflicted and having trouble sorting out her real emotions. She wasn't sure how to feel about Phyllis. She didn't want to be bitter. After all, she had no reason to be. Carolyn had had her chance with Paul. She resolved to hope for the best and to pray for them. They were two good people who deserved a happy married life, especially him.

Still, something tugged at her conscience. Something she was having a difficult time processing. Phyllis had never expressed even the slightest interest in Paul, and she certainly never pictured him with her. Why now? They didn't seem to fit, but maybe that was her pride talking. After all, Carolyn knew her opportunity was long gone. For now, she was going to have to be satisfied with labeling her emotions as bittersweet. Emotions that took a while to parse out. Images of Paul and Phyllis occupied Carolyn's reflections for the better part of that fall—especially when she received the shock of her life.

CHAPTER FORTY-TWO

Barely had she absorbed the revelation of Paul and Phyllis's marriage when she received news that made her gasp for air. It came by way of certified mail. The envelope bore the seal of the United States Army. She held the troubling package in her hands for a long time. *Is this from Gus? If so, why was it sent to me and not to my parents?*

Carolyn beckoned back to her childhood fears about not being good enough or someone going away. The government seal alone made her nervous, as if she were about to get some terrible information. She stood paralyzed with fear, while her thoughts ran wild with doom. *Oh, no! Oh, no!* Her hands felt hot holding it. Instinctively her fingers fell open, and the package dropped.

Mary Catherine bounded inside from playing with the younger Hamilton children. "What's the matter, Mama? What's that big envelope on the floor?"

Taken by surprise, she joggled back to reality. "Oh, nothing, honey. Mommy's clumsy." Carolyn hid her emotions in a drawer with the mail. Once she was sure her daughter was asleep, Carolyn retrieved the envelope, walked outside and around the house, and knocked on the sisters' door.

As soon as the door opened, Carolyn handed the package over. Her hands were shaking so badly that Sister John Patrice could hardly grab it. "I received this from the Army, but I'm afraid to open it."

"Well, child, why don't we carry this back to your place and open it together?" Since religious women were not allowed to go alone into the dwellings of the laity, the sister beckoned one of her housemates from her quarters. Sister Clare Benedict accompanied them around the back of the house into Carolyn's kitchen.

Carolyn first sat at the table, but not for long. Her legs were shaking horribly. She jumped up and held onto the sink. Sister John Patrice agreed to read the letter to her. Carolyn groaned and paced back and forth in the tiny kitchen, while the good sister read in a steady, measured tone:

10 October 1963

"Dear Carolyn,

I am sure this letter will come as a shock to you. In no way do I want to upset you or make your life any harder than it has been.

I deeply regret having taken advantage of you the way I did. I regret all the times I used women for selfish gain.

I was a lost soul, but I have repented. I pray God will spare me from the ravages of hell. I heard His call to commit my life to His Son, Jesus, which I have done.

I was injured in a hostile incident during the crisis in Lebanon, where I have been stationed. The injuries are severe enough that they are taking my life from me as I write this. It will be a slow and painful death, so I am told. But I willingly suffer it.

It is my wish that all my monetary assets be left to you and to your child, whom I have come to learn is my own.

Upon my death, you will be informed by the United States Army, and a check will be issued in your name. You will be free to use the money however you wish to assist you in raising your child or toward some other good and holy venture.

If you do not wish to take my money, I understand. Should that be the case, I ask that you then donate it to a charity of your choice, so that someone else may benefit from it. For all the bad I've done, I want to try to make it right somehow, in some way.

I regret all my sins, especially those against you. You would bring this repentant sinner a lot of peace if you would accept the check when it arrives and use it for good. Again, my sincere apologies and unfeigned wishes for all beautiful things to come into your life and the life of your daughter.

I am unworthy of the Lord's mercy and your forgiveness.

Sincerely and sorrowfully,

S. Jergen, Staff Sgt.

United States Army"

By the end of the letter, Carolyn was moaning and shaking, partly from relief that he wasn't coming to take her little girl away, and partly from reliving the nightmare of six years ago. She searched her jumbled brain to understand how Skip had even found out about the baby.

Sister Clare—afraid that Carolyn was about to pass out—braced her firmly against the counter by the sink. Sister John Patrice set the letter down and came over to lend support until she was stabilized. "Let's sit."

Carolyn was so numb that she had to be physically moved by the sisters. She let them lead her to the sofa in the living room. She allowed them to position her body. She was vaguely aware of where she was, but nothing inside her moved. She stared blankly off into space, fixing her eyes on nothing.

"Poor thing, she's in shock," she heard Sister Clare say. The underwater voice was warbly. *Am I drowning? Why can't I breathe?* She was aware that a black habit had stood up, *but who's wearing it?* She heard the water running at the kitchen sink, but she didn't know why. A cold cloth was positioned on her forehead, but she couldn't respond.

The patient sisters waited, with moving rosary beads in hand, until Carolyn came back to reality. They kept her company until she could pull herself together enough to call her parents. "We'll be in to see you tomorrow," promised her father. "Try to get some rest."

"We love you," her mother said. "We'll be there first thing in the morning."

The sisters made some tea and stayed with Carolyn until she fell asleep on the couch.

As promised, her mom and dad, along with Anne Hildegard, were at her apartment at nine sharp. Carolyn answered her door, feeling somewhat back to herself. She walked with her parents and the two girls over to the school. The two scampered around the playground. The adults sat on benches and talked about the ramifications of Skip Jergen's letter.

Mary and Anne ran around to all the various swings and slides, squealing with happiness. It was a delight watching the little aunt and niece be carefree and cut loose around the schoolyard. Anne was adept at climbing due to living with so many older siblings. Mary Catherine was proficient at swinging. She could pump high for her age. The two of them tried their hand at going up the slide backward, as they both had seen older kids do. Mary couldn't quite make it to the top, but Anne could. Mary raced around to the ladder and tried to get to the top before Anne. They laughed and giggled as they chased each other. Their excitement was contagious, and the mothers on the bench couldn't deny getting caught up in their daughters' joy.

"They are so darling," her mom said.

Carolyn nodded in agreement. No matter how serious things seemed, life would go on.

And then she heard Anne ask Mary a question. "My dad is your grandpa, but where's your dad?"

Carolyn's head whipped around to see Mary's face scrunched up. Her little girl was searching for the answer. In all the busyness of making a good life for her daughter, Carolyn had not yet addressed the obvious— always procrastinating until a more appropriate time. And there never seemed to be one. Carolyn was so mortified that she couldn't think of an immediate response—not a good one anyway, but she saw Mary descend the slide and head toward the bench where Carolyn was sitting with her parents. Her mom's hand pressed on her shoulder to keep her in place, while her dad ventured toward his granddaughter.

He crouched down to both girls, for Anne had joined them. "Well, sometimes dads aren't nice to their families and don't live with them. And sometimes people die. You remember, Anne and Mary, when my dad died?" Carolyn's Grandpapa Fandel had recently passed.

"Yeah," they said.

"Did my dad die?" asked Mary. Carolyn saw her daughter glance in her direction, so she stood up and walked to where her dad and the girls were sitting on the ground. "Was my dad nice?"

Carolyn's father continued, "Well, wee doll, I'm very sorry to have to tell you that your dad was not a kind person. He was not nice to your mommy, and he would not have been nice to you."

Mary's little face grew sullen.

"Honey, instead of living with us, your dad became a soldier in the army. He needed to fix whatever was wrong in his life—whatever was making him a bad man. The good news is—" Carolyn's throat closed.

Her dad finished for her. "So, the good news is your dad fixed whatever was wrong and chose to love God before he died."

It wasn't a lie. Skip—if his letter was honest—had accepted Jesus, had apologized and had atoned before he was to die. He just wasn't dead yet.

"I'm glad he fixed it," said Mary. "Everyone should love God. It's the only way we can be happy. Come on, Anne, let's go play." In a flash, the girls were off and back to their game.

Carolyn and her dad got off the ground. "Thanks, Dad. You've rescued me again."

"How children process is pure. What we told her has sufficed. She might ask again, but at least you have a framework."

By the time her parents left in the afternoon, Carolyn felt better. She had even begun a mental list of options for how to use the money. One idea came so expediently and so soundly that she knew it was God calling.

Alas, the one person she was dying to call, she could not! For there was no way she was going to do anything to come between Paul and Phyllis and their new marriage. *Neither one deserves that, nor is it their problem.*

For now, all these things were going to have to be kept close to her soul. She reflected on the Blessed Mother and how Scripture had said, "She pondered all these things in her heart." This was her only choice, as she had no idea when Skip would die or when the future package might arrive.

CHAPTER FORTY-THREE

That fall, the week of Thanksgiving on November 22, 1963, John F. Kennedy was assassinated in Dallas. With the news of the president's death, the restaurant closed down. Carolyn sat transfixed at her television. On the verge of tears, she was horrified as she watched Walter Cronkite deliver the news bulletins as they were received. It seemed like a nightmare listening to the accounts of eyewitnesses who watched the president being gunned down. She knew she would remember this day forever.

***

Christmas of 1963 was in full swing. The Fandels, indeed all of America, were still reeling from the tragic assassination of their president. "It'll be a long time before American citizens begin to relax back into normal life," her dad said.

Carolyn and Mary had been in Grand Lake for a few days over Thanksgiving, and they were there again now to celebrate the yuletide. Families held one another close that holiday season, and the Fandels were no exception—especially since they were missing one of their own across the Atlantic.

Carolyn, her mom, Adeline, and their two grandmothers had baked up a storm. They were packing up a huge box of Christmas goodies— including a batch of Kristin Sherman's holly wreaths—to send to Gus, stationed in Germany.

"For now, our boy is safe," her mom sighed. "He's even getting to explore the native country of the German Fandels and Wagners."

Carolyn imagined traveling the world as she packed up the final tin, which held her grandmother's specialty—sour cream cookies. The package of sweets would be a welcome surprise to Gus's unit, so far away from home.

There was also a newcomer to the Fandel celebrations. Silvester had met the love of his life, a spunky redhead named Lucie Van Hockstra.

Sil had been at Van Hockstra Furniture now for about five years. He had proven himself to be a valuable, innovative employee. The Van

Hockstra brothers, Willis and Ervin, had offered him a job as assistant manager of production.

"No doubt it is your diligent and intuitive work that led to your promotion," Carolyn noted. "Congrats, brother!"

"And that hickory table," Lucie said, pointing to the sofa table Sil had made in high school for their mom.

"The table?" inquired Carolyn.

"Yeah, I snagged a photo out of an album the day I applied. Since I was going to a furniture company, I figured it might be an advantage."

"It sure was! My father tells the story whenever Sil meets one of his friends." The fiancé continued her gushing, "And you ought to see Sil's house now. My guy is both handsome and pretty darn handy." Lucie leaned into Sil's shoulder with a lovesick expression.

"Thanks, Hon." Turning back to Carolyn, "I can't wait for you to see it." Silvester had purchased a small three-bedroom bungalow in Holland, in a tidy, tulip-lined neighborhood on the outskirts of town. He continued with the story, "I had no idea who the ginger-haired, freckle-faced beauty was. But I became interested when I caught the flounce of that pretty green skirt out of the corner of my eye. I knew it wasn't one of those middle-aged secretaries."

They all laughed.

"Yeah, I could sense him staring at me," said Lucie. "So, I waved. When he waved back, I bounded over to his office."

"All of a sudden, there she was!" said Sil.

"And he had nothing to say," laughed Lucie. "He didn't even remember me."

"Remember you?" queried Carolyn. "Had you met previously?"

"We had," Sil threw in. "But I didn't remember because it was the day I got hired. I was too nervous to notice girls that day."

Lucie was laughing, and it was infectious. She had the whole room roaring.

Sil resumed, "Anyway, so then, she says, 'Hi, I'm Lucie Fay Van Hockstra' in her cute voice, and it dawned on me that I was talking to my boss's daughter."

"But here's the kicker," Lucie said. "Catholic boy here wasn't going to date me because he thought I wasn't a Catholic."

"So, you began taking instructions in our faith so you could date Sil?" asked Carolyn.

"Nope. She already was," Sil said. "Which I didn't know until I spotted her in Mass the following Sunday at St. Peter's."

"And the rest, they say—" Lucie began.

"—is history," the three sibs finished in unison.

"That's a great story!" gushed Carolyn. "You two are so cute together." Sil had found an awesome match for himself. Where her brother sometimes took things too seriously, Lucie sprinkled in an element of optimistic, carefree fun. A balance of personalities.

Adeline agreed, "I'm so happy you found my brother, Lucie."

Carolyn and Adeline were both living vicariously through Sil. Neither sister had a dating relationship in the works, but they had shared they were ready for that day to arrive. "Don't worry, Adeline. Our moment for romance will come." She yearned for this to be true more than she was willing to admit.

Carolyn was thrilled for her brother. He was such a good guy. He had been there for her in her darkest days. She was determined to show him support in his brightest ones.

***

The entire bunch woke with excitement the morning of Saturday, April 11, 1964, for the wedding of Silvester James Fandel and Lucie Fay Van Hockstra.

The boys had all received fresh haircuts early that week, except for Gus. The best man was home on a two-day furlough, with his hair buzzed in the familiar military style.

Out the door they went, with the fashionable female Fandels piling into the station wagon for the half-hour trip to St. Peter's. Adeline sat in back with the two girls, while Carolyn took command in the driver's seat. They agreed their mom was too nervous to be behind the wheel. The nattily clad brothers—Gus, Wally, and Frankie—crowded a moment later into the back seat of Sil's car. Silvester had spent his final night as a bachelor back in his old room with his brothers, for old times' sake. Their dad hopped in to drive while the groom rode shotgun.

"They're milking these last few moments of guy time," Carolyn said, smiling. "The brothers aren't little boys anymore."

It was to be a simple affair to respect the wishes of Lucie's good parents. Some of the Van Hockstra relatives had put up such a fuss over Lucie's conversion to Catholicism that her parents included only immediate family for the event. Therefore, the guest list was comprised of the parents, siblings, nieces and nephews, and grandparents, twenty-three guests in attendance, with the Fandels representing well over half.

Because Lucie was now a Catholic, there was a full nuptial Mass. To blend the two families of differing Christian views, the priest had extended an invitation to the Van Hockstras' pastor to give a marital blessing at the end of the nuptial Mass, which he did, and they appreciated it.

There was no huge party after the ceremony, for that was not the Dutch style. Instead, Ervin and Janet Van Hockstra chose to host a cake and punch reception in honor of the newlyweds. It lasted just over an hour by the time Lucie and Sil had opened their last gift.

As the new Mr. and Mrs. Silvester Fandel waved and drove away to their honeymoon, tin Pabst Blue Ribbon cans rattled and rambled from the back—compliments of Gus, Wally, and Frankie.

Carolyn was so happy for her brother and his new wife, though she couldn't stop dreaming of a day when such a blessing might come her way. Until Sil's engagement, she had put such visions on the back burner, fearing that dating would take away her focus. But now, she was ready for something more.

It had been several years since that fateful night, and she had moved on. Carolyn had proven herself capable as both parent and provider. She had begun to yearn for her personal life to be more complete. That was, if she could find a decent man to take on her situation and be a compassionate father to her daughter.

CHAPTER FORTY-FOUR

Carolyn had decided it was about time she took full responsibility for getting herself and her daughter back and forth to Grand Lake on their own accord. She began looking for used cars she could afford. Mr. Hamilton scouted for a safe vehicle on her behalf.

On a Tuesday, he called Carolyn into his office. "Please close the door and come have a seat." He swiped his arm toward a wooden dining chair across from his desk. "I was studying your file, and I noticed you have some experience with auctions."

"Yes, some. My Pa Wagner—er, my grandfather—used to take my older brother and me to sales when we were teens. I learned quite a bit." She regaled her boss with her knowledge. He was impressed.

"I knew I could count on you. Since I've bought the adjacent building and plan to expand, I'd like you to be my buying agent at estate sales."

Carolyn was speechless, but she was smiling. She pulled herself together as soon as she could. "Oh, Mr. Hamilton, I'm flattered." She was enthused about her modified job responsibilities. The prospect invigorated her. "I'd be honored to do this work for you!"

It now became apparent that she also needed a vehicle for work. At first, Ward Hamilton allowed her to use his station wagon. As her experience and travel distance increased, along with the size of her purchases, it became impossible for him to allow her so much use of his family car. A friend of his was selling a red 1958 Chevy Pick-up for four-hundred bucks. It was almost five years old, but, to Carolyn, it was brand new. Mr. Hamilton offered to pay half since she was going to use it part of the time for work. It was odd for a woman to drive a truck, but it fit her lifestyle. And Carolyn was thrilled beyond measure with her two-hundred-dollar automobile.

She enjoyed putting to use all that wisdom she had garnered from her grandfather. He had taught her how to determine the value of unusual pieces and that she should go one day in advance of a sale to preview potential purchases. He had rattled on and on about what to look for so that she could determine which items were authentic. Pa had also cautioned her that she should always keep a poker face so as not to give away her interests. She learned when and when not to get into a bidding war. His priceless tips would serve her well in her new role of locating, bidding, and buying furniture pieces and artwork for the expanding establishment. *God bless Pa!*

Her parents offered to keep Mary on some of the weekends when Carolyn had to travel for estate sales. The businesswoman's side of her was in her element on these missions. If there was an auction or two coming up, Fridays were used for scouting and Saturdays for buying. Scouting consisted of making notes and even drawing a diagram of where hoped-for purchases were located, allowing her to go straight to the object the next day to maximize her time.

***

In early May 1964, Carolyn had to go to an auction near Aunt Hildy's. "Come on, Mary Catherine, we're headed on an adventure." They left Friday after lunch, planning to spend the night at the farm. After Carolyn previewed the sale, the two of them parked along the roadside to pick a bunch of wild daffodils. They divided it in half, one part for Aunt Hildy and the other part for Elaine. The first stop was to their former landlord.

Knocking on Elaine's door, Mary was ready with the yellow flowers extended in her hand. "Oh, my goodness, thank you! Mary Catherine, you're so grown up!" Elaine smiled from ear to ear. "Come in, you two!"

They visited about an hour and then headed out to the farm. They were due for supper.

Hildy, her arms wide, beckoned them in an excited voice, "Come, give your old aunt a giant hug." Surveying Mary Catherine from head to toe, she announced, "You're going to be a tall one!" The midwife always sized up everyone. "You have your mommy's features." Mary Catherine took the comment in stride. She and Carolyn were used to people saying that wherever they went.

The two were ushered into the kitchen and told to sit. So, they sat. The table already held a stack of toast. From the stove, Hildy shlepped over a large saucepan of Carolyn's favorite Friday meal. Carolyn smiled broadly as she ladled the creamed tuna onto the toast and spread it around. It was warm and velvety with chunks of albacore. The gravy was peppery, which married well with the salty butter on the toast. "Yum!"

Mary Catherine agreed. "I love it when Grandma makes this for us."

The visitors cleared the table and did the dishes. Carolyn was proud of how her little girl meticulously dried the silverware. Aunt Hildy noticed, too. She went into her candy jar and offered her great-great niece her choice of gumdrops.

"Red, please!"

"It's so good to be with you, Aunt Hildy. And to be at the farm." Carolyn hugged her aging aunt. "Thank you so much for dinner and the overnight."

"My pleasure, Girl."

"Aunt Hildy, how about some tea? It's my turn to serve you for once." Carolyn approached the stove and turned the knob, igniting the burner under the kettle. The familiar chirp of the bluebird reminded her of her time there. Sweet memories.

The three of them sipped, chatted, and played a few games of Crazy Eights before lights out. Carolyn and Mary Catherine cuddled upstairs in the creaky double bed.

"This is the room where you were born, honey."

"It is?" Mary Catherine's eyes were wide and full of wonder.

"Yes, it sure is. The day you were born was the happiest day of my life."

Mary snuggled closer to her mom. "It's cozy. Sleepovers with you are fun, Mama."

Carolyn agreed and smooched her daughter on the top of her blonde head. They said their prayers, pulled up the covers under their chins, and slept.

In the morning, they stayed long enough for a nonnegotiable cup of coffee and a bran muffin. Mary Catherine's coffee was mostly milk and sugar. "Well, Aunt Hildy, this has been delightful, but I suppose I'd better get to work."

"Where are you headed on this adventure, child?"

"I've got to go up the road to the Spitzley farm and bid on some items for the Water's Edge."

"Oh, the Spitzleys. Nice folks," Hildy remarked, "They run quite an operation. You ought to find some good buys up there."

The two waved and blew kisses to their elderly aunt as their truck rambled away from the farmhouse.

They arrived at the auction at seven-forty-five. People were starting to pour in, so Carolyn had to make good time and scope out her hoped-for purchases. "Mary Catherine, stick close. We're going to have to hurry."

The previous day she had spotted a luxurious, red velvet settee that would make a great piece for one side of a walnut table that she had procured the previous weekend. Now she envisioned finding two wooden ladder-back chairs—or something similar—to complete the four-top for the restaurant.

Carolyn had come to appreciate how the Hamiltons used real furniture to set up the Water's Edge. Customers acknowledged it, as well, for they often had their favorite tables. On a given night, she could pretty much guess which patrons were coming, what time they would arrive, and where they preferred to sit. It was part of the charm and comfort. So homey that it was hard to believe it was located in the center of a bustling city.

Carolyn spotted two chairs on the far side of the yard. It was hard to tell if they were fitting until she got closer. She noticed a man standing with his back toward her. He, too, seemed intent on the same. "We'd better pick up our pace, Mary Catherine, or that guy is going to get first dibs on those chairs." She grabbed her daughter's hand, and they started across the large yard in a jog.

The closer she got, the more clearly she saw. She was no longer focused on the chairs because the man had rotated. She stopped dead in her tracks with certainty that she wasn't ready to see *him*.

"Come on, Mama," Mary Catherine urged, tugging forward on her mom's arm, "we can't miss out on those great chairs."

"Um, they're not that good after all." She turned around to head the way they had come—but not quite in time.

"Carolyn, is that you?" said the familiar voice behind her.

She halted but then kept going.

The voice was emphatic. "Carolyn!"

"Mama, someone is calling your name," Mary said quite loudly as if her mother might be deaf.

Carolyn gradually turned around and met him face to face. She hadn't seen hide nor hair of him since before his wedding to Phyllis. "Why, hello, Paul. What brings you up here?" She tried to sound casual, but she was nervous. She wasn't sure what to do with her hands, so she folded them behind her.

"I'm hunting for some things for my new apartment. This is my great uncle's place, and my mom said I'd be able to find some solid pieces here."

"Oh, how marvelous you and Phyllis have a new apartment." Carolyn tried to sound genuine.

He corrected her in a tone that said he was not pleased. "It's not our apartment. It's mine."

It took a minute for the gravity of his words to sink in. Carolyn thought she understood, but she was almost afraid to acknowledge it. "I'm not sure I understand."

"The marriage didn't last. It should never have happened." He added, "I can't talk about this here. Not now. Not with you. Let's finish our business. It was nice seeing you."

Carolyn didn't deserve to ask for more from him, so she let it drop. "Oh, Paul, I'm very sorry." She hated to see any marriage fall apart. She cleared her throat in a way people do when they attempt to clear the air. "It was nice to see you, as well."

Before departing, she called over Mary Catherine, who had become intrigued with some old toys.

"Honey," Carolyn said, bending down to her daughter, "This is Mommy's friend, Paul."

Mary Catherine stuck her hand out like a businessperson and said, "I'm pleased to make your acquaintance, Mr. Paul."

The two adults chuckled and agreed this was a brilliant way to part.

Carolyn clasped onto her daughter's hand. She watched Paul Johns walk away, longing to go after him—or that he would come back to her. But obviously, with things being such a mess with Phyllis, she had to let him go. Bittersweet nostalgia and a legion of what-ifs filled her. *You had your chance, Carolyn.*

Back at her truck, auction hands loaded up a few pictures, those two chairs, and the red settee. Its legs rested on the dropped-down tailgate. The men used some strong rope to secure it and, if she were a careful driver, she could get it back to the city with her purchases in fine shape.

As she drove away, pangs of guilt pestered her. She said out loud, "I should have insisted Paul have those chairs."

"But, Mommy, Mr. Paul said he didn't want them. He wished for you to have them."

"Yes, honey, but I still feel bad."

"Maybe it makes him happy that you have them."

"Yes, maybe." *Man, it was good to see him! Really, really good.*

CHAPTER FORTY-FIVE

In the coming weeks, Carolyn offered a few short prayers for Paul, but she had precious little time for more than that. When not with her daughter, Carolyn threw herself into the newest Hamilton business project, the expansion of the Water's Edge. She barely had a moment to give her chance-meeting with Paul any real consideration. It was crunch time to get the project completed and opened by Memorial Day weekend.

As an addition to their expanded menu and seating capacity, the Hamiltons decided to open an ice cream window for walk-up guests. With wide coverage from the *Grand Rapids Press* and a plug from a local television news reporter, it had become the talk of the town. Nothing could compare in the near vicinity. People walked or rode their bikes from all over to get an ice cream concoction via that window.

A sweltering June evening proffered a line longer than usual. Joanie, the teen who worked the ice cream window, had called in sick with a broken arm from a water-skiing accident. Since Mary was away on an overnight at her grandparents' house, Carolyn offered to stay late and work the crowd through to the end of Joanie's shift.

She was having great fun, as all the customers at the ice cream window were wearing happy summer smiles. They were patient with Carolyn as they chatted and watched her fill their orders with cold, luscious goodness of all combinations of the six Hudsonville ice cream flavors: Butter Pecan, Orange Pineapple, Tutti Fruitie, Chocolate, Strawberry, and, of course, Vanilla.

Carolyn was a fanatic, running around trying to complete orders as speedily as she could. She was handing cones, sundaes, and malts out the window faster than she could count. She was so busy that she didn't even have time to look at the customers. She kept her head down, ready to write out the next sales slip, turn, fill it, collect the payment, say 'Thank you,' and move to the next order. Dozens of times. For hours. Carolyn's feet ached. She could barely hold herself up.

She stepped back up to the window and handed three chocolates and one vanilla to a busy mom of three. Her head down, she wiped the sweat

181

from her brow. For the millionth time with waning enthusiasm, "What can I get you?"

"Double butter pecan, Miss." The reply stopped her cold. *That voice again.*

She gulped. Her eyes cautiously scanned the customer from the ground up. Standing in front of her were tan legs in sockless loafers, blue plaid shorts, and a white short-sleeved button-down shirt. At the sight of Paul Johns, Carolyn was no longer exhausted.

"Yes, sir, coming right up!"

"What time do you get off?"

"Nine."

"I'll be back then," he said as if she had no say in the matter.

She nodded and smiled, noting the time on her watch. *Almost an hour.* Her heart ticked faster than her Timex.

She continued waiting on sweaty customers as exuberantly as she could, but there was no getting around it. She hadn't minded taking Joanie's hours, but now the last place she wanted to be was stuck behind that ice cream window. Even though the line was still long and kept her busy, the next fifty-seven minutes seemed to slow to a crawl.

She was elated to close that darned pane of glass and venture outside to where he waited for her. As she approached him, she didn't want to assume anything. She simply grinned and said, "Hi," and waited for him to tell her.

"Carolyn," Paul began, "I need to tell you what happened between Phyllis and me, if you'll hear me out."

"I'm open to anything you want to share with me, Paul. I've wondered ever since I saw you at the Spitzley auction, but it wasn't my place to ask."

"May we go somewhere private?"

"Sure. Mary Catherine is on an overnight at my folks'. We can go to my place."

"That'd be great. I'd like to see where you and Mary have been living."

They started for Carolyn's apartment, walking side by side, careful not to touch. It's not that she didn't long to. She chose to be sensible until she could sort out what was going on.

She purposely sauntered the long way around the rental house, so she and Paul had to pass by the sisters' apartment. It wasn't right to hide anything from them, as they had been so good to her and her daughter.

Sister John Patrice was on the front porch with an iced tea and her Bible. "Hello, Sister," called Carolyn as they got closer.

"Well, hello, Carolyn," returned a voice that revealed interest.

"Sister, this is my good friend, Paul Johns. Paul, this is Sister John Patrice."

"I am pleased to meet you, Sister."

"Happy to meet you, Mr. Johns."

Around the back of the house, the two stepped up and into Carolyn's kitchen. From over her sink window, she noticed Theresa Hamilton standing at hers, so Carolyn waved. Theresa waved back and nodded. Carolyn contemplated closing the kitchen curtains, but she didn't dare. It didn't seem prudent. She should stay at least within eyesight so no one could claim unsavory behavior. After all, the Hamiltons had been so gracious to rent Carolyn this sweet apartment, and they had no idea who Paul Johns was. *I can explain it tomorrow after church.*

As the two settled into the tiny kitchen, Carolyn put on the tea kettle. She grabbed some glasses and filled them to the top with ice. The hot tea caused the cubes to crack and send the glasses into a sweat. Paul took a seat, and Carolyn sat his chilling brew on a paper napkin in front of him. He offered an enthusiastic, "Thank you," and then instantly added, "Man, is it ever good to finally be here!"

She sat at the other end of the table. "What do you mean, 'finally'?"

"I've been trying to get up the nerve ever since I saw you at that auction. How in the world was I going to explain a failed marriage after only a few months?" He blushed. His eyes revealed sadness and embarrassment.

"I've wondered about it, Paul. And I've prayed. Don't be embarrassed. You can tell me. I'm a pretty good listener."

"That you are."

"Well, here I am now. Explain away. I'm not going anywhere."

"Marrying Phyllis was a huge mistake, most especially since I still had feelings for you."

Carolyn smiled. "You did?"

"Naturally. You were my first love."

"Then why did you marry Phyllis?"

"She was persistent."

"Always has been."

They both laughed.

"She did not give up, so I finally asked her out. After all, we had quite a bit in common."

"Right. Same schools, same religion, your parents were friends with her parents. I can understand that."

"There was one thing, though, that I was in the dark about. And it became the deal-breaker." He paused, and his face scrunched up like he had eaten something awful.

Carolyn sat motionless, respecting his timing.

After a span, he ventured forth. "Phyllis was cheating on me with an actor from the theater. Pretty cliché, eh?"

"Oh, Paul. How awful!"

"You're telling me! I was committed to her and the sacrament of marriage. Apparently, she wasn't. I had no idea. I was a fool," he chided himself.

"How could you have known?"

"That's the thing. I didn't. I mean, I knew she was withholding something from me because we stopped having meaningful conversations, but I did not imagine in a million years what was going on." Paul scoffed in disgust. "Things weren't right from the get-go. We went way up to Copper Harbor at the tip of the U.P. for our honeymoon, but there wasn't the spark that should have been. Things seemed merely functional. She wasn't forthcoming, as you can imagine. I thought it was wedding jitters and that things would get better once we got to know each other better, you know, in that way." Paul stopped himself and apologized. "Oh, my word, Carolyn, I am so sorry I just said that!" He hung his head with shame for blurting out such intimate details.

"Don't worry about it. We're not sixteen anymore."

"No, I guess we're not, but still…" He paused as if to muster up more courage. "So, after our honeymoon, we moved into our apartment downstate. We went on fine for a couple of weeks, or so I believed. One day I surprised her by coming home for lunch, and—" Paul stopped again.

But he didn't need to continue, for Carolyn had filled in the rest. "He was there with her?! Oh, my word! Paul, I am so sorry." Carolyn had tears in her eyes.

"I had failed. But with the pastoral guidance of Father Fedewa and a good counselor, I worked my head around to comprehending that her sin wasn't my fault. Because we were married for such a short time and because of the intimacy thing and, because shenanigans were going on before we married, an annulment was granted expediently."

"Where is Phyllis now?"

"I heard she moved back to the Upper Peninsula. His people are from there. They've known one another since childhood. But, honestly, I haven't cared to find out exactly where she is. I needed to cut my losses and move on. I had recently moved into my place when I saw you at the auction. Things were still too raw. I'm sorry I cut you short or made you wonder all sorts of bad things about me."

"Oh, Paul, I could never wonder all sorts of bad things about you. But I have prayed for you."

"And I for you, Carolyn. I believe those prayers are part of what led me to you here."

"I believe you're right about that, but it was still a shock to see you standing at that window. I don't understand how you happened to be there."

"Silly girl. I couldn't stand it anymore. I found out where you worked because I had to see you! I had to talk to you and disclose everything."

Feeling foolish now that he had stated the obvious, she said, "I'm glad you did." 'Glad' was an understatement. She was over the moon. Her heart was fluttering, but she kept that to herself. Her emotions were conflicted. She ached for Paul and his doomed marriage, but she was also secretly happy his marriage failed. *I'm awful and need to hit the confessional.*

Paul ventured, "It hasn't been that long since my marriage and annulment, but I've had something important to say for about six years, and if I don't try one more time, I'm going to regret it. Do you think we could start seeing each other again?"

She didn't know what to say—for about two jiffs. "Yes! I would like nothing more!"

"My prayers have been answered!" He reached across the table and took her hands in his. Peering directly into her eyes, he said, "Carolyn Joanna Fandel, I do not intend to let you slip through my fingers ever again."

"Paul Joseph Johns, I wouldn't let you, even if you tried." Her spirits soared. He had always been her one true love, even if she couldn't admit it to herself all these years. "I do have one question, though."

"Shoot." The way he said it told Carolyn he was open to any questions.

185

"Who gave you the extra push to come to see me?"

In unison, they said, "Silvester," which caused them to burst out laughing.

Paul admitted, "I ran into Sil after I got back to town. I told him what a wreck Phyllis was and about the divorce. He looked straight at me and said, 'Johns, if you don't go get my sister, I'm gonna clean your clock.'"

Carolyn chortled out loud. "He's been working on me, too. I was too set on my independence to hear it. But I'm ready now." She had proven to herself that she could be a good mother and also a good businesswoman. And a woman worth marrying. At last.

After Paul left her apartment, Carolyn sat awake for hours, smiling. She grinned so wide and so long that her cheeks hurt.

CHAPTER FORTY-SIX

Within six weeks, the two became engaged. Paul and Carolyn were ready to confer the most Holy Sacrament of Matrimony upon each other forever. By the end of August, they were sitting in the Saint Michael parish office, waiting for Father Fedewa. They were excited to begin their pre-marriage counseling at their home church in Grand Lake.

"Well, this has been a long time in coming," said the affable clergyman with a wink in his eye. "I witnessed you two grow up. I observed your sweet glances across the church during Mass. I doubt either one of you got much out of my homilies in high school." He howled with laughter.

It caused the pair to do the same. "You're right, Father. We barely heard a word you said," admitted Paul.

"I've also watched you both make tough decisions and move away from your families." Looking at Carolyn, he said, "I've been impressed by your bravery, young lady. You accepted your unconventional circumstances and have become a wonderful mother."

"Thank you, Father Fedewa. That means a lot coming from you."

He turned to Paul. "Young man, I watched you marry someone who was not the best match for you. But God has a way of working things out if we stay close to Him. You have always been faithful, and that is commendable."

"Thank you, Father." They both felt his confidence in them. He was wise and jovial, but he called a spade a spade in loving truth. And for this moment in time, there were no spades. Only hearts.

The priest flipped open his calendar. "So, what date do you have in mind?"

"As soon as possible, Father. We've wasted enough time apart," Carolyn said.

"Oh, child, no time is wasted searching for God. He's not on our timetable; we are on His."

They smiled and nodded.

"Soon as possible, eh?" Father Fedewa repeated Carolyn's words.

"Yes, Father," Paul agreed. "To be honest, it is unbelievably burdensome for us to be separated now that we have found each other again."

"Well, let's see," said the reverend glancing at his calendar. "There are a few things to do before you are to be married. This will take some study and some time. How motivated are you?"

"Very!" Paul and Carolyn replied with gusto.

"Well, then. How about the end of November? That gives you three months. How's that sound?"

"That sounds good to me," Paul said. He turned toward his fiancée. "Carolyn?"

Grinning ear to ear, she said, "My mother and I can pull a small wedding together in twelve weeks."

"It's settled then. How about a Saturday morning, right after Confessions? Say, eleven a.m.? You could have a luncheon after in the church hall."

"Sounds wonderful, Father. Thank you! I like the idea of a morning wedding." Turning toward her future husband, "Do you, Paul?"

"Sounds good to me. I'm a guy. I don't have to do much, other than put on a suit and show up, right?" He winked.

"Smart man," Father Fedewa winked back. He handed over a booklet and then continued, "Okay, here's a copy *Casti Connubii*, an encyclical written by Pope Pius XI. Truly, it's one of the best things I have read on the subject of Christian Marriage. It will reaffirm the goodly things you've seen in your own parents' unions, as well as bring to light the importance of a marriage being rooted in Christ and His Church. It's not long. Read it together. Discuss it. Take it section by section. Write down any questions you might have, and let's meet again. Call me."

"We will do that." Paul said, "Is there anything else?"

"Yes. There is a couple in Carolyn's current parish, St. Mary, who teaches a natural form of birth regulation. The Church is against any form of contraception because it puts an obstacle between the spouses and God. The marital embrace is a renewal of the marriage vows to be free, total, faithful, and fruitful. However, there might be a time when one of you, for serious reasons, decides it is not prudent to bring a new life into the world. The Church allows postponement of pregnancy in such cases. In the past, it has been up to the woman to figure it out, hoping the rhythm method worked or, at times, they even separated into different bedrooms—not ideal. Anyway, this pair at Carolyn's church is on the cutting edge of natural family planning. Set an appointment to go see them."

"I'm open to that," Carolyn said.

"I am, as well," Paul said. "I've been reading and studying about why there has been concern over the Anglican Church's acceptance of artificial birth control. The pill is becoming more popular with women of all denominations. I've read that there appear to be higher rates of infidelity in contracepting marriages. Increased infidelity will lead to more divorce and more children being raised by single parents. What the Holy Father is saying makes a lot of sense to me."

Carolyn stared at him. She was in awe of his taking charge of matters such as these. She loved him even more at that moment, for she became convinced that he would be an excellent spiritual leader of their family.

She wished they could be married tomorrow, but she was an obedient daughter of the Church. Besides, marriage preparation was nothing to be rushed, no matter how phenomenal the love between Paul Joseph Johns and Carolyn Joanna Fandel happened to be.

They were more elated and content than they ever had been. After going into the sanctuary to kneel for a prayer, they locked hands, floated out of the church, and headed toward the beach for ice cream and a long stroll. Paul called dibs on butter pecan. "Chocolate for me," said Carolyn.

CHAPTER FORTY-SEVEN

Paul drove back and forth to Carolyn's apartment two or three times a week. They searched for houses to buy, studied the marriage encyclical, talked about their future, and enjoyed watching TV together after Mary Catherine had gone to bed.

America was riveted by the present-day evening news. Paul and Carolyn listened to the following report from Walter Cronkite on CBS:

"Earlier this month, two U.S. destroyers stationed in the Gulf of Tonkin in Vietnam radioed that they had been fired upon by North Vietnamese forces. In response to these reported incidents, President Lyndon B. Johnson requested permission from the U.S. Congress to increase the U.S. military presence in Indochina. On August 7, 1964, Congress passed the Gulf of Tonkin Resolution, authorizing President Johnson to take any measures he believed were necessary to retaliate and to promote the maintenance of international peace and security in Southeast Asia. By the end of this month, the Johnson Administration believes that escalation of the U.S. presence in Vietnam is the only solution. Therefore, we will be sending more U.S. troops onto the soil of Vietnam."

Cronkite then ended with his standard, "And that's the way it is, Tuesday, August twenty-fifth, nineteen sixty-four."

Paul wrapped Carolyn in his arms. Neither said a word because they knew what this might mean. Gus, already in the military, could get deployed to Nam at any moment. And, with Wally's recent graduation from high school, he could be shipped there, as well, once he enlists.

Paul tried to be reassuring. "We can't be positive that they will have to go."

Her phone rang. They ignored it at first, as they were deep in conversation. Paul was trying hard to convince Carolyn that everything would be okay, no matter what. The phone kept on ringing and ringing, and Paul finally answered it.

"Hello, Robert, how are you?"

"I've been better, Paul. Is Carolyn nearby?"

"Yes, she's right here," Paul replied. "It's your dad."

"No!" was her first response. She pulled away as Paul tried to hand her the phone's receiver. Paul put it in her hand and moved her arm up to her ear for Carolyn to acknowledge her father. "Oh, Dad. Gus has to go, doesn't he?"

"Yes, Doll, he does. He called us today from Germany."

"When? I mean, when does he have to go?"

"Soon. Probably the end of the week."

"For how long?" inquired Carolyn, who already knew it was a selfish question.

"Carolyn, I'm afraid you're going to have to face the fact that Gus won't be there for your wedding."

"Yes, Dad, of course. I'm sorry to be so self-centered. How inconsiderate of me! How's mom taking it?"

"Not too well, as you might imagine, but she's got company. The Clark, Huhn, and Miller boys are all being sent, as well."

"Lord, have mercy, Daddy! Poor guys. Poor families of these guys."

"Those boys are going to need our prayers to be strong, and we have to put on a brave face for their sakes."

"Right, Dad, I hear you. If you talk to Gus, please tell him I love him and am praying for him. And give Mom my love. This must be killing her."

"It is, but we'll get through it together. We always do. God is faithful."

"Amen, Dad. Any word on Wally yet? He must be nervous."

"Most assuredly. A couple of buddies have been sent already. He hasn't quite reconciled with whether he can muster up the courage to go back to the recruitment office and fill out the remaining paperwork."

"I can't say that I blame him. I've been praying for him, too. Tell him I love him."

"I will. And tell Paul, 'Thanks,' in advance, for any and all prayers."

"Will do. Bye, Daddy."

"Bye, Doll." She heard the click of the phone. Carolyn gripped the receiver. Putting it down somehow made her feel as if she was losing connection with her brother. She burst into tears.

Paul took the receiver from her hand and hung up the phone. He held her for a long time. Then he went into Mary Catherine's room where she was playing to give Carolyn time alone to process the news.

Carolyn could hear Paul and Mary making noise in her room. They were having a pretend tea party. Carolyn smiled inwardly, as she imagined Paul sitting on the floor wearing one of Mary's dress-up hats. Later, she heard the two rummaging for the toothpaste in the bathroom. Mary was brushing her teeth, and Carolyn could tell that her daughter was laughing through the foam in her mouth. Soon, her little girl ran into the living room for a goodnight hug and a kiss. "Mama, Paul is going to read stories and tuck me in tonight!"

God had led him back to her. She treasured that her little girl could be so carefree with him. The way he interacted with her daughter made Carolyn treasure him even more. *Lord, I praise you.*

Paul left around ten p.m., honoring the curfew they had set for themselves. It was agonizing to let him go. Carolyn felt safer with Paul near and lonely without him. Not only that, she yearned to share her bed intimately with him. The closer the wedding got, the more their desire for each other grew. And it was almost too powerful.

CHAPTER FORTY-EIGHT

The newly engaged couple took to the task of going through the list of topics—things such as their families of origin, finance, religious beliefs, and any past mistakes that might hinder a full giving of one another. They had most definitely discussed in length Paul's failed marriage. Obviously, religion would not be an issue. They were also on the same page regarding finances. Having families in the same town was a big plus. Paul and Carolyn had most things in their favor for a successful marriage.

There was one topic they had not discussed. And that was Paul's missionary experience. Carolyn speculated there was something he was not telling her. He always skirted around the topic. She had tried to let it go because she was meant to be married to him, but it gnawed at her conscience. She could no longer ignore it.

Paul was scheduled to come to her place after he was done working. Carolyn thought it prudent to have her facts organized before she confronted him. She went into her bedroom and retrieved the envelope that had come from the military. She hadn't read Skip's letter in months. Her hands shook as she unfolded it. Her eyes watered, reading his signature. But one word kept popping out at her. "Lebanon." The more time she gave it, the more betrayed she felt. Her shoulders stiffened, and a fury kindled in her gut.

That evening after Mary had fallen asleep, Carolyn stood by the couch with her arms crossed and said point-blank, "Paul, we need to talk."

"Well, that sounds serious," he said flippantly.

"Don't you dare patronize me." She was fuming.

Paul raised his brows in a surprised fashion. "Whoa, there. Settle down."

"Settle down? Are you kidding me?!"

Paul's sheepish face told her that he realized telling her to calm down wasn't the best plan. He appeared scolded. Because he was. Paul changed his course. "I'm not sure why you're mad at me, but please tell me. Whatever it is, we can work it out."

"I'm not sure we can!" She turned her back on him and strode to the kitchen, hearing his footsteps close behind her.

"This is no way to work through things. We can't fix it if you won't even tell me why you're so upset."

She spun around and thrust the letter at him. "THIS! This is why I'm upset."

Paul took the letter and sat at the table to read it. He stared at it for a long interval. "I understand now. May I explain?"

Carolyn ran into her room and slammed the door. She wanted an explanation, but she was so hurt. She couldn't believe he had kept this from her. Or that he had acted so innocent just now. She was reeling. Her emotions within were raging out of control. She took deep breaths to no avail. She was pondering breaking off the engagement when there was a knock on her bedroom door.

"Carolyn, please. I love you. I can explain it."

She made him ask to come in a few more times before she got up and opened the door. She reluctantly let him take her hand and lead her back to the kitchen where they could talk. She sat down, plunked her elbows on the table, and glared in his direction. "Okay, explain away," she said stiffly.

"My uncle and I were accompanying the U.S. Army chaplain to minister to the severely wounded in the V.A. hospital in Beirut. One day on our rounds, I pulled back the curtain surrounding one of the soldiers to discover the bed held Skip Jergen."

Hearing his name made her tremble. To know Paul had had contact with him was too much. "You ministered to my rapist? You put him ahead of me, even after what he had done to me?" She could not sit here and listen to his rationalizations. She got up from her chair and tried to leave the kitchen.

Paul put his arms up to block her exit.

"Let me through!" she demanded.

"No, Carolyn. Hear me out. We've come too far to let this wreck everything."

His words rang true, and she knew it. She couldn't see how he was going to justify it enough to make it better, but she had worked incredibly hard. No longer willing to abandon her dreams, she sat back down at the kitchen table. "Okay, you're right. I deserve to know, and you deserve to be able to tell me. But lay out all the details." She pointed and wagged her index finger, "Don't you dare hold anything back!"

"I won't," Paul promised. "So, there he was. I wanted to strangle him,

Carolyn. I was so furious that I had to leave for a while and walk around until I simmered down. My uncle made me go back. He said, 'Jesus ministered to a multitude of the greatest sinners. You can minister to this one.'"

She nodded, and her mind finally slowed. The storm inside of her had quelled, and she relaxed.

"It was obvious he was in excruciating pain. He looked pitiful. He hid his face when he saw me. I sat down and waited for him to speak. The first words out of his mouth were pure regret for what he had done to you. He kept apologizing and apologizing. Then he rambled off all of his life's regrets. Believe me; there were many."

"What else happened during the days you were with him?"

"He expressed his need for faith. He told me he wasn't raised to believe in anything. My uncle told me it was my job to teach him. So, that's what I did. I sat with him, read from the Scriptures, and taught him about Christ. He had a true conversion, and Fr. Mark baptized him a Catholic."

Carolyn put her head in her arms on the table. The tears poured. Paul stood behind her chair, rubbing her back.

"How did he find out about Mary Catherine?"

"One of my last days there, he got up the courage to ask how you had been. He was searching for some assurance that he had not destroyed your entire happiness—some restitution for his crime. I could tell his sorrow was great. So, I told him. I told him about Mary."

"I see."

"He wept, Carolyn. He broke down and sobbed as I have never seen anyone cry in my life. His hollow eyes stared deep into mine, and he said, 'Hearing she at least received a beautiful child is a balm to my wretched soul.'"

Carolyn gasped. "Wow. That's profound. Why didn't you ever tell me this, Paul?"

"Because it was missionary work, Carolyn, and I regard the things that happened there sacred."

"But I'm going to be your wife. You knew what he had done to me!" Intellectually and spiritually, she understood. Emotionally, she did not. She could not. She fell silent. For a long time. She got up again and marched straight to her bedroom. She shut the door. Hard.

Paul left her alone. He had learned that space and time were allies.

Carolyn glanced at her watch as if she were timing him. A quarter of an hour had passed. She could hear his chair scrape away from the table. His footsteps moved closer to her room. She was taken aback when he didn't even bother knocking. He came right in and breathed a huff. But she continued to lay face down on her pillow.

The mattress sagged when he sat down beside her. He rubbed her back some more. "Honey, I am so sorry that I never told you. I should have. I should never have kept this from you. I am so sorry. Will you forgive me?"

She was annoyed that she couldn't stay angry at him. His touch was so gentle yet manly. Her heart fluttered. She loved him so much it was almost painful. She slowly rolled over and gazed at him with both devotion and exasperation. Even though it still stung, she managed to say, "Yes, I forgive you. I'm just so hurt. The best phrase I can use to describe it is 'extremely betrayed.'"

"I can understand that. I'm so sorry."

"Were there any other reasons you didn't tell me?"

"Yes," he admitted. "I didn't tell you because I couldn't bear for you to relive the horror of so long ago. I was trying to protect you. I was doing it for both you and Mary."

"Did you know Skip had written me?"

"Not for sure. Not until now. Why didn't you tell me?"

"Oh, Paul, I wanted to right away, but you were married to Phyllis. I didn't want to do anything to cause trouble between the two of you."

"Well, you had no idea that Phyllis and I already had bigger trouble than that," he smiled.

"I guess we both were keeping secrets."

"Yes, I guess we both were."

Her passion for Paul had grown strong. She reached up around his neck and pulled him down on top of herself. One by one, his shoes thumped the floor.

They kissed passionately, their breathing rapid and bodies moving until Paul bolted off the bed. "I'd better leave, or we are going to end up in the place we promised to wait for."

CHAPTER FORTY-NINE

Carolyn sat going over the wedding plans spread around her kitchen table. She was determined to finalize the guest list today. It was too long. Which names she should cut had her rapt attention. A knock at the door startled her enough for her to knock over her coffee. "Darn it!" she said aloud. "Who could that be?" She grabbed some napkins and threw them upon the spill to sop it up before it saturated her papers. Whoever it was kept knocking, which annoyed her. *Geesh! I'm coming!*

It was the door by the living room. *No one ever comes to that door.* She stopped cold. It was the door where she accepted the certified letter from the military. *No! Not now!*

Carolyn sat frozen at her table, unable to face the news at the door. Whoever was there was insistent. The knocking continued until she could no longer avoid it. She cautiously pushed her chair back and walked through the apartment to answer it. She pulled back the drapes and peeked out the window. Her breath caught. She peeked again to make sure.

Phyllis was standing on Carolyn's porch. She was wringing her hands and trying to peep through the window in the door.

Carolyn cracked open the door to her long-lost friend. "Hello, Phyllis. What are you doing here?"

"May I come in?"

"Well, I guess. Sure." Carolyn swung the door wide to let her in. "Please sit down. May I get you something to drink, a cup of coffee? Tea?"

"Thank you. Plain water will be fine." Phyllis's voice wavered, "I won't be here long."

Carolyn made her way to the kitchen, glancing back at Phyllis, who had remained standing. She kept her eye on her as she filled the water glass, not sure of what to make of her visit or her behavior. Phyllis took a seat on the couch. Her knees jittered up and down, causing Carolyn herself to become nervous.

Carolyn walked back into the living room and offered her the glass of water. "Here you go, Phyllis. You seem upset. Please tell me why you're here?"

"I think you know why."

"No, Phyllis, I don't. If I did, I would tell you."

Phyllis took a sip of her water, searching Carolyn's face as if trying to read whether she was telling the truth. Carolyn stared back, waiting for Phyllis to say something.

Her friend stood up again. "Are you sure you don't have any idea what I'm about to tell you?"

"Phyllis, I'm sure. And I'm busy. Can you please get to the point?" Carolyn was growing annoyed. She wanted to get back to wedding planning.

Phyllis lowered herself onto the couch. Then she rose again and walked over to the end table that held Mary Catherine's kindergarten picture. "She's beautiful. You are so lucky." Phyllis picked up the frame and stared into it, swaying back and forth.

Carolyn's voice trembled. "Yes, I am blessed, Phyllis, but that's not why you're here, is it?"

"Sort of."

Carolyn's old fears wormed their way in. She was concerned over the amount of focus Phyllis was giving Mary Catherine's photo. "Who sent you here?" Carolyn demanded an answer.

"No one."

"I don't believe you!" Carolyn shouted. "Tell me why you're here!"

Phyllis turned and must have seen the fright in her eyes. "Oh, Carolyn, I'm so sorry!"

Carolyn's armpits were moist. Her voice crackled, and she shrieked, "About what?! What are you sorry about?"

"About scaring you. Let me try to explain." Phyllis's demeanor had switched.

Carolyn relaxed. "Sure. But put down my daughter's picture first and come sit on the couch. Please."

Phyllis obeyed, and Carolyn sat beside her to prevent her from standing yet another time. She was going to get to the bottom of this surprise visit before it took another detour.

Her friend hemmed and hawed and then began to cry.

Carolyn wasn't sure what to do or say. She softened her voice. "Phyllis, we were good friends for a long time. Whatever it is, you can tell me. I won't judge you." This was true. After what Carolyn had been through, she was the last person on earth who had any cause to judge people for what had happened in their lives.

Phyllis stared at her with desolate eyes, full of regret. "I'm so sorry for hurting you. You were my dearest friend. I couldn't see another way. I was such a mess."

"What are you talking about, Phyllis? Do you mean when you abandoned our friendship? If so, yes, I was deeply hurt."

"I'm sorry. I just couldn't be there for you, and I have finally come to terms with it all. You deserve to know the reason why I left you high and dry."

Carolyn couldn't imagine what explanation Phyllis could offer to explain years and years of a friendship being stripped away in such a sudden motion. But she was curious. "Okay, I'm listening."

"You remember how I broke it off so suddenly with Hank?"

"Yes."

"What you didn't know is why. My parents made me."

"They did? How come?"

"Because I was pregnant."

Carolyn could not believe it. "You were pregnant?"

"Yes. I was. But not for long."

"What do you mean? 'Not for long.' Did you have a miscarriage?"

"I wish!"

"What happened, Phyllis?"

"Hank and I connected. We were moving fast. Too fast after Spring Formal. You knew that. I knew that, but we lost control of ourselves. He started coming over in the afternoons while my parents were at work, and one thing led to another. Everything was going great. My parents were allowing me to date. They had no idea what we were up to in the afternoons. But I loved him. You have to believe me," her friend pleaded.

"I do believe that. Go on."

"Well, as I said, one thing led to another, and I got pregnant."

"Oh, Phyllis, I had no idea!" Carolyn felt the sting in her eyes. She bit her lip to keep from crying. This was about her friend right now.

"How could you? You were going through your own hell."

"What do you mean?"

"Oh, Carolyn, I know about what happened with Skip, and I am so sorry!"

"Paul must have told you, huh?"

"Yes, he did, after we started dating. I'm so sorry, Carolyn. One of the biggest regrets in my life is that I did not go with you to the bathroom that night. If I had, Skip would never have hurt you."

"It's not your fault, Phyllis, and it is long in the past. Right now, I want to know what happened to you? And I don't mean with you and Paul. I mean, what happened to your baby?"

"My mother took me up north to that place. She told me a baby would wreck my life and hers. She threatened that if I had the baby, I would never be able to come back home. She made me have an abortion." By now, Phyllis was a sobbing mess. Her cheeks were covered in tears. When she wasn't crying, she was gulping for air.

Carolyn handed her a handkerchief and put her hand on Phyllis's knee. It was bobbing up and down, so Carolyn was trying to steady it by pressing on it. She put her arm around her poor friend and drew her close. Phyllis responded by weeping in her arms. Carolyn rocked her back and forth till the crying stopped.

"So that's why. That's why I couldn't be your friend anymore." Phyllis appeared to be waiting for Carolyn to respond.

But Carolyn couldn't. She was thinking about that poor baby at the hands of the abortionist. She was so horrified she couldn't even speak. She also realized for the first time in her life that not all who have abortions have a choice. Instead of Phyllis's parents shielding the baby—their grandchild—they forced their frightened daughter to have it killed, something Phyllis never asked for. She wanted her baby. "Oh, Phyllis, I am so sorry for your loss. Your unimaginable loss."

"You have no idea what those words mean to me."

"Does Paul know?"

"No. You are the first person besides my counselor and my mother. She did not even share this with my dad. He is in the dark, and I rarely speak to my mom anymore."

"Wow."

"'Wow' is right. You have no idea, Carolyn. My life has been an absolute mess. All these years. I started drinking and jumping from guy to guy, trying to make it all go away. I'm so ashamed of that."

"I take it all that is behind you now?"

"Yes, I've been to Confession about it."

"That's good, Phyllis. But—"

"But you're wondering how Paul came into the picture?"

Carolyn nodded.

"Yeah, so when I heard Paul was back in town after the missions, I assumed pursuing him was a good move. I was convinced he would improve and rectify my screwed-up life. But, the only thing I accomplished was making a mess of his life, too."

"Oh, Phyllis. I'm so sorry. Paul's okay, though. You've heard about us, right?"

"Yes, and I am so happy for you guys! Truly."

"Thank you. That means a lot. But you must realize I cannot keep this visit from him."

"Right. That's why I came. I sought out a pastor who could minister to me in all this. He recommended that I begin to heal myself by trying to make amends with all those I've hurt in my brokenness. I'm not courageous enough to tell Paul face-to-face about my abortion, but he should know. I came here to ask you to do it for me. It's a lot to ask."

Carolyn trusted the sincerity of her friend's request. "Surely. I can do that for you, Phyllis."

"Thank you, my friend. I cannot begin to tell you how much I appreciate that. Please tell him my bad behavior had nothing to do with him. It's on me. I screwed it up because I did not think of myself as worthy of being happy."

"I understand. We get confused sometimes when life throws us curveballs."

"We sure do," Phyllis agreed. "One more thing. I am going away for a while to get my head on straight. There's a retreat center in Chicago that has opened up for women. For women with my issues. It's a month-long therapy program. My mother is not interested in discussing her part in this, so I have to get away and try to heal on my own. I can't live my life holding it against her. She is remorseful enough, especially once she was able to admit that not only was that my child but also her grandchild. She just isn't ready to face how much it devastated me. She's yet to apologize."

"I'll pray for her."

"Please do. And pray for me, Carolyn. I need all I can get."

"I will, but can I ask you something, Phyllis?"

"Sure. I've dumped a lot on you. Ask away."

"Is the abortion the reason you pulled away? I'm guessing it is."

Phyllis nodded. "I couldn't risk being close to anybody. And, not to hurt you more, but I couldn't stand that you had a baby and family support when mine was dead." She started crying again.

"Oh, Phyllis, I understand. I get it. No need to explain more. Please, your secret is safe with me. I will never tell another living soul besides Paul, I promise."

"Thank you. You're a real friend. I've always felt that. I wish you and Paul all the best. You both deserve it. And I hope you two have a lot of babies together because you're bound to make adorable ones."

Carolyn smiled. "What a lovely thing to say, Phyllis. That is our prayer, too."

"Well, I've taken enough of your time," Phyllis said as she rose from the couch. "I leave tomorrow for Chicago. I'm hoping that by the end of this program, I will be strong enough to become a counselor for those who have suffered my same fate. Wish me well, and please pray for me whenever you think of me."

Carolyn hugged her friend. "I will. And your desire to offer solace to others pleases God very much, Phyllis." A thought struck. "Wait a second! I'll be right back." She went into her dresser drawer and grabbed something. It was the pewter dragonfly Elaine had given Carolyn when she first moved into the garage apartment. Carolyn read the etching at the bottom one more time. "I am beautiful and strong." She smiled because this moment felt right. Returning to her living room, she extended her hand. "Here you go. This was given to me at a life-changing moment. When you are seeking encouragement, hold it, and read it. Let it be a safety point. And, then, a few years from now, God will send you someone who needs it. Pass it on."

Tears flooded Phyllis's eyes as she accepted the memento. "Thank you. You've always been my dearest friend, and you've made this way easier than I deserved it to be." She hugged Carolyn once more, opened the door, and waved goodbye as she walked to her car.

That night, Carolyn filled Paul in on her surprise visitor. The whole story gave him clarity on why Phyllis found it hard to keep her marriage vows. There wasn't anything to be done about that, but he promised to pray for her and keep her secret.

CHAPTER FIFTY

November 1964

Carolyn was an exuberant bride, standing in the church narthex with her dad and Adeline. One of the side doors was ajar, so she could secretly see the guests waiting for the wedding to start.

She also saw Paul, in a black suit with an ivory carnation boutonniere, emerge from the sacristy with his brother Mike as his best man. The sight of her groom made Carolyn take a deep breath. *That's MY man. So handsome!* Her head danced with joy.

The Johns brothers took their places next to the two priests in white chasubles at the foot of the altar. Paul was standing tall and beaming. He and Carolyn had waited years for this moment. She could see him teetering back and forth on his feet as if he were impatient for the main doors of the church to open. Carolyn giggled. "Look at him, Dad. He's a wreck."

"Men in love often are," came the reply. "He's head over heels for you. I've known it for years."

"Me, too," said Adeline.

Carolyn smiled from ear to ear. She was so happy. Beyond happy. She was ecstatic.

Soft music wafted—Adeline's cue to enter. Her brunette hair touched the shoulders of the mid-calf, satin emerald green dress. As maid of honor, she carried a half dozen ivory carnations tied together with an emerald-green ribbon. She winked at Carolyn and initiated her slow procession toward the altar, taking her place to wait for her sister.

Following were the two almost seven-year-olds. Mary and Anne proceeded in their matching emerald velvet dresses, white tights, and black patent leather shoes. They were adorable in how seriously they took their jobs of tossing rose petals onto the white aisle runner. When they reached the front pew, they climbed on its bench and leaned way over into the aisle to get a better view. Carolyn was charmed as she watched the shoulders of the four black-habited sisters moving up and down, indicating they were laughing at the girls' spontaneity.

With gusto, the organist in the balcony blared the famous Bridal

Chorus. Carolyn could see her mother rise and face the back of the church. It was a signal that all others in the pews do the same. The aunts and uncles were grinning at each other. Her mom mouthed "at last" to Paul's mother, who nodded in agreement.

The cousins craned their necks like geese. It was as if no one was breathing. Carolyn almost wasn't. To her, it seemed they were all suspended, waiting for the doors at the back of the church to swing fully open.

The heavy wooden doors finally widened to reveal the love of her life. Paul's immeasurable smile matched hers. Simultaneously, their eyes welled, causing a ripple effect in the congregation as several reached into pockets or purses for handkerchiefs.

Carolyn was poised with her left arm entwined with her dad's right. His eyes were moist. "Doll, your mother and I are beyond thrilled for you."

"Not nearly as thrilled as I am, Dad."

Carolyn was radiant in her mid-calf, ivory satin gown. Its lacy sleeves draped over her arms. Her bouffant-styled hair held an ivory pill-box hat with a short veil over her eyes. Over her right arm lay a cascading bouquet of ivory carnations, roses, and babies' breath, wrapped together with an ivory satin ribbon and adorned with the rosary her mother had carried on her wedding day. Together the bride and her father processed toward the altar, where Carolyn handed her bouquet to Adeline and then turned to face her man. Her tearful father took her hands, kissed them, and placed them into Paul's. "She's yours now." He patted her groom on the back before taking his seat next to her mother.

Paul and Carolyn both knew that the theological implications of a Catholic wedding were profound. The scripture readings and music couldn't have been more fitting, talking about the themes of forgiveness, patience, and charity. Paul's uncle, Fr. Mark, proclaimed the gospel, and Fr. Fedewa gave the homily. The two priests did an excellent job of making it both a personal and holy occasion.

With God and the witnesses present, they pledged their free, total, faithful, and fruitful love till death would part them. They partook of the Eucharist for the first time as husband and wife. And they carried a bouquet of red roses to the alcove of the Blessed Virgin Mary. Both had sensed that the Mother of God had interceded to Her Son on their behalf. They had been led to Matrimony—a sacrament of service to encourage each other to heaven. The new Mr. and Mrs. Johns were ready to take on that covenant commitment.

The November nuptials were commemorated with a few pictures taken by Paul's sister, Susan, who happened to enjoy photography as a hobby. She took several shots of the bride and groom, one with them and their attendants, one of the pair with both sets of their parents, one with both sides of the family including, of course, Mary Catherine, but missing Gus, and one last picture of the newly married with their two favorite clergymen and the four benevolent sisters. It seemed right, though, that the new husband and wife be flanked in a photo alongside their two spiritual fathers and their four spiritual mothers.

The reception was simple—warm ham sandwiches, German potato salad, and a large two-tiered white cake with buttercream frosting. "The food smells delicious, but I have way too many butterflies to eat right now," Carolyn told Paul. He filled a plate for himself, offering his bride a few bites.

Potted mums in fall colors from Ma Wagner's and Grandmama Fandel's gardens adorned the tables. Toward the end of the reception, Carolyn and Paul approached the gift table and began unwrapping the assortment of warm wishes inside the many boxes. Two gifts made Carolyn cry.

One was from Adeline—an ivory picture frame containing a photo of Paul and Carolyn on the evening of that spring formal so many years ago. Paul and Carolyn both teared up when they saw their own two radiantly happy, younger faces smiling back from behind the small pane of glass. Carolyn stifled any bad memories of that night by turning her face up to Paul's and staring into his dark brown eyes. He gave her a sweet kiss on her cheek and whispered in her ear, "Our remarkable journey continues!" They then gleamed toward their parents and noted all four were sporting broad grins.

The other tear-producing present was from Gus, sent from Germany before he had flown to Nam. Carolyn started to cry, and she hadn't yet even opened the gift. Inside was a beautiful, hand-carved wooden crucifix. Carolyn accessed the hatch on the back to reveal a bottle for holy water, a white linen cloth, and two candles. If the crucifix were removed from the base, it could be placed upright. This enabled the priest to say Holy Mass in someone's home or to have the proper sacramentals, should he be called to visit someone gravely ill or near death. She hugged it to her chest, as Paul placed his arm around his new bride.

"What a thoughtful gift!" Carolyn said, holding it up for all her guests to see.

"Father Fedewa," Paul spoke up, "will you bless this for us now?"

"Absolutely!"

Guests blew kisses and tossed rice when the bride and groom exited the church hall, pure joy radiating from their faces. Carolyn and Paul stooped to give Mary Catherine one last hug. "Be a good girl for Grandpa and Grandma."

Their honeymoon was to be a short two-night, three-day trip to a lakeside village in the northern lower peninsula of Michigan, famous for its breathtaking views, classy boutiques, and quaint diners. The new Mr. and Mrs. Johns stepped into Paul's car and zoomed away with a "Just Married" sign taped to the back window headed for the Perry Hotel in Petoskey.

CHAPTER FIFTY-ONE

Paul had eagerly adopted Mary as his own, giving her his last name. They had met with an attorney prior to the wedding to get all the paperwork lined up. The final step was to see the judge and have him make it official, which was done the first week of their return from their honeymoon. It was an immensely proud moment for Paul, and a glorious day for Carolyn, when the judge pounded his gavel and issued a new document listing Paul as the father of Mary Catherine Johns.

The new Johns clan had settled nicely into their new home, a reddish-brown brick craftsman near the same neighborhood as Carolyn's apartment. Paul had purchased it once his Uncle Scott gave him the go-ahead to move his portion of the insurance business to Grand Rapids. With four bedrooms and a backyard sunroom, the house would accommodate a growing family, something they both desired.

They had acquired some used items from both sets of parents and a few pieces from the Water's Edge—those that the Hamiltons decided had run their course. Included among the truckload were the two chairs haggled over between the lovebirds at the Spitzley auction.

With first-grader Mary back at school all day, Carolyn's mornings were allotted to her household duties of cooking, cleaning, laundry, baking, and paying bills. For two hours each afternoon, Carolyn afforded herself the luxury of delving into creative projects.

Carolyn and Paul had transformed their basement into a go-to place for home improvement. She had repainted the ladder-backs in a buttercream enamel. Once dry, she took them from corner to corner in the sunroom, trying to decide on the best position. They ended up at a small round table painted similarly in sky blue. Carolyn could hardly wait for spring as she envisioned sipping early morning coffee side-by-side with Paul and facing the gorgeous sugar maple and a row of daffodils.

Because of her interest in sewing, Carolyn had inherited Auntie Dora's fabric bag, along with her Singer push-pedal. Her entertainment in these early weeks of being an at-home mom had consisted of sifting through the fabric to create accents to spruce up their décor—tiebacks for curtains, throw pillows for the couch, and cloth napkins for dining.

Today, she dug through the duffle, pulled out a roll of orange and blue paisley broadcloth, and sewed two small placemats for the porch set. *Thank you, Auntie Dora!*

Even though she was thrilled to be a homemaker, she needed to wean herself from the ridiculous schedule she had been obligated to. She couldn't quite let go of it. Even on days when she was less than energetic, she kept to a strict agenda. Her days were full, and by evening, she was ready for bed.

Within weeks of the wedding, Carolyn began exhibiting signs of illness. She couldn't shake whatever it was that had overcome her. She was having headaches and digestive issues. And she was plagued by fatigue.

She finally made a phone call. "Mom, I'm concerned. I haven't been well since Petoskey."

"Might you be pregnant?"

"No, I'm sure I'm not. I've had a period."

"Hmm. You still might be, but I can hear that you're worried."

"Yeah, I don't remember feeling so awful with Mary Catherine. I'm scared, Mom." Carolyn started to cry. It felt as if her dreams were potentially crashing to an end. "What if it's something dreadful? I just got married!" Carolyn wailed into the phone.

"Breathe, Doll. Just breathe. Try not to panic. There's a good chance nothing is wrong with you."

Carolyn wanted to trust that was true.

Paul had been wanting her to see a doctor and finally put his foot down. "Carolyn, I have made an appointment for you. You're going tomorrow at two. I'll be home early from work to stay with Mary."

Carolyn assented, and the next day she sat in the doctor's office waiting and dreading for her name to be called. She tried to keep herself occupied by perusing old copies of Woman's Day and Life magazines. She scanned recipes without actually reading them. She skimmed over articles on politics she couldn't have cared less about. She was daydreaming and about jumped out of her skin when the nurse yelled, "Mrs. Johns. Carolyn Johns."

Carolyn obeyed, going through the motion of being weighed and supplying a urine sample before returning to the examination room to wait for the doctor.

"So, you've not been well? Headaches? Digestive trouble? Fatigue?"

"Yes, Doctor."

"Well, Mrs. Johns, I can tell you what is wrong with you." Doctor Hickner made eye contact. "Why such a worried look, Mrs. Johns? Don't you and your husband want more children?" Carolyn cocked her head at the physician. "Mrs. Johns, you're not sick; you're pregnant."

It took her a while to process what he had said. Carolyn put her hand low on her abdomen. "I am?!"

"Yes, how does that resonate with you?"

"Besides feeling foolish, I'm absolutely fine with it!" A huge smile beamed across her face. *I'm carrying Paul's honeymoon baby.* "Since I had had a period, I presumed I couldn't be pregnant. But you have no idea how thrilled I am."

"Well, that settles it then. You best get going and tell Mr. Johns the happy news. I'll see you in a month."

She headed out of the office on cloud nine. She couldn't wait to get home.

Paul was waiting by the garage. He opened the car door for his crying wife. "What's the matter? What did you learn?"

"I learned that I'm not sick," Carolyn sobbed.

"Then, why are you crying?"

"Because…because I'm pregnant. These are happy tears! We're going to be parents again!"

Paul picked Carolyn up and spun her around. "Seems we've got another wee project in the works." He kissed her on her forehead, her cheek, her neck, and her lips. They smooched for a long time.

It was quite a while before the two parents realized they had an audience. Finally, the young onlooker fake coughed a few times to get their attention.

"Oh, Mary Catherine! You're going to be a big sister. Mommy's having a baby!" Carolyn said.

"Hip hip hooray!" shouted the happy big-sister-to-be, and then she exclaimed, "Now we have two pregnant mommies, you and Aunt Lucie! I can't wait to tell Anne that she's going to be an aunt—again!"

"And I can't wait to tell your Grandma Fandel!" Carolyn kissed Paul a few more times and then ran inside to call her mom.

CHAPTER FIFTY-TWO

Carolyn soldiered on during the pregnancy, even though the summer of 1965 was blistering hot. She was able to travel well, including a trip to Derby Lake, where her parents had rented a cottage for a short vacation. The young Johns clan was invited up for a day of fun. Anne and Mary had a blast swimming and playing together from dawn till dusk, and the boys had an equally good time rowing across the lake to catch bullfrogs. It was the respite Paul and Carolyn needed before baby number two emerged.

***

In the lazy, hazy days of August, on the fifteenth of the month—the Feast of the Assumption—Carolyn's long labor debuted to the world a son born at Saint Mary's Hospital in Grand Rapids.

The two parents stared in wonder at their first child together. Paul leaned over and kissed Carolyn's sweaty forehead, ignoring the fact that her hair was plastered to her scalp. "I couldn't love you more than I do at this moment. You are so brave and so beautiful!"

After the nurses cleaned up the little guy and Carolyn put him to breast back in her room, she and Paul thanked God for another safe arrival.

It was a dream come true for Carolyn—to be married to Paul and to bear his children. She felt blessed to have conceived on their honeymoon, for joining her body to Paul's was, indeed, the one-flesh union spoken of in Genesis. The marital act was the literal renewal of their wedding vows so recently promised amidst those closest to them. Carolyn cherished these thoughts.

They were ready to be parents. After all, they already had been. Paul had settled right into the role of father to Mary Catherine even before they were married. That was part of what was so gut-wrenching when she had first turned down his proposal. Carolyn knew he loved both her and the baby she had borne from the rape.

***

Later that day, her parents brought Mary Catherine to the hospital to meet her new little brother. "He's so cute!" the big sister squealed.

"He is a handsome little lad," said her mom.

210

Her dad had tears in his eyes. "Seeing you two together with these children is a beautiful sight."

The new big sister was infatuated. She couldn't wait to touch the baby. Mary mounted the hospital bed to take a turn holding her brother. Carolyn remarked, "I can't believe how grown-up you seem, Mary Catherine. You're such a wonderful big sister."

"Thank you, Mommy! I love him to pieces!" She kissed the baby all over his head and squeezed him tight.

"Okay, gentle, honey," Paul said. "You might love him to pieces, but we don't want him broken into pieces." The room chuckled.

"Too tight, Daddy?"

"Just a tad."

The nurse came in to check on the new mother and infant. "May I take him back to the nursery, Mrs. Johns?"

"Oh, no, not yet. We love having him here. In fact, may I have a bassinette?"

"What about your rest, Mrs. Johns? Let us give him a bottle during the night."

"Oh, how kind of you," said Carolyn, even though she thought the nurse was insane. "I plan on breastfeeding him and not giving him formula."

"Well, Mrs. Johns, a lot of moms are bottle feeding with formula now. It frees them up to do other things. And we're told the formula is about the same as mother's milk."

The new mom forged ahead. "That may be so, but I am going to nurse my baby, and I could use a bassinette to place him in when I am finished. Can you make that happen, or shall I speak with the charge nurse?"

The nurse's face reddened. Message received. "Oh, no, Mrs. Johns, it isn't necessary to speak with the charge nurse. I will make sure you have the bassinette. I will make sure the baby is brought to you for each feeding."

"Thank you."

The nurse clarified. "You're choosing circumcision, correct?"

"Yes, we are," said Carolyn.

"Yes, ma'am, Mrs. Johns. I've got it. I will be back with the bassinette and to see if there is anything you might deem essential."

"Thank you," said Carolyn to the nurse, who was on her way out of the room.

"Well, good job. I had to bite my tongue," said her mom. "I'm proud of you for sticking to your guns. Not that I see anything wrong with a mother bottle feeding her baby formula if that's what she and her husband decide is best, but moms today must be strong about breastfeeding."

Her dad laughed. "I felt sorry for that young nurse. She had no idea about the strength of the women in this room."

Paul guffawed and agreed, "No, she didn't, but she does now."

For the rest of the visit, the adults talked about the baby's baptism and when it might be. Finally, Carolyn's dad spoke with a wink, "I suppose that for this baby to be baptized, though, the first thing you might want to decide is his name."

The new parents laughed, realizing they had forgotten to tell them. Paul looked at Carolyn, and she gave him the go-ahead to be the one to share their son's name. "We've named him Robert Augustine," Paul said, handing the baby boy to his grandfather, who beamed with pride at his namesake.

"What an honor! Thank you. Gus will be so proud, too."

Her mom's eyes glistened. "Yes, your brother would be enormously proud."

"I hope he's able to come home soon," said Carolyn. "Our son ought to have his godfather present for the Baptism."

Her dad agreed. "Right now, Gus thinks he will earn a furlough around Halloween sometime. Check with your pastor to see if you can delay the Baptism till then."

"Great idea, Dad! We'll ask Father George at St. Mary's on Sunday."

"Usually, it's best to baptize as soon as possible, but we do have a special case," offered Paul, who gave an empathetic nod to his mother-in-law.

Carolyn's parents gathered Mary Catherine to depart from the hospital. Her mom leaned over to kiss her daughter and wee grandson. Then she straightened and kissed Paul on the cheek. "I told you to be patient and not to give up on her." Indeed, she had. Way back when Paul announced his journey to Lebanon.

"Thank goodness I'm a little more stubborn than your daughter." Paul and her dad laughed, while Carolyn rolled her eyes and feigned oblivion.

CHAPTER FIFTY-THREE

September 1965

With second grade in full swing for Mary Catherine, Carolyn walked her daughter to school every day and dropped her by the flagpole with her teacher and classmates for attendance, the Pledge, and the Morning Offering. Carolyn continued to the church for daily mass, waving at several other mothers with tiny tots.

She observed the school children enter single file, each class behind their teacher. Grade by grade, they genuflected and filled the front pews for Mass. Hearing their young cherub voices made Carolyn's soul swell. *Such purity, innocence, and trust.*

She prayed for her daughter and her classmates. They would be making their Solemn First Holy Communion in the spring. She sat in her pew and pictured what they would wear on that blessed day—white dresses and veils for the girls and black suits for the boys.

Carolyn chatted with some of the other moms before strolling home to face her mounting household tasks. It was hard to get much accomplished with a newborn, but Carolyn enjoyed the challenge, and she cherished her time alone with the baby. All the breastfeeding hurdles had been overcome, and Robby was nursing like a champ. There was nothing better than sitting with her newborn son and cuddling his warm, full-of-life body. She soaked up the time she was able to hold and rock him, breathe in his fresh baby smell, kiss him, and listen to him breathe or hiccup against her chest. To her, it was a slice of heaven to be gazing at another beautiful baby, this one the result of a lifelong love affair with his daddy.

Carolyn stared at her wedding ring and smiled with fresh tears in her eyes. She was filled with gratitude to God for putting up with her stubbornness and bringing Paul back to her. *Thank goodness my man never gave up on me!*

Carolyn's musings drifted back to that earlier time with her first baby and how hard she had worked. Her days had been spent on her feet at the Log Slide up north, and at night she had to care for Mary, sometimes all through the night. And then she was back at it the next day, and the next, and the next. She had internalized Saint Augustine's advice, praying as if everything depended on God and working as if everything depended on her. For seven years. Seven long years! Carolyn wondered how she even kept her wits about her. *By God's grace, did I do all that!*

She wasn't sure how long she had been daydreaming, but Robby had zonked out halfway through the second breast. She gathered him closer and walked into the kitchen.

She glanced at the clock and poured from the percolator the last cup of coffee, which was too hot to drink. "Well, Robby, it's ten a.m. Time for your nap." She tee-heed to herself, finding it funny that she often talked out loud as if the baby understood her, even if he were sleeping in her arms. She carried him to the cradle and lay him down. She watched his tiny chest breathe up and down. She marveled at it, lost in the wonder.

"What was I going to do?" Carolyn whispered aloud. "Oh, yeah, my coffee." She went back to the kitchen and decided it was still too hot, so she set it back down on the counter. Walking through the living room, she opened her front door and stepped onto the porch, and descended around to examine her side garden.

The sun shone brightly, but the summer flowers were fading. The Shasta daisies and daylilies had few blooms remaining. The mums were budding, though, and full of the promising rust color soon to appear.

She heard "Boogie Woogie Bugle Boy" coming up the street and waved to Steve, the whistling mailman. He took her porch steps two at a time and stuffed her mail into the box.

"Thank you. Have a great day, Steve!"

"You, too, Mrs. Johns." He whistled back into the song mid-verse as if he had never been interrupted.

She walked up the stairs and opened the lid. She put her hand in to discover the day's envelopes. As she pulled out the wad, she nearly stopped breathing when she saw the white package. She sank into a nearby colorfully-webbed lawn chair, her mood sinking simultaneously. *The package I've been dreading for two years.* She held it in her hands and stared at the United States Army seal that seemed to be staring back at her.

Immediately, Carolyn prayed. "Lord, give me the strength to accept what's in this envelope and the wisdom to use it for Your glory. Mother Mary, make haste to aid me." She added a prayer for Skip Jergen, "Eternal rest grant unto him, O Lord, and let perpetual light shine upon him. May his soul, through the mercy of God, rest in peace. Amen." She had forgiven him. A single tear ran down her cheek.

With a deep breath and a long sigh, Carolyn sat on the porch, forgetting about her coffee. She started to peel back the tape that sealed the long-awaited envelope. She did so in pensive slow motion, not wanting to open it but knowing she must. The package would reveal what she already knew to be true. He was dead. Skip had met his Maker. *And mine as well. What a sobering reality.*

Carolyn read the letters, blurred because of the tears in her eyes. One was a formal notice from the United States Army. "My, they use a lot of words to inform that someone has died," she said to no one. Then she read the letter from Skip. It was his last written correspondence to anyone, it had said. Carolyn pondered that for a long time. *I am the last one on earth he reached out to.* How weighty that truth was! Her hands felt heavy holding the package. Even though Skip's missive reiterated what his original letter had said, still it was very humbling to hold a dying man's last words in her hands. She was the recipient of that dead person's last bit of written communication ever. So profound was this that she momentarily forgot there was one last thing in the envelope.

She pulled out an official-looking check, flipped it over, and gasped. "Oh, my word." It was all she could say in that bittersweet moment. Carolyn was astonished by the amount that was written out: Fifteen thousand, two hundred dollars and forty-one cents. "That is a lot of money," she mouthed out loud.

At a snail's pace, she put the check and both letters back inside the package and held the bulky envelope to her chest for a long while, deciding what to do. She would wait for Paul to get home from work to break the news to him. After all, she had known this day was coming. *I can handle this.*

To keep herself occupied, she added more chores to her list, providing Robby cooperated and let her do them. He was a good baby, but he loved being right next to his mommy. He could suckle for up to an hour or more, several times throughout the day, as newborns are prone to do. Luckily, Gus had sent her a *mei tai*—a sling he had seen Asian women use to carry their babies. Carolyn considered it a prized possession. She could even do the ironing and nurse him while he was in it if she took the time to position the baby well. It was a great gadget, that *mei tai*!

As soon as Paul pulled into the driveway from work that evening, Carolyn ran out to the car. "It came. Skip is dead," her voice cracked.

Paul held her and reassured her. "It's okay; it's okay. It's over now."

"May he rest in peace."

"Yes, amen to that," Paul said.

As soon as Mary and Robby were asleep, Paul and Carolyn retreated to their bedroom. Spooning on top of their quilted floral bedspread, with Paul behind her, Carolyn talked about the ramifications of this final letter and the check that had been sent with it. Paul told Carolyn he was all-in on her idea of how to use the money. "The Holy Spirit has inspired you, my love." He kissed the back of her head.

She turned over, lay her head on his chest, and squeezed her husband. He tightened his arm around her. She loved lying in his arms—so protective. She tilted her head back and observed his jawline—so strong. He rolled her over and returned her affection with a full-on kiss. The time they had spent lying together and talking things through had soothed and abated any remaining doubts of the past. They dove under the covers—tossing clothing aside—both of them fueled with a sudden, strong desire to recommit their marital bond of love.

CHAPTER FIFTY-FOUR

It had taken a year for the preliminary plans and design details to be ironed out, but the new house was now in its finishing stages.

On a chilly October day in 1967, Paul and Carolyn—obviously pregnant again—put fourteen-month-old baby Robby in the wagon and said, "Mary Catherine, grab your jacket. We're going on a family stroll to see our project." Mary climbed in behind her little brother, while their daddy pulled them down the sidewalk.

Departing from their home on Jones Street, they walked several blocks. With each street they crossed, excitement grew. They wondered how close the house was to being completed. As they rounded the corner of Fremont onto Marnon Avenue, the two-story frame rose in front of them. "Wow! They've got the exterior pretty much done," said Paul. "Now they can take the whole winter to finish the inside."

"It looks good, doesn't it, Mr. Johns?" Carolyn was teasing.

"It looks great, Mrs. Johns!" Paul teased back.

Mary expressed her approval by showing two thumbs up. "It's so pretty." Leaning over her brother in the wagon, "Isn't the house pretty, Robby?" The baby babbled back as if he understood, and Mary scrambled out.

They surveyed the large wrap-around porch. *Perfect for evening chats,* Carolyn imagined.

"Be careful as we go inside," Paul said, "it's going to be messy with all the construction going on."

After taking Robby out of the wagon, Carolyn and the rest of her Johnses ascended the wide stairs together and opened the front door into an expansive, two-story foyer. "Ooh, I love it!" Carolyn exclaimed.

To the right was a spacious living room with framing for several large double-hung windows, still in boxes. To the left was an ample dining room. Beyond it was a cozy sitting room for reading or reflecting.

"It's so airy and welcoming!" Carolyn felt the baby kick and held out her hand. "Come here, Paul. Our new child approves."

He placed his hand on her stomach. "I agree!"

Paul took Robby from her arms as he and Carolyn explored more of the beautiful structure. Mary followed. It was shaping up exactly how she had hoped it would.

"They're going to love living here," said Mary Catherine. "The new mommies are going to love it here!"

"I hope so, honey," said Carolyn.

"It is obvious that in all the meetings with the architect and the builder, they listened," Paul said. "The carpenters and sub-contractors are putting a lot of detail into their work."

They stepped over some two-by-fours and tools in the dining area on their way to the massive kitchen, which would house another family-style table. Carolyn pictured the residents sitting around it while she taught them how to make cinnamon rolls and donuts.

Behind the kitchen on the left side was a full bathroom with a commode, sink, and shower, which connected the kitchen to a small bedroom where the housemother would live. Through the kitchen to the right, the house boasted another sizable living area with a huge picture window that faced the backyard. French doors opened up onto a patio.

Upstairs, they saw the outline of four bedrooms and another bathroom, this one with a tub and double vanity. All of the rooms were generous enough to hold a twin bed, a dresser, and a crib. The wide landing at the top of the stairs would house one changing table and four rocking chairs. Beside each rocker would be an end table with a dim lamp. Carolyn could picture it in its entirety.

Paul wanted to check out the basement level to make sure things were laid out to specification, mainly daylight windows and a door leading to the street. There were some other plans in the works, and the basement had to be ready to accept any changes to the house that might be made.

Once he rejoined Carolyn and the kids on the main floor, the Johnses knelt and offered prayers of Thanksgiving. What a great gift had been given to them! They were so pleased and blessed to be able to build this house, which would be a sign of hope for many in the greater Grand Rapids community. Young women who might not have anywhere to go during their unplanned pregnancies could live at this residence and call it their own.

"They'll be able to take their children across the street to Westside Park," Paul noted.

"And have a safe place to nourish their souls and their babies while they prepare for motherhood and the bittersweet times sure to come,"

Carolyn emphasized.

"Surely," said Paul, "Skip would approve."

"I hope so. I want to facilitate that repentant soul's yearning to spread goodness in the world, as was his dying wish."

Mary Catherine had overheard. "I'm sure my first daddy is happy."

Carolyn and Paul nodded and scooped up their daughter and son into a long group hug.

The estimated completion date was about six months away. It was hard to believe that Carolyn's dream of turning her sorrow into a long-lasting joy would soon be here.

The dwelling would be able to take in up to four young women whose families had abandoned them. Girls of any faith could apply. They had to sign declarations of commitment to God, promises to continue their educations, and agreements to care for the home as if it were their own.

Once there, they would receive regular tutoring in the evenings by the four good sisters on Broadway Street. One was a licensed counselor, so she agreed to meet individually with them to make sure spiritual and emotional paths were strong.

They would also acquire job training skills, giving them a solid shot at gaining employment. They would have up to three months after giving birth to establish a bond with their babies and get used to being new mothers. Then, they were expected to work and save for their futures, as well as provide groceries for the house. They would have up to a year after that to organize a plan for independent living.

During that time, they would be advised to refrain from dating. They were to focus instead on building a solid foundation for their children. The sisters reasoned this might be a good way for the girls not to find themselves in another similar situation as might have gotten them there in the first place.

A large benefit was free medical care for the young moms and their babies throughout the first year by Doctor Rachelle P. Matthews, a faithful Catholic physician who had volunteered her services.

It was going to be a win-win for all involved. Paul, with his background in insurance, gave him enough credentials to oversee the project. Adeline volunteered her accounting skills. Carolyn managed the practical side. She had found a warmhearted widow, Mrs. Marguerite Hanley, to move into the house and act as housemother to the young women. Her job included setting the training and chore schedules, as well as supervising the comings and goings of the moms and their babies.

Carolyn and Paul had hired a retired art and home economics teacher to lead and oversee all the practical studies. Mrs. Arlene Finnis was going to be a great asset. She had taught school for ten years after she had raised her own family. With her children grown and Mr. Finnis deceased, she had been looking for a golden opportunity to use her skills. She would show the residents how to cook and sew. For those who already had these abilities, they would be expected to demonstrate for the others. Arlene was also willing to offer watercolor and oil painting lessons for an incidental fee.

The Hamiltons were both financial and practical benefactors to the home. During the initial phases of the project, Ward had run an idea by Carolyn.

"Mr. Hamilton, an eatery in the lower level will be a tremendous opportunity for acquiring employable skills!" The breakfast establishment would provide excellent job experience, allowing the new mothers to earn money and be close to their babies while they worked. Carolyn and Paul had a kitchen and restrooms stubbed in. Daylight windows and a wide stairwell leading outside were integrated into the building plans. Already, Magnificat Café had a reservation list two pages long for its grand opening slated for the following year.

Karlene and Karenna Hamilton, the twins, had long since graduated from high school, but they offered extra tutoring services in their free time. Theresa Hamilton herself, along with her younger teenage children, volunteered childcare. The Hamilton boys had already been donating their time for light construction and outside chores.

Others stepped forward, too, in assuring the full outfitting of this new home of hope. Standard Goods delivered several boxes of cleaning products, personal care items, and even new kitchen appliances. The Fuller Brick Company, where Paul's dad was now president, gave the contractors the deal of the century on any exterior brick used. Van Hockstra Furniture promised to supply most of the furniture from their clearance warehouse. Even their childhood priest, Father Fedewa, believed so strongly in this mission of life that he had told them his estate would be bequeathed upon his death.

The largest benefactor, sadly, had died prior to the home's completion. Aunt Hildy had gone to her reward during the building project's final stages. Carolyn and Paul were sorry that she was never able to see it, especially since she had practically paid for it. Scarcely did anyone in Kalkaska realize, but Hildegard Wagner's farm had been sitting on Michigan's solitary oil field. It was discovered the year Carolyn was staying there. Hildy made all involved promise that no word of it was to be leaked. She garnered the undying, silent loyalty by promising big dividends to the secret keepers, a promise she made good on later.

None of the Fandels had any idea how secretive and strong and stubborn their beloved German aunt was! She had announced after the fact, "There was no reason for wrecking a good farm until I was done with it." She lived sparsely all those years, while sitting on an enormous pile of black liquid money.

***

Near the end of her life, Aunt Hildy had become too frail to live alone and too proud to live with anyone else, so she retired to a small independent nursing facility that had connections to St. Mary's Hospital. Carolyn and the children went to visit her often, for Saint Anthony's Acres was not too far from Paul and Carolyn's house.

It was when Hildy was settled into her final residence that she gave the go-ahead for the drilling to be done, and she informed Carolyn of it. "Remember that day when those two men showed up to inspect my property?"

"Yes, I do," said Carolyn with a skeptical tone. She wondered what deep dark news Hildy was about to spring on her. Although her fright had long disappeared, her gut twinged.

Aunt Hildy continued, "Well, those men were prospectors. There was oil on my land. A lot of it."

Carolyn laughed. "Oh, Aunt Hildy, I used to have these fears of being kidnapped or something. When I saw those men that day, I got worried. When I inquired about it, you told me that it was none of my business."

"Well, it wasn't. But I wasn't privy to those fears of yours, Girl. I suppose you were worried. But there was no occasion for it."

No worry was warranted at all because a couple of million dollars were the result of that drilling. Hildegard, the family learned later at the reading of the will, had set aside some for each of her nieces and nephews. She gave a good portion of it to the Catholic Church, and she gave well over half to Carolyn and Paul to be used solely and strictly for the unwed mothers' project.

***

Paul said, in a bright voice, "Our venture in faith is garnering demonstrative support from so many great people."

"I pray this haven will be a beacon of hope for so many scared young girls as they face their most grueling life challenge," vocalized a humble Carolyn. "I can hardly believe all of this."

"God's blessing," Paul said as he placed Robby back in the wagon for the return walk. Mary Catherine skipped ahead of them.

An unexpected check was waiting in their mailbox when they got back home. It wasn't a large amount, but it was from Phyllis with a note that read:

To Paul and Carolyn:

Thank you for your vision in building this haven of hope for young, scared, and abandoned women. They need you more than you realize. Thank you for doing everything in your power to make sure they do not feel pressured to make a fateful choice for their children.

To the benefactors: Thank you for your generosity. Thank you for your witness to LIFE. Thank you for not judging the young women for whom you have built this dwelling. Thank you for loving them in their hour of need. For your love is the greatest gift you can give them beyond this home.

To the young women who will live here: Be grateful to God that He has sent you this particular place. Learn all you can. And enjoy your first go at motherhood. I'm praying for you.

Kind regards,

Phyllis Norton, MSW

Specialist in post-abortive care for women and their families

Upon receipt of Phyllis's extensive sentiments, both of them teared up. They had a revelation at that moment how powerful God is and how active the Holy Spirit is if only individuals are open to it. They prayed that God would someday send Phyllis an amazing man with whom she could have at least one baby. They decided to name the rocking area upstairs the Norton Nursing Nook. They would frame Phyllis's touching letter and hang it at the top of the stairs.

The lessons were clear. Life was precious, even in the midst of tragedy. Souls needed nourishing, especially in times of tragedy.

CHAPTER FIFTY-FIVE

On that great opening day, May 1, 1968, Paul, clad in his black suit, and Carolyn, her hair in a French twist and donning a knee-length navy dress with heels to match, stood proudly outside the newly built, newly blessed home of life and love. Next to them were their three children: nine-year-old Mary Catherine, twenty-one-month-old Robert Augustine, and three-month-old Rose Patrice.

Nearby were all four of their parents, most of their siblings, and all their nieces and nephews spilling into the side yard. Even Elaine had driven down from Kalkaska. She waved at Carolyn, who waved back.

Susan Johns was poised, like she was on Paul and Carolyn's wedding day, with her camera ready to capture the highlights on film. So, too, were journalists from the *Grand Rapids Press* and reporters from *The Michigan Catholic*.

The entire Hamilton clan was gathered in full force, as well. Carolyn and Paul smiled wide at Patrick Hamilton and Adeline. The two had been dating for well over a year. Their arms were wrapped around one another's waists, with Adeline sporting a shiny new engagement ring on her left hand.

All those present were certain it was a happy day in heaven and on earth when Madonna Maternity Haven was officially opened. Side by side, the first four unwed residents were the four good sisters, who had each agreed to adopt one of the young ladies and become her spiritual mother for the journey.

Father Fedewa, Father George, and the priests of several city parishes accompanied the prelate of Grand Rapids, Bishop Karl Ryerson, in the blessing of the house, named for Mary the Mother of God. The Blessed Mother's presence had been with Carolyn throughout her entire life, especially in those bittersweet times when things were kept close to her soul. It was fitting and right that the house should be consecrated to Her.

The bishop and the priests entered first and processed throughout the home, blessing all the doorways and rooms with holy water. The reflection room held beautiful walnut bookcases built by Carolyn's dad and brothers. They were filled with donated books and various religious statues. In the foyer, Mrs. Finnis had stenciled a scripture citation across the arch that led into the dining room. It quoted Romans 12:12, which was a sublime message for those who came to reside at this house. Bishop Ryerson read it aloud: "Rejoice in hope, be patient in tribulation, be constant in prayer."

Carolyn's soul took flight, for those words were a consummate way to describe not only the hardships that had gone before her but also all that she and Paul would face together.

Back outside with the entire crowd, Carolyn noticed the sun radiating down magnificently onto each person there. She couldn't help but lift her eyes toward heaven when the bishop invited the congregants to pray in unison the closing line of the dedication blessing, "Glory to God in the highest, for He is the author of Life and Love! Amen."

Carolyn was beaming as she turned to survey her supporters, especially her Fandels. She was bursting with pride, and her eyes pooled with tears of joy and not just for the house. There was another reason.

Among the crowd was a soldier in uniform. Upon eye contact, Gus broke stride and ran straight into the arms of his older sister and spun her around. The crowd burst into applause.

The entire Fandel clan stood smiling and crying at the same time. From that awful night in 1958 to now, God had watched over them all, safeguarding both their bodies and their souls.

Carolyn caught Paul gazing at her. She returned it with the warmest devotion. Through their grit and God's grace, they were together. That alone would have been enough.

Her life's vocation had been made clear, and her heart was full. She marveled at how God had authored her path and kept her straight, even though the lines were wavy at times. She had kept her faith and discovered a mission. She was ready to mentor countless young mothers, showing them how to navigate the rougher waters of their lives and how to keep their focus close to their souls as they did so.

EPILOGUE

Fewer than five years after Madonna Maternity Haven opened its doors to women facing unplanned pregnancies, the United States Supreme Court legalized abortion up through the ninth month in all fifty states. It did not take long for more women to need assistance. Some still came because their parents had banished them. But many more were now seeking haven because they were being coerced into having abortions by their parents or their babies' fathers.

Madonna Maternity Haven expanded its outreach. Generous donors from all faith traditions allied. The vacant lot next door was purchased with some of Hildy's funds. A two-story addition was built to accommodate four additional bedrooms, as well as the offices of Mother's Choice, a free clinic that offers pregnancy tests, ultrasounds, parenting classes, and any other needs women in crisis have. In 1993, the two partner missions merged and formed the Alpha and Omega Institute of Life and Love.

Carolyn retired as CEO in 2011 at the age of seventy. She turned the reins over to her thirty-year-old granddaughter, Joanna, the daughter of Mary Catherine.

To date, thousands of women and their babies have been given a chance for life and love because one sorry soul repented, and another chose to forgive.

Acknowledgments

I appreciate you—my readers—more than I can express. I pray all is well with your souls. Thank you for taking the adventure through my first novel.

Close to the Soul has been a labor of love. Those who know me might recognize familiar names and places and even some events. This is my way of giving little shout-outs of grateful remembrance.

For the writing of it, I am indebted to the encouragement that I've received, along with the boatload of help. No novel gets published without an army. Every author says this, and now I know how true it is!

To Ellen Gable Hrkach of Full Quiver Publishing: When I reached out asking if you would be interested in reading my first novel after providing you a snippet, you did not hesitate. Thank you for that! You read it and then critiqued it like it needed it to be critiqued, offering clarity about what you thought I needed to do to make *Close to the Soul* worth reading by a lot of people. I can never repay you nor the other editors and proofreaders at Full Quiver. You are incredible!

To Lori Nelson Spielman (international best-selling author of *The Life List*, *Sweet Forgiveness*, and *The Star-Crossed Sisters of Tuscany*): a huge thank you for reading one of my early drafts and following it up with a forty-five-minute phone call. I will never forget your words: "Mary Jo, a lot of people say they want to write a novel, but you actually wrote one. It has all the constitutive elements." You never stopped teaching me, helping me, and encouraging me to get *Close to the Soul* published, and I appreciate all you've done for me.

To Jenn Fox, fellow author, long-time friend, and my first writing mentor as a novelist: I have learned so much from you! Thank you for your patient indulgence. Thank you for painstakingly editing one of my early drafts. Thank you for gently trying to tap me on the head about Point of View. Seeds were planted! Thank you for agreeing to reread another version, even though you could see I wasn't there yet. I cannot begin to enumerate the lessons you taught me about writing a novel. I pray every success will be yours.

To my husband, John: You're amazing. I could stop there, but people need to know more. You have listened to excerpts of chapters and acted genuinely interested in my characters. You read the whole book on one of our vacations. You came to me with real tears and good questions. Thank you for always encouraging me. I love you! I've loved you since 1975.

To our daughters, Karen DeVries and Jenna Jonaitis, my initial two readers, and our sons, Mark and Scott: You have no idea how much confidence you gave me as you nudged me to get *Close to the Soul* published. I love you more than words can express.

To my grandchildren, those already born and those yet to come: I love you. I love my Catholic faith and believe it to be true with all my heart. Be a lover of Truth. It's yours for the taking.

To my birth family—the descendants and relatives of the Irish family of Grand Ledge, Michigan: you are the cast of characters I am proud to love and call mine. Enjoy finding some of your names in the pages of *Close to the Soul*. Our parents, Ward H. and Adeline R. cooperated with God to bring us into the world. We were taught the tenets of our Catholic faith by them, and we received their unconditional love. May they, and all our siblings who have gone before us, rest in peace. May God hold us all close and our beloved dead closer.

In all things, I encourage everyone to "rejoice in hope, be patient in tribulation, be constant in prayer." (Romans 12:12) Your life, no matter what comes, is a gift. You are a gift!

Close to the Soul Discussion Questions

1. What is your first impression of the Fandel family? Did your impression of them change once you had read the book? If so, how? Did they remind you of any families you know?

2. Beyond the flirting and drinking, is there any other reason you think Carolyn believed the rape was her fault? If so, explain.

3. Adeline was always supportive of Carolyn, but the rape affected Adeline's life, as well. In what ways?

4. How have societal standards affected or contributed to women's impressions of themselves?

5. What do you think led to Carolyn's need to be independent?

6. What, if anything, surprised you when Carolyn turned down Paul's first proposal? Could you empathize more with Carolyn's feelings or Paul's? Why is that?

7. How important is Aunt Hildy's role in this story? What are some of the things she could give to Carolyn that others could not?

8. Were you frustrated with Silvester that he did not tell anyone about Skip's supposed rape of another girl the previous year? How heavy might that weigh on your conscience if you knew something of that magnitude and kept it to yourself?

9. How did your impression of Phyllis change throughout the story?

10. How did you feel about Gus's enlisting? Do you think Wally should have? What memories, if any, do you have of the Vietnam Era? How did it impact you?

11. What feeling did you get when Anne Hildegard asked Mary Catherine about the identity of her dad? How might you have answered that question for a child?

12. Were you surprised to learn of Phyllis's reasons for pulling away? What impression do you have of Phyllis's parents? Can you identify with them?

13. What were both the positive and negative ramifications of Adeline's wedding gift of the ivory-framed photo to Carolyn and Paul?

14. How has legalized abortion made it easier for men to shirk their responsibilities to the families they create through sex? How has legalized abortion made it easier for men to use women as objects?

15. What would be your feelings if you found out that your mother had chosen to end the life of one or more if your unborn siblings? Could you have sympathy and empathy for her?

16. Why should we have empathy for women who've chosen abortion, no matter our personal views? Why do they deserve our love?

17. What can society do to make it easier for women to choose adoption or to keep their babies? What do women need in this regard? Make a list and decide how you can help.

18. How critical was it that Carolyn retained her faith throughout her life? Could she have achieved the same goals without it? Why or why not?

19. Skip is a character people might enjoy hating. Eventually, Carolyn found a way to forgive him. Why is forgiveness of infinite value to the victim?

20. *Close to the Soul* is a story of sexual assault from a faith perspective. It is also a story about the infinite worth of every single human person. Which part(s) of the story touched your soul? Why do you think this is a story that needed to be told?

Resources

If you or someone you know is grieving the loss of a child through abortion, or having self-harming thoughts, know that you are not alone. There is help for those who share this special kind of grief.
https://hopeafterabortion.com/
Nationwide toll-free helpline: 888-456-4673
Nationwide Suicide Prevention 1-800-273-8255

https://www.rachelsvineyard.org/
Rachel's Vineyard Ministries
808 N. Henderson Road 2nd Floor
King of Prussia, PA 19406

(610) 354-0555 (office)
(610) 354-0311 (fax)

If you or someone you know is facing an unplanned pregnancy, there are generous organizations around the world who will help mothers and their children.

National Right to Life

https://www.nrlc.org/

Crisis Pregnancy Center U.S. Map

UNITED STATES **https://crisispregnancycentermap.com/**

CANADA **https://priestsforlifecanada.com/prolife-canada-index**

EUROPE **https://prolifeeurope.org/**

ASIA **https://www.facebook.com/ProLifeAsia/**

AUSTRALIA **https://righttolife.com.au/home**

LATIN AMERICA **https://aul.org/latin-america/**

AFRICA **https://www.achpr.org/legalinstruments/detail?id=10**

If you or someone you know is the child of rape, please know that you do not have to feel alone.

Save the 1

https://www.savethe1.com/

Jennifer Christie (pregnant through rape)

https://www.jenniferchristie.org/

If you or someone you know are an abortion worker who wishes to leave the industry but could use help in finding another job, this organization was founded by a former abortion worker.

https://abortionworker.com/

If you or someone you know wishes to get more involved in the pro-life movement, there is a place for you.

Sidewalk Advocates for Life

https://sidewalkadvocates.org/

40 Days for Life

https://www.40daysforlife.com/
info@40daysfor life.com
4112 East 29th Street
Bryan, TX 77802
888-543-3316

About the Author

Mary Jo Thayer is drawn to stories with relatable characters and educational opportunities, which she hopes is apparent in everything she authors, whether it be a novel, an article, or a speech.

In 2014, she began to spill *Close to the Soul* into a word document and wrote the novel's skeleton of 50,000 words in ten weeks. Two moves, three weddings, her husband's retirement, lots of travel, the birth of six grandchildren in six years, and a couple of life catastrophes later, she is beyond proud to have it published.

A teacher and public speaker by trade, with a master's in curriculum and teaching, her open classroom of love goes wherever she goes. She is ever at the ready to sprinkle in humor and doses of reality. Or throw on a pot of coffee for a good chat because family and friends are irreplaceable treasures.

She resides in Grand Rapids, Michigan, with her high school sweetheart husband, John. The Thayers split their time among the city, the lakeside, the tropics, and wherever a plane might take people. *Close to the Soul* is her first novel, but she thinks she has at least one more rambling around in her brain.

Contact Mary Jo at her website: maryjothayer.com

Published by
Full Quiver Publishing
PO Box 244
Pakenham ON K0A2X0 Canada
www.fullquiverpublishing.com

Made in the USA
Monee, IL
23 July 2021

73880594R00142